NO WAY IN

NO WAY IN

Freedom is the greatest addiction of all

Richard R. Fernandez

Contents

The Passenger 1
One for the Road 10
The Weakest Link 18
Loose Ends 30
A Bowl of Laksa 34
Small World 48
Night Ride 53
The Perfect Couple 61
Lyndon Johnson Slept Here 67
Shadows 71
The Road South 77
Confluence 95
Breakaway 103
Parry and Thrust 111
The Man From Singapore 115
The Plan 120
Race for the Key 126
The Roof of Australia 130
Looking for Gaps 135
Justine 144
Ramon Delgato 156
Cindy 163
Wanted: Dead Or Alive 170
Vanished 176
The Happy Jacks 179
Pincer 188
Sixth Sense 201
The Promised Land 215
The Last Valley 223
Head On 228
Winchester 232
The Last Rebels 236
Night Moves 249
Last Stand Lake 253
And Last 259
Afterword and Acknowledgements 266

THE PASSENGER

Alex Francisco turned at the sound of the voice and looked up at a man who looked like a doll. The man's hair was welded by gel into a single shiny surface parted in the middle to reveal a white slash of scalp. The haircut and round face gave Governor Johnny Fortunas a cartoonish appearance entirely at odds with his notoriety. But since one of Alex's community forestry projects was located in the Governor's province, he rose to his feet to shake his hand.

"Ah, Francisco," the governor said, "so you're going to Sydney. So am I. Are you on vacation?"

"No, I don't think I can afford a vacation in Australia on my salary at the Institute," Alex said. "I'm going to a conference on community forestry sponsored by the Australian National University."

"The ANU is in Canberra," Fortunas said in an oddly nervous manner. "I've often been as a guest of members of Parliament. Know it well?"

"My first time, but I'm hitching a ride with a friend who's been there. It's cheaper that way and we can reimburse the gas from the conference organizers."

Alex instantly regretted mentioning the gasoline reimbursements. It made him seem even more down at heel than he really was. Fortunas, who was the right hand man of the Philippine President, made so much from rackets that he probably regarded $100,000 as petty cash. That made him a widely admired figure in the Philippines where what counted was how much you made, not how you made it.

Alex chided himself for being so obsequious to a crook. At any rate, his teaching job paid enough to meet the mortgage on a small apartment overlooking a gray, dirty street in Metropolitan Manila that flooded when it rained. And he had enough respectability to prompt the doorman at the Institute to address him as "Dr. Francisco".

But he knew enough to realize he was only a big fish in a small pond, a point that was driven home when everyone in the faculty lounge congratulated him on being selected to attend the Canberra conference, all expenses paid – Economy Class. It depressed him to think an invitation to a minor conference should merit such congratulations. It confirmed what he had long suspected: that he had reached the stage in life when plaques of appreciation given to guest speakers at the Rotary Club counted as badges of achievement.

Occasionally, he wondered where all the old panache had gone. Then the memory of his cheap car and dingy little condo brought him back to earth. No, this was it. He glanced at the walls of the Economy Class waiting lounge and the cheap suit-jacket draped over the plastic chair, and sighed. This was where he belonged: going to forgettable conferences and spending his remaining years hacking out feasibility studies for grant-funded projects in dusty, god-forsaken places.

He looked at Fortunas again. The governor's face was glistening with sweat despite the air-conditioning. Then, almost as if he was just mouthing the words, he said to Alex.

"Renting a car? It's faster to take the plane. There's a shuttle flight from Sydney to Canberra, you know. Australia's a great place to enjoy cattle, horses, honey and fruits. And sometimes you can find the best of it in some nest in the hills. I'll be staying at the Westin Sydney."

Even as he uttered that strange and stilted string of words, a furtive expression flashed over Fortunas' features. His eyes flickered from side to side, as if he was on the lookout for danger.

Alex watched the facial display with some puzzlement but it soon passed. The governor composed himself, turned on his heel and walked wordlessly away toward the First Class lounge, leaving Alex to wonder what the entire conversation was about. Fortunas seemed jumpy, simply eager to talk to someone and Alex was the only one available.

He folded his frame into the plastic chair and returned with renewed energy to pondering the meager consolations of Third World academia. Not for the first time, he wondered where it all went bad. There was a time when he would have thought it wrong or at least distasteful to deal with people like Fortunas, but the power to laugh at the world came with youth. At fifty-two, an academic with a small reputation and an income to match, he couldn't really laugh at anyone but himself.

Just then, the boarding sequence was announced. Alex stayed seated, knowing that Economy always boarded last. Some twenty minutes later, he picked up his laptop computer bag and walked to the gate.

The 747 took off and began its turning climb south. As the aircraft gained altitude, the grimy streets of Manila briefly wavered through the tiny airline window. Finally, a brilliant Pacific emerged from beneath the wing. It stretched to the horizon in varying shades of blue. On its surface, vessels crawled like distant toys.

Alex snapped the cabin window shade shut. The sunlight was so harsh it made the conference documents hard to read. Never mind. He knew what they said. Soon the buzz of take-off conversation dwindled and the whine of engines dominated the darkened cabin. Alex was in no mood to watch the in-flight movie projected on the bulkhead. After dinner and three glasses of wine, he slipped the small airline pillow behind his head and tried to sleep.

Nearly six hours later – two hours after the flight had crossed over the Australian north coast on its southeastern track to Sydney – Alex began to sense in half-sleep that something was wrong. The sensation began with a tattoo of hurried footsteps. Alex opened his eyes to see what the commotion was about and saw the stewardess standing over him with a clipboard.

"Dr. Francisco, there's a passenger who's very ill in First Class. Could you come forward and have a look at him?"

Alex shook off the cobwebs and immediately understood the stewardess' mistake. "I'm sorry. The 'Doctor' in front of my name stands for a doctorate in management. I think you're looking for a doctor of medicine."

"Oh, I'm sorry to have bothered you," she said. She walked back to the bulkhead, pulled a handset from its cradle and made an appeal over the speaker system. "We have a very sick passenger in First Class. If there's a doctor, paramedic or nurse aboard, we need your help urgently. Please come forward."

A short-haired, muscular man in his early thirties immediately stood up and joined the stewardess at the bulkhead. They disappeared behind the Business Class curtains. Later, Alex learned from scuttlebutt that the man was a medic in the Australian Army heading home from a holiday.

Though only minutes had passed since the passenger showed distress, he was near cardiac arrest when the medic reached him. They laid him on the First Class aisle to work on him but forty-five minutes of intensive effort by the medic and crew failed to raise a pulse or a heartbeat. Alex saw the medic walk back to Economy, disappointment written all over his face. He knew the patient didn't make it.

The "patient" was then laid in the crew rest area. He would remain there until landing, when he could be examined by an official doctor and pronounced legally dead. Until then, the flight crew would only say that the passenger was "ill". But rubberneckers returning from the front of the plane brought back additional news: the deceased was a Filipino. That got Alex's attention. He knew of only one Filipino in First Class – the man he had met at the departure lounge – Johnny Fortunas, the governor of a province in northern Luzon.

When the plane landed in Sydney, Alex told airport security that he wanted to speak to someone about the man who died in-flight because he might know him. He was given directions to the airport branch of the New South Wales Police. Once past passport control, he made his way to the cop at the desk. He was a very large man in a light blue, short-sleeved shirt whose florid face wore a look of professional boredom. Its immobile features changed instantly when the cop heard what Alex was asking.

"You say you knew the deceased?" the cop said.

"I do if his name is Johnny Fortunas. He's a well-known politician in the Philippines. I know him slightly and he spoke to me shortly before take-off in the pre-departure lounge. I'm just a fellow countryman and if there's anything I can do … well I thought I'd ask."

The policeman picked up the phone on the desk, spoke a few terse sentences into the mouthpiece, then listened to a lengthy answer.

"Well, that's his name all right," he said to Alex. "We're treating it as a natural death – so far – and we're trying to contact the Philippine Consulate to help with next of kin, but if there's anything, we'll call you. You can leave your contact details with me and thanks for your help."

All of a sudden, Alex realized he had said too much. The phrase "we'll call you" was never good to hear from a cop and it made him want to be somewhere else. But he could hardly back out now. He wrote down his cell phone number on a form and walked quietly toward the door.

"Wait!" the cop shouted from behind him. Alex stopped and turned slowly to face the cop, who only said, "mate, do you have anyone driving you into the city?"

"No, I don't."

"There's a van that goes into town I can get you on. Save you the cab fare."

The cop picked up the phone, spoke some words into it, then told Alex where to wait for the van. Alex mumbled a sincere thanks and said goodbye. A complimentary van into the city would save him about forty bucks, a sum he would rather keep, even though conference organizers had promised to refund airport cab fare. Alex kicked himself again: he was getting into the habit of thinking like a loser. He walked to the appointed place and waited. The van pulled up on schedule and he got on, bound for downtown Sydney.

Alex figured that Fortunas' death would be in the news within half an hour. Consular officials would be calling ahead to their political patrons to scoop the press. On the status-mad Manila cocktail circuit, advance access to the news was a surer sign of importance than a diamond-studded Rolex. Well, if diplomats could do it, why couldn't he? On impulse, Alex decided to give his friends the scoop and play the big man for once; it would make him forget the memory of pinching pennies. He took out his cell phone and sent out the news by text message to a dozen friends.

Alex sent off the SMS just as the van descended into the tunnel beneath the Royal Botanical Gardens. The green vistas of Sydney and the rows of skyscrapers towering against the amazingly blue sky were replaced in an instant by yellow tunnel lighting and the whir of huge ventilation fans. The tunnel blacked the cell phone signal out. Three hundred meters into the tunnel, the van began to slow to a crawl. Ten minutes later, they passed the cause of the delay: a car had smashed into the tunnel wall and a tow truck was pulling it away. When the van popped back up onto the surface after the brief delay, Alex's phone was ringing urgently.

"Alex Francisco, speaking," he answered automatically.

"Alex, listen carefully. Who else did you send a text message to about Fortunas' death?" He recognized the voice of Rodolfo Barcelon, the dean of his Institute and a former Philippine Secretary of Defense. Alex was surprised by the question, but replied matter-of-factly.

"To you and the distribution list you were on. Why?"

"Because when news of his death becomes public in a few minutes, all hell is going to break loose."

"It's shocking that he died," Alex said, "but kings, queens and presidents die and the world keeps turning. Why should all hell break loose?"

"You may not know it but for the last 12 hours, Fortunas has been the object of the biggest manhunt ever. The police have been looking for him everywhere. By sending out that text message, you have not only solved the mystery but also advertised that you were on the plane with him. Your message is now being forwarded everywhere and it's going viral. In half an hour, you're going to be at the center of the biggest shit-storm ever. Just about everybody is going to want to know what you know about how he died."

Alex hadn't expected this twist. It left him momentarily speechless. Barcelon spoke again. "Tell me, did he say anything to you before he died?" Something about Barcelon's tone and his sudden change of tack worried Alex, but he could not put his finger on it.

"Nothing beyond small talk in the pre-departure lounge," Alex said, looking out the window as the van drove the last few blocks into downtown Sydney. "He came up to me in the departure lounge and started a strange and aimless conversation, like he just wanted to talk to somebody. He told me to fly to Canberra instead of renting a car, to try Australian wine and sample all kinds of goodies I probably couldn't afford. Weird stuff like that. It was like listening to a parrot squawk. I didn't know then he was on the run, but I should have guessed something was wrong from the way he was acting."

"Fortunas had been called to testify before the full Senate to reveal what he knew about the ballot-box swap that supposedly stole the election for President Licban," Barcelon said. "When Fortunas didn't show up, calls were made to his office, his cell phone – anywhere he could be reached. It soon became clear he had vanished. There was an uproar. Finally, the Senate President restored order and declared Fortunas in contempt for running out on the subpoena. The cops were ordered to arrest him, but nobody knew where to start looking. Now we know he got on the plane to Sydney, probably in collusion with a contact in passport control that let him board without question. Now that he's dead, nobody's going to answer the Senate investigator's questions. People are going to ask the last man who saw him alive."

"Look, I was just a passenger on the plane. He rode at one end of it, I rode at the other, along with 300 other people. Just because I was on the plane with him when he died doesn't mean I know anything."

There was a momentary silence on the line.

"I know," Barcelon said, "but his testimony was the key to the impeachment of President Licban. When someone who can bring down a president flees and dies in the process, people stop believing in coincidences."

Personally, Alex wouldn't altogether mind if Fortunas' death lit a fire under Licban. That crook of a president proved even worse than his predecessor. President Ulysses Licban was called the Malignant Midget at cocktail parties in Manila for his unusually short stature and freakish features. He came to power after a campaign of civil disobedience toppled a TV star who rose to the presidency on a wave of populism and fell, before his term was over, on a wave of disgust over his incompetence. Licban, then the vice-president, had actually orchestrated a smear campaign against the actor-President behind the scenes. The change was swift. The Supreme Court, for the sake of domestic peace, declared the actor-President mentally unfit to serve and declared Licban president. Within a year of the new government, the public realized they had exchanged a stupid and venal president for a cunning and even more venal one. Licban began to loot the country with a thoroughness no one could ever imagine.

"Licban should be glad Fortunas had croaked," Alex answered finally. "Who's going to finger him now? Look, Dean Barcelon, if you're saying that the press will be hounding me for a scoop, I'll switch off my cell phone after this call."

"That won't be all you'll have to worry about. There will be political pressure for Australia to investigate any possibility of foul play. They're going to start looking, and they're going to start with you."

"In that case, I'm safe. The Australians are sane," Alex said evenly. "They're not conspiracy addicts like the politicians in Manila. They will turn over the rocks, but I won't be under any one of them. The Aussies will do this by the book and in the end they'll buy me a beer."

"Sure they will," said Barcelon, "but remember, maybe it's not the Australians that you should be worried about."

Alex was turning that curious remark over in his head just as the van reached the Queen Victoria Building in downtown Sydney. The driver opened the door and motioned Alex down onto the curb. Alex told Barcelon he had to hang up.

"I've got to go," he said. "I'll be in touch." Alex stepped onto the sidewalk pulling his luggage after him. He stood for two minutes on the pavement beside the bronze statue of Queen Victoria thinking about Barcelon's call before it finally dawned on him just who he should be worried about.

ONE FOR THE ROAD

Fortunas died before the plane took off, though he didn't know it at the time. Death came via a "bartender" who dropped poison into his drink in the First Class lounge. The assassin was smuggled into the secure section of the airport on orders of President Licban. In his pocket was an ampoule of toxin developed specifically for covert assassinations by Lab 12 of the former Soviet Union, now under Russia's FSB. It cost $50,000 in the underworld black market.

The planners knew of Fortunas' fondness for liquor so the "bartender" had been trained to drop a 0.5 cc of toxin into the victim's drink from its glass container. When the governor went into the First Class lounge, he headed straight for the bar.

"I want a *mojito*," Fortunas said, as he glanced up to watch the lounge TV.

"Very well, sir."

The "bartender" put crushed mint leaves and lime slices in a tall glass. He added a teaspoon of brown sugar. Then he snapped the ampoule's stem with an opener that looked like a small aluminum tube and shook the contents into the mixture. He added crushed ice, rum and club soda and stirred it. Finally, he put a festive little flag in the *mojito*, screwed his face into a toothy grin and served it to Fortunas.

"Your *mojito*, sir," he said. Fortunas took the glass without looking down from the TV. He took a sheaf of peso bills from his pocket and without counting it, flicked it with his hand across the counter.

The toxin was harmless outside the human body and required no special handling. Once in the stomach, however, the body's metabolic chemistry converted it into a cholinesterase inhibitor similar to the nerve gas VX. According to the toxicological tables supplied by the Russians, in four hours after ingestion, the victim would have metabolized enough poison to feel giddy. From there, the victim would become progressively disoriented and slide irretrievably into cardiac arrest.

Fortunas sipped the *mojito* and absentmindedly watched a beautiful European clay-court star play a match against an Australian newcomer. Behind the bar, the killer watched in fascination as Fortunas, a man immeasurably his social superior, slowly drank his life away. He was waiting to see how long he would last but he was to be disappointed. Fortunas kept drinking imperturbably on and nothing happened. He decided that poisoning required too much faith for an old-fashioned killer like himself.

He had done his job and as agreed sent a text message confirming mission completion. In his head, he was already counting the promised five thousand dollars. But something about the impending death of his victim, which would come in stages over four long hours, warned him never to be too certain about anything.

The *mojito* and the fact that the flight was nearly ready for boarding calmed Fortunas down. He had been nervously watching the doors but no arresting team came crashing through. It looked like he was going to make it to Australia after all.

The boarding call sounded. He moved like a seasoned traveler up the jetway into First Class, settled into the full-length recliner with ease and adjusted the lighting to suit his mood. Fortunas fingered the complimentary box of chocolates and toiletries from habit and reveled in the primitive rush of being at the top of the food chain.

From his earliest years, Fortunas believed the only place for him was at the top and that the only way to get there was to take all he could. What distinguished him from ordinary thugs was his unusual discipline. He had the cunning to calculate and the patience to wait until the prize was his. Now it looked like his planning had paid off, even against Licban. Fortunas leaned back in his First Class seat and considered whether to order the lobster bisque or the caviar before dinner.

He thought back to the events that led him here, to his wife Carol Ann, whose suicide had ironically given him an entrée into the inner sanctum of the President. He met her at a teenage beauty pageant he had been asked to judge. Unlike his fellow panelists who were content to ogle the girls, Fortunas had marriage on his mind and Carol Ann fitted his desired profile to a T. She was half-white, beautiful and poor, the perfect trophy wife as far as he was concerned. When she spotted her among the nubile contestants, he saw his chance to take the next step up the ladder.

Like some changeling stalking in the wild, Fortunas had a knack for transforming himself into what his victims wanted to see. In the case of Carol Ann, he assumed the guise of a self-made businessman who had made his fortune and finally wanted to settle down. He courted her the old-fashioned way, calling regularly and taking her out to dinners at fancy restaurants, never forgetting to send her flowers and gifts on special occasions. He was a perfect gentleman and every inch the devoted suitor. When he finally got around to proposing marriage, he could see she had been stripped of all her defenses and trusted him with all of her heart. She happily agreed to marry him but he saw she was worrying about something.

"What is the problem Carol Ann?" Fortunas asked.

"My younger sister. Ever since Mama died, she has had only me to look after her. If we marry, I'd have to leave her and she'll have no place to live."

"Oh, don't worry about that," he said smoothly, "she can move in with us."

Fortunas dropped the mask right after the wedding. Immediately after Carol Ann and her sister moved into Fortunas' mansion, they noticed the armed guards patrolling the grounds, the exits and the heavy, armored doors. The two girls looked at each other, unsure what to think and felt very afraid. That night, Carol Ann's doubts were laid to rest. Impatient with her questions and finally relieved to give vent to his true sadistic nature, Fortunas administered the first of his many

12

beatings. He believed doing it on the first night helped to set the tone in a marriage.

From then on, Carol Ann lived in a state of terror. Whenever she accompanied him to official functions, Fortunas displayed her like a prize horse. When among his political friends, he referred to her as "Whitey". It was not long before she snapped under his relentless abuse and sought refuge with the nuns who ran her old high school in Manila.

It did not take long for Fortunas to find her but he was thwarted in his attempts to see her by the 90-year-old Mother Superior of the convent who had once hidden Filipino guerillas from Japanese soldiers during the war. So he tried blackmail. He sent word to Carol Ann that without a wife to service him, he had no choice but to use her younger sister. He knew this would bring her back running, and it did. When Carol Ann finally returned to their luxury apartment in the city, she was made to wait by the guards outside a bedroom, from which Fortunas emerged with her sister. Yet Carol Ann showed no emotion, even when he began to beat her minutes later. Fortunas wondered what the catch was.

Later that night, both sisters sat on the balcony, laughing and reliving all the dreams of their girlhood. Then, by agreement, they walked off hand in hand to the ledge of their 23rd-floor apartment and jumped. Fortunas' bodyguards quickly wakened him to tell him the news. As he stared down at the two red splotches on the pavement, he felt a moment of rare defeat. Whitey had foiled him. But he didn't let that fact depress him. He was quick to revert to form. He knew the saying that one should "never let a crisis go to waste" and he would never let a tragedy go to waste either. It was time to arrange a period of ostentatious mourning and play the part of a bereaved husband.

Fortunas' gestures of grief and bereavement seemed so authentic they proved providentially useful. At a routine Palace reception, the President approached him to offer his condolences.

"I'm sorry for your loss, Governor," the President said, holding out his hand. At that moment, Fortunas saw his chance to make his pitch. He

13

had always wanted to cut into the immense river of graft that flowed past the Presidential office.

"Thanks for your condolences, Mr. President, but there's something else I want to say. I know how you can stay in office for as long as you want," the governor whispered.

President Licban, who was just four feet and eleven inches tall, perked up at these words. His lips widened in a mirthless smile. Fortunas felt the hairs on the back of his neck rise. He had met many rough characters in his career, but nothing frightened him as much as that presidential grin. The President nodded, signed to his secretary and told him to calendar the governor for an appointment the next day.

Ulysses Licban was the only son of a former senator. He had every notable feature of his father's handsome face reproduced in a mutated way. Even his intelligence seemed a twisted version of his father's. He liked clever conversation, but mainly of the scheming variety. As a child, he showed a disturbing talent for creative cruelty: once his father beat him for shooting all the pet birds in the family aviary with a BB gun. From that, he learned never to let his father catch him being himself again.

He followed his father into government with little apparent interest in electoral politics. However, that indifference hid a burning ambition and a gift for crime and intrigue. By his late 30s, Licban had become, behind his blank expression, the political patron of several major drug and gambling syndicates.

He rose inexorably through the bureaucracy, going from the Bureau of Customs to running the Department of Finance, propelled by seemingly invisible backers. Then, in a political masterstroke, Licban persuaded a popular actor to pick him as his vice-presidential running mate, lending his familiar name and so-called management skills to the movie star's charisma. It netted him the Vice-Presidency. In the shadow of power, in line of succession to the highest office, he worked his backroom magic. When the Supreme Court declared the actor-President mentally incompetent, a process in which Licban played no small part, the Malignant Midget simply stepped up to the presidential chair and sat on it.

Even Fortunas was impressed by the audacity of Licban's conspiracies and looked up to him with a kind of villain-worship. Yet Licban's labyrinthine mind could not find a way out of his current political dilemma. He was the most hated politician in the country and no amount of spin seemed to be able to change that fact. Poll after poll showed him trailing the other candidates. As far as the people were concerned, he was the most corrupt president they've ever had and they were determined to boot him out in the next election. How could he win a new term of his own?

Nor was he any good at campaigning. His real talent was backroom dealing and conspiracy. Despite the best speechwriting, performance coaching and camera angles that money could buy, Licban on the stump had all the charm of a ventriloquist's dummy.

Declaring Martial Law was out of the question. The Cold War was over and he knew those pesky Americans would not support another dictator in Manila. He had to win the election somehow, yet did not know how. Fortunas' whisper promised a solution, and the next day, Licban sat down to listen.

Fortunas described a plan that was breathtaking in its dishonesty.

"We're going to steal the election by being more crooked than anyone can imagine," Fortunas said. "Most election fraud schemes fail because they only corrupt part of the system. The trick is to corrupt the whole system, to cheat on the largest scale, to suborn the *entire* voting process, not just parts of it. Otherwise, the real parts will give away the faked parts. There can be no loose ends."

Fortunas sensed that Licban had taken the bait. The President picked up the phone on his desk and cancelled all other appointments for the day.

"Go on," he said.

Fortunas' plan was to buy off the members of the Commission on Elections and blackmail the holdouts. He explained how a topnotch computer programmer could create a backdoor into the vote-tallying algorithm to produce any margin of victory Licban desired. Then he addressed the problem of how to fix the paper ballots themselves.

Paper ballots were assumed to be immune from fixing because it seemed impossible to alter millions of pieces of paper. But Fortunas thought otherwise. "Most analysts think the sheer number of paper ballots makes it impractical to corrupt an audit. But they are wrong," he said. "To steal an election, you don't have to fake all the paper ballots, just any given *sample* that may be taken. The auditors can never recount all the ballots, only a sample."

He proposed creating a ballot factory where forgers could produce any distribution to order. It only remained to find a way to switch any sample of real ballot boxes with the faked ones. "That can be done by corrupting the custodial process," he said. He explained that recounts were based on samples stored in the basement of the Senate Tribunal, usually under an armed guard drawn from the Philippine Scout Rangers. "So, to switch the ballots, all we have to do is co-opt the Scout Ranger commander. Then we can substitute any sample we want. You *will win* the coming election, and by any margin you want."

The proposal – a corruption of the entire system – was so completely dishonest that it appealed to Licban immediately. Once Fortunas had spelled the plan out, the President saw the whole scheme clearly. He buzzed his secretary and ordered two glasses of champagne brought into the Presidential office. Licban wet his teeth with the French bubbly like a man gargling with Listerine, then began drafting an executive order that would give Fortunas the means and authority to carry out the plan. The governor knew he had finally made his way into the innermost circle of presidential graft, but his flesh crawled at the thought that he was now in the sights of the monstrous President. Licban would watch him like a hawk. The first slip would be his last. Fortunas picked up his glass of champagne and drank it all down.

Fortunas was roused from his reverie by an air hostess placing a cup of lobster bisque before him. The plane was now at 40,000 feet, carrying him away from Licban at just under the speed of sound. He sipped at the bisque and congratulated himself for getting away.

THE WEAKEST LINK

When Fortunas and Licban were putting the finishing touches to their election-stealing scheme, neither imagined that totally unrelated events that started three years earlier in the office of a Marine Colonel would fatally derange their plan. That day, two dozen Philippine Marines and Scout Ranger officers gathered in the office of Col. Jeremiah Bayani to discuss what they believed was an inevitable attack against the vast Muslim rebel fortress of Camp Abu Bakr on the southern island of Mindanao. The assault would eventuate, change the career of an officer and bring him into a collision course with the President of the Philippines three years hence.

The 25,000-acre bastion of Abu Bakr had grown into a Muslim stronghold in between ceasefires agreed by the post-Marcos governments in Manila and the Muslim rebels in Mindanao. While negotiations took place, the rebels stockpiled arms, built fortifications and conducted training under experts from Saudi Arabia, Chechnya and Pakistan.

For years, the so-called rebel 'partners for peace' had used safe-conduct passes and money diverted from government development aid to fortify a swath of west-central Mindanao in full view of the Philippine military. The Army, forbidden by their political masters to act, watched helplessly as the rebels constructed bunkers, armories, training centers and live-fire ranges for the inevitable next time. But now it was clear to the officers in Bayani's office that "next time" was imminent. The rebels had set up roadblocks and 'toll booths' on the National Highway, shaking down everything that passed through. With provincial governors, town mayors and hundreds of businesses clamoring for help, they realized that even the government's "peace" faction could no longer prevent a new round of hostilities.

As they stared at the map of Abu Bakr, the officers in the room wondered if they could successfully carry out an attack when the government, headed by the actor-President, finally ordered it. On paper, Philippine ground forces had almost the same numerical strength as the US Army, but most were merely garrison units with little ammunition and even less training. The only effective ground units were a few Army brigades, the Philippine Marines and the Army Scout Rangers.

"Gentlemen," Col. Bayani began, "one of our biggest challenges is how to counter the Chechen-inspired tactics of the enemy. I have here with me Navy Lt. Commander Carlos Brillantes who has made a special study of these problems. He will brief us on these tactics and the difficulties we face." Brillantes got up, strode to the front and began to flash a series of slides on a screen.

"Here's what we're up against," he said. "On New Year's Eve six years ago, separatist forces in Chechnya, which was part of the former Soviet Union, declared independence from Moscow. Russian President Boris Yeltsin dispatched a large armored force to suppress the rebellion. Due to a lack of coordination, one armored brigade – the *Maikop* brigade – arrived in Grozny, the capital of Chechnya, ahead of the others and deployed around the city's railway station to wait for the other units. The Chechens let them through."

The men in the room listened politely to this apparently irrelevant historical digression. Almost nobody had heard of or was interested in the Chechens. They had come to discuss problems in Mindanao. Why should events in the Caucasus have any bearing on the coming operation?

Brillantes continued. "Then the Chechens, using small, specially trained 'hunter-killer' groups consisting of snipers, machine gunners and RPG grenadiers, surrounded and swarmed the Russian unit. They destroyed the entire *Maikop* brigade over the next 24 hours. Even the brigade commander was killed."

"Do you mean to say," a Scout Ranger colonel interjected, "that these Chechens destroyed an entire Russian armored brigade in 24 hours? How could irregular forces armed with hand weapons destroy a Russian armored brigade dug in at a train station? That's hard to believe."

"Well, they did," Brillantes said. The *Maikop*'s losses were 800 men, 26 tanks and 102 other armored vehicles. Except for a handful who managed to escape, the brigade ceased to exist."

Brillantes had caught the attention of the officers. The idea that an entire armored brigade could simply vanish in a 24-hour onslaught was frightening to men who knew that the entire Armed Forces of the Philippines could not muster as many armored vehicles as the *Maikop* lost in a single day.

"For the last four years, our enemy in Camp Abu Bakr has been training under the same Chechen veterans who destroyed the Russians. We are going to fight the students of the men who destroyed the *Maikop*. Also the Chechens have been augmented by another group based in Pakistan called al-Qaeda about whom we know very little. We hope to get more background information on them from US intelligence liaison, but available reports suggest they are fanatics who will not hesitate to strap explosives around themselves to strike civilian targets – or the men in this room. The Chechens and al-Qaeda together are a training team. They will have prepared the defense of Abu Bakr. Unless we understand their tactics and counter them, we may suffer heavily."

The reassuring sound of Philippine Marine trucks and the formations of marching men outside came through the glass windows that kept the air-conditioning in. The meeting was being held in what was possibly the best-guarded spot in the Philippines, but the tone of Brillantes' briefing seemed to darken the brightly lit room.

"We estimate the Chechens have trained about 100 Grozny-style 'hunter-killer' teams at Abu Bakr, each team consisting of RPG men, light machine gunners and snipers, plus associated infantry. They are flexible, miniature combined armed packages that can be assembled into bigger units at need. Three to five such 'hunter-killer' teams might support an enemy company-sized formation. I've prepared a primer on their tactics which you can read later. After you've studied it, we'll reconvene for further discussion. Right now, I will give the podium back to Col. Bayani." Brillantes switched off the slide projector and returned to his seat.

"So, gentlemen, that's what we're up against if the President gives the order to take Abu Bakr," Bayani said. "I don't need to tell you that in our present state of readiness, we'll have difficulties. The forces assigned to lead the assault would probably be the 1st and 3rd Marine Brigades and the 1st Scout Ranger Regiment. The 6th Infantry Division will provide the main force. These units are the best we have but I don't have to remind you we don't have all the small arms ammo we want nor nearly the amount of artillery shells we need. And until recently, we had no dedicated sniper units."

"And we've got snipers now?" the Scout Ranger colonel asked with surprise. Bayani nodded. "Where did you find the money to buy sniper rifles? The Department of Defense can barely keep us supplied with rifle ammunition."

"How else do Marines get things except by cannibalization and conversion? We just built the rifles ourselves," Bayani said.

He described how the Philippine Marine armorers decided to modify stock M16s into an acceptable sniper rifle type, a task not unlike converting a family sedan into a NASCAR racecar. The result was an M16 with a competition-quality trigger, free-floating barrel, and a Tasco variable power scope. The weapons used hand-loaded, match grade ammunition. While it could not compare with the M40 used by US Marines, the modified M16s could accurately hit out to 800 meters with a good man behind them.

"We got our USMC counterparts to train our new sniper unit. They helped us buy hand loaders second-hand in the US. They may not be well-equipped by Western standards, but if we go up against Abu Bakr, the enemy will be in for a surprise."

Bayani closed. "I've started devising tactics to counter their hunter-killer teams. We are equal to the enemy in organic weaponry and we will have an overwhelming advantage in air and artillery. Now so did the Russians but unlike them, we're not going to underestimate the opposition. Our enemies are tough but I am sure you, gentlemen, will be tougher. Please study the briefing material provided by Lt. Brillantes. Submit your training plans and operational suggestions within 72 hours."

The succeeding weeks were a blur of activity as the commanders raced to prepare for the coming battle. It came soon enough. The President finally gave the order to reduce Abu Bakr.

Three months later, Col. Bayani was commanding the lead element of "Operation Dominance", the understrength 18th Marine Battalion Landing Team, against strongpoint Barira on the approach to Camp Abu Bakr. Opposing him were 800 men of the grandly named 703rd Brigade, 3rd Field Division of the Muslim force under the command of Hashim Sabaya. Sabaya's men were dug in the foothills controlling access to a central mountainous mass with 3,000-foot-high peaks. The Marines aimed to take the strongpoints to the immediate east of the road, a position known as Fort Abdullatif.

Abdullatif was located on a series of low successive ridges, each defended by interlocking positions equipped with machine guns, mortars and rocket launchers designed to provide mutual support. To cover the gaps between the strongholds, Sabaya had numerous hunter-killer teams of the Chechen variety and more light infantry in mobile reserve.

But the Marines had an ace in the hole. The night before Bayani's scheduled assault, Lt. Brillantes led a Naval Special Operations Squad – the equivalent of US Navy SEALs – to an observation post behind Abdullatif. The small group of Naval Special Operators stealthily took position on a hill some distance behind Sabaya's positions, from which they would direct artillery fire onto the reverse slope positions. Despite the woeful lack of ammunition, artillery was the Philippine Marines' trump card. When dawn broke, Brillantes and his men overlooked the battlefield from a God's eye view. Then they rained down the shells.

Sabaya's field fortifications erupted in a spray of broken timber, wire, weapons and men. While the enemy was still in shock, Col. Bayani gave the signal for the main force to advance.

But the wily rebel commander kept his cool. He let the Marines get halfway from their jump-off positions on the highway to the ridge before opening up from dozens of hidden positions. Medium machine guns, mortars and snipers raked the leading elements advancing from the road. A dozen Marines went down almost immediately. The rest were pinned to the ground. Another commander would have stalled under the withering fire but Bayani knew he had to get his men out of the kill zone. Moving forward with his command group, he pressed his company commanders to attack, hoping to get his men out of the fire-beaten zone as quickly as possible. To cover his advance, he called Brillantes to direct yet more artillery onto the newly unmasked enemy positions. Once again, the enemy bunkers dissolved into gouts of mud as the shells landed on them.

With the enemy machine guns temporarily beaten down, Bayani shifted his strength to his right while keeping up the pressure on the center. He planned to roll up the enemy bunker line from right to left. But Sabaya planned to beat him to the punch with a flanking move of his own. Two companies of rebels felt their way around the left flank of the Marines to cut it off from the highway, with teams of hunter-killers in support.

Brillantes warned Bayani of the flank attack, who reacted by sending a Company-minus force up to block the enemy flank attack. He put his own command group into a 360-degree perimeter and continued the attack on the right. Soon, a rising crescendo of fire to his left told him that his lead Marine platoons were in contact with the Chechen-trained hunter-killer teams. The sound of machine-gun fire and RPG explosions rolled across the entire front. Then Bayani heard the Marine 105s slamming into the rear of the enemy attack.

Sabaya cursed as he watched the airbursts walk through his companies. "The bastards have an observation post somewhere," he told his second-in-command. "They are killing us. Somehow, they can see every move we make. Take a company and beat out that ridge over there. That's where any hidden OP is bound to be."

Brillantes saw rebel infantry peel off and head directly for his ridge. They advanced in an extended line and when they found his little unit, it would be game over. The textbook defense was to bring the 105s in around his position. But he had another idea.

He called down artillery fire on the Muslim units advancing on the far end of the ridge. By defending the wrong position with fire, he hoped to bluff his way out of a corner.

When Sabaya saw the Marine 105s slam into the platoons advancing on the eastern ridge, he interpreted it as protective fires for the artillery spotter team.

"That's where they are!" he said. Sabaya instructed his western platoons to hook around to the east and concentrate on the knoll surrounded by artillery bursts. The rebels pressed ahead, unmindful of the shells which landed among them and threw *Jihadis* around like dolls. Brillantes had foxed them, but for how long?

For the remainder of the day, small-unit engagements raged between the highway and the slopes of Fort Abdullatif. Rebel rockets and 40mm grenades passed each other in flight. Philippine Marine machine guns dueled with rebel RPDs. The Chechen-trained snipers attempted to engage the Marines beyond 500 meters but to their horror and surprise found their Dragunovs answered by accurate fire from hidden positions.

By the afternoon, Sabaya had run out of mobile reserves; his men were either in flight or dead. Fort Abdullatif was taken. The door to Abu Bakr was open.

When the forward elements from the Battalion Landing Team reached Brillantes' hill, they found the surviving naval Special Forces soldiers inside a small perimeter surrounded by a large number of dead enemy. Sabaya's men had realized their error too late. When they switched their attack to the opposite end of the ridge, the battle had already turned against them and they had to flee for their lives before they could destroy the OP. But only two men in the Special Operations Squad remained unwounded. Brillantes himself was lightly wounded, and nearly incoherent from exhaustion. Three critically wounded men lay in the center of the perimeter, in a gap formed by two rocks.

Bayani came up himself and called for a helicopter to evacuate the wounded men. But when minutes passed and no chopper came, Bayani ordered the radio operator to raise the Air Force control center and took the handset himself.

"Alpha 713, this is Col. Bayani. We have three urgent surgical WIA. Where is the helicopter? Repeat, where is the helicopter?" There were some seconds of silence on the other end of the circuit. Finally, the Philippine Air Force liaison came on.

"This is Alpha 713. Negative medical evacuation. Repeat. Negative medical evacuation. All helicopters are unavailable."

"What do you mean no helicopters are available?" Bayani asked incredulously. "We have men dying here."

"Our helicopters are currently being used by Vice-President Licban as VIP transport for a golf tournament in Zamboanga City. Repeat. Negative medical evacuation."

With an effort of will, Bayani remained calm and asked the controller to put him through to the Air Force commander-in-charge who was his roommate at the military academy. The commander's adjutant came on instead.

"Sir, Col. Lapida is out trying to rent a civilian helicopter with his own money. He told me he would steal one at gunpoint if there's anything to steal. That's the Colonel's message. Over."

"Over," Bayani said.

Bayani and Brillantes looked at each other and gave the orders to carry the wounded men to the nearest trucks. Brillantes walked beside the stretchers to keep their spirits up. He told them to hold on, to think of their families, their friends, their buddies, but by the time they loaded the blood-stained stretchers aboard the trucks, the men were too far gone from shock to hear anything at all. He stood on the road for a long time after the trucks had vanished down the road.

Two weeks later, Bayani and Brillantes attended the funerals held at the Philippine Marines base in Ternate, Cavite. The dead were mostly from dirt-poor backgrounds and their families sat awkwardly through the pomp and ceremony. Brillantes, still stiff from his stitches, sat beside Bayani. The President sent his regrets, which was just as well. Drunks did poorly at funerals.

A seven-year-old boy seemed confused by the ceremony around him. He stared mostly at his father laid out in his dress uniform in a coffin. He seemed to think that his father might actually get up until the soil began to be shoveled in around the coffin. Brillantes' final recollection of the event was of a child standing over his father's grave, crying "Daddy, Daddy!"

Having tended to the dead, Col. Bayani now turned to the living. In the period after the funerals, he pulled strings over the informal network of senior field grade officers to get Lt. Brillantes transferred to non-combat duty. He thought the junior officer had temporarily become too brittle for command. Soon enough, an easy joint posting was found with a Scout Ranger unit based near Manila. Unknown to Bayani, he had put Brillantes on a fateful collision course with Fortunas' election-stealing machinery. Instead of giving the brave officer a respite from danger, Bayani had actually dropped him into a vortex of intrigue.

Brillantes spent an uneventful year at the joint billet until shortly after the presidential elections, when the Scout Ranger unit received orders to saddle up for the city on an unspecified mission. The only thing that Brillantes thought was unusual was that the Scout Rangers were issued two complete units of fire, enough ammunition to last through a couple of days of intense combat. Why would they need that in Manila? But orders were orders, and so they headed into the capital loaded for bear.

When they got to the Senate Building, Brillantes assumed their mission was to guard the ballot boxes that were stored there. For the first few minutes, things appeared to move along those lines. They set up checkpoints and barricades, just as if on routine security. But at 2:00 in the morning, Presidential Assistant and Governor Johnny Fortunas arrived without fanfare and signed to the Scout Ranger commander who responded with a nod. Brillantes sensed something seriously amiss; he knew the mission was about to take an unwelcome turn.

As if by pre-arrangement, the commander ordered Brillantes to take all the men upstairs and remain there until further notice. Brillantes was stunned but obeyed without a word. He looked backward from the stairs in time to see a group of masked men entering from the side door carrying ballot boxes.

The Rangers remained upstairs until it was nearly dawn. Then their commander called them down individually to a back room. Each was handed a brown envelope and told to resume normal duties. They were to say nothing to their reliefs and return directly to barracks, where papers for a week's leave awaited them. When Brillantes walked out of the back room and opened the brown envelope he was handed, there were two hundred thousand pesos in crisp notes inside. That afternoon, everyone was told to go away and have a good time. Brillantes and one Ranger First-Lieutenant he knew from Camp Abu Bakr days were sickened to their stomachs. They decided to get drunk.

They went to one the most expensive nightclubs in Quezon City and tried to get totally soused. But try as they might, they stayed sober. The world sat, brooding, like a weight on their chests. Finally, the two men left the bar in the small hours of the morning and sat down on the sidewalk on Quezon Avenue, their spit-shined shoes in the gutter, paying no attention to the stream of dirty water gurgling around their feet. Even inebriated, they exuded such menace that the petty thieves who normally rolled drunks gave them a wide berth.

"What's the craziest thing we could do?" Brillantes asked.

"Rob a bank? Go back to Mindanao? Dunno, maybe we could bust Sabaya out of jail and ask him to a drink."

"I mean something even crazier than that."

The Ranger First-Lieutenant kept his mouth shut. He sensed where the conversation was going and didn't like it. He knew what Brillantes meant because the same thought had crossed his own mind. That didn't make it any less insane. But he knew that going directly against the bee that Brillantes had buzzing in his bonnet wouldn't work. So he tried another tack.

"What good would it do, sir?"

An itinerant vendor approached, offering them a basket full of peanuts and fried pork rinds. The two men shook their heads.

"Well, it wouldn't do any good at all but it would make me feel better," Brillantes said.

He took a sheaf of pesos from his pocket and began balling them up and throwing them into the middle of the road, one by one. A small crowd of vendors and vagrants gathered around them, too scared to make a move for the money but too greedy to leave it alone.

"Sir, that's nuts. I've got a better idea. Let's just take all this money," he counted out his own bills, "and give it to the men's widows and their orphans. Then, let's go to Mindanao. Come to think of it, I like it better back there."

"It's damned sight cleaner," Brillantes said, "in more ways than one." He looked up at the overcast sky. It had been a long time, he reflected, since anyone in smog-blanketed Manila had seen the stars.

"But I don't feel like going to Mindanao today. What I want right now is to go down to that five-star hotel by the US Embassy. Go spend some of this money on coffee there, real five-dollar-a-cup coffee. Maybe, do the breakfast buffet while I call my orderly and have him bring over a fresh uniform, a toothbrush and a bottle of mouthwash. I need to get all cleaned up."

The hotel, not coincidentally, was close to the Senate.

"Alright sir, I could use a five-dollar cup of coffee myself."

By mid-morning, Brillantes had sworn out a complaint before the Senate Blue Ribbon committee. He told them flatly that "I will testify that the ballot boxes were switched before the Electoral Tribunal met, because I saw them switched."

Brillantes' walk-in testimony touched off an immediate call for Licban's impeachment. The President brazened it out by suggesting the naval officer was suffering from post-traumatic stress disorder. But the senators wouldn't be stopped. The impeachment proceedings gathered momentum like a landslide working up to full force. The senators put Brillantes under protective custody and subpoenaed the Scout Ranger commander, who gave up Fortunas. The spotlight moved up the chain to the governor.

Then Brillantes heard that the governor had skipped on the subpoena. After a day of desperate searching, news came back that Fortunas had died suddenly on the plane to Sydney. Brillantes knew he would be next. He picked up the phone and called Col. Bayani.

"Colonel, Fortunas is dead."

"I know."

"Been nice knowing you."

"Don't tell me you've come all this way just to lie down and die," Bayani said. "The Brillantes I knew didn't quit – ever." Then he hung up.

LOOSE ENDS

Barcelon put away his cell phone after Alex Francisco rang off and reached into his drawer for another. The phone he produced was a cheap, disposable model of the kind sold in third-rate Manila shopping malls equipped with pre-paid SIMs. He punched in a number which was answered in a few rings by a special assistant in the Office of the President.

"Vicky. This is Rodolfo Barcelon. I just spoke to Alex Francisco."

"Did Fortunas say anything to him before he died?"

"No. They met briefly in the departure lounge. Fortunas apparently engaged in nervous small talk, which Alex thought strange but attached no importance to at the time. My assessment is that Alex suspects nothing. All the loose ends have really been tied up."

"I disagree. There's always a chance, no matter how small, that he knows something he's not sharing. We can't afford to take any chances in this matter. The stakes are too high."

Something in Barcelon rebelled at the sinister implication. For a moment, the younger version of himself – the young officer who had fought against the NPA in the 1960s, the Harvard Business School graduate and, later, the hardworking chief of Logistics Command – took over. "Don't be unreasonable. There's a point beyond which a cover-up creates more danger than it prevents. Don't start anything in Australia. It may lead to an investigation we can't control."

"All right. I'll convey your advice to **him**. But it's **his** decision. It's our professional duty to head off all threats to **him**."

Barcelon had been as much of an advocate for Alex as he dared, but the special assistant to the President had hung up. His opinion no longer mattered. What happened next was out of his hands. He extracted the SIM card from its slot in the disposable phone and put it in his pocket. He would ditch it on his way home. A SIM was the soul of a cell phone, the electronics which gave the device its identity. It was nice to know that phones had souls, he thought. That was more than he could say for some people he knew.

Bill Greer, who sat some six miles from Barcelon in a skyscraper by Manila Bay, knew all about cell phone souls. He had made a career out of subverting them to his purposes. Greer was assigned to provide intelligence support to the Joint Special Operations Task Force-Philippines. Officially, his job was to provide an assessment of threats to the mission. Unofficially, that meant spying on Filipino officials before they could create enough mischief to stop the show. To do that, Greer and his predecessors had developed a network of clandestine taps into all the phone providers in the Philippines. Practically any conversation of interest could be diverted in real-time for analysis. Just now, his software had been scooping up Barcelon's conversation.

Greer's monitor displayed a diagram of the intercepted message represented as a network diagram, consisting of circles and lines. The circles represented people or "nodes". They were connected to other nodes by lines called "edges", and the thicker the line, the heavier the communications traffic between the nodes. In short, the tangle of circles and lines was a map of who was talking to whom and how often. By looking at the diagram, Greer could see the network of political conspiracy at a glance. Some circles seemed connected to everything with the thickest lines. These were the "hubs"; in criminal terms, they represented the masterminds who gave the orders and made things happen.

At the center of the web was the President's office: the biggest hub, the origin and terminus of the biggest conspiracies. So many lines led to it that it looked like a monstrous tumor on Greer's computer display. It took Greer's analysts a considerable amount of time to disentangle and identify each of the many threads that went in and out of it. Then they named what each of the threads did.

Some nets were relatively innocent: channels to distribute patronage, channels to manage the system of bribes and kickbacks, the kind that supported dirty politics anywhere. But some networks were purely criminal: those that manage murder, blackmail and extortion. In there somewhere, Greer discovered, was the network dedicated to election cheating.

Greer gave that network his special attention because anyone who would try to steal a whole country would sooner or later become a problem to the Task Force. The election cheating network reported back to the President through a young woman whose modest title of Special Assistant belied her real importance. From her desk came and went a stream of encrypted phone calls and other electronic communications that Greer's intercepts sucked up, broke and analyzed.

After Brillantes' testimony to the Senate, something changed in the signal patterns. New channels were emerging to undertake a cover-up. The established murder and intimidation skeins began to merge into the cover-up thread. Not only had the cheating and murder nets come together, they had spread into places they had never gone before. A new line of message traffic opened between the Presidential Palace and an obscure travel agency in Paris, France. A check with the intelligence database listed the travel agency as a front for a criminal organization of indeterminate extent with connections throughout Southern Europe, Africa and the Middle East.

News that the star witness of the Senate investigation into the ballot box switch had died of cardiac failure on a plane to Sydney triggered a flurry of messages between the Palace and Paris. Greer knew something had been turned loose to silence whatever might lead back to the President. His immediate problem was that the cover-up threatened to destroy the work that the Joint Special Operations Task Force had taken so long to complete. President Licban was sure to go after Brillantes now and, without Fortunas to corroborate the naval officer's revelations, the Senate eventually would tire of protecting him and throw him to the wolves.

Greer knew that Brillantes' liquidation would touch off an officer's revolt among those in the Philippine Armed Forces who loathed

President Licban. When this revolt was put down, as it would be – the State Department would insist on it – the damage would undo everything the Task Force had worked so hard to build. All the elite units it had so painstakingly nurtured would be smashed, and smashed hard. Washington would never allow another Marcos. It would act to suppress any coup attempt against the "democratically elected" leader of an allied country. In the worst case, the Task Force itself might actually have to help President Licban destroy or capture the very men they had trained. It would be a nightmare of the first order.

Greer ground his palms against his temples. Somehow he had to find a way to stop the train wreck. That meant keeping the Senate investigation going. As long as it kept going, Brillantes would live. The problem was that the Senate had just run out of witnesses.

Fortunas had probably gone to Australia to hold something over Licban's head, something to prove the President was guilty, and thereby insure his survival. But they got to him before he could put his plan into action.

Did Fortunas reveal anything of the plan to Francisco? Greer re-read the transcript of the phone intercept between Dean Barcelon and Alex Francisco and realized that nobody had asked him the right questions. The real mystery was where Fortunas was going, because that is where the insurance policy was. Perhaps Francisco had the key and did not know it.

Francisco probably would not get the chance to remember. Greer knew that President Licban's special assistant had just sent an encrypted message to the travel agency in Paris. The message had not yet been broken, but he knew what it would say, from the context alone. It would be a death warrant for Alex Francisco.

A Bowl of Laksa

Alex looked at the three men heading toward him. From his left came Marvin Lee, a Singaporean professor who was once a Visiting Professor at the Institute in Manila. Marvin was also going to the conference and had asked Alex to split the cost of a rental car to Canberra. From the other direction came two men about six feet four inches in height and 250 pounds in weight, whose suit jackets and sunglasses could not hide the fact that their primary interests had little to do with business. Only five minutes had elapsed since Barcelon warned him that he would face trouble, and it was here already. It was a safe bet that the two bruisers heading his way were not only cops, but Australian Federal Police. Alex sighed to himself, kept his hands in full view, relaxed and turned to the two cops. They spoke first.

"We're from the Australian Federal Police. Are you Professor Alex Francisco?"

"I am," he answered. "What can I do for you?"

One of the two cops looked past Alex's shoulder at the approaching Singaporean, indicated him with a nod of his head, and asked, "Who's he?"

"Marvin Lee, a professor of business from Singapore," Alex answered matter-of-factly. "We worked together in the Philippines and were going to drive up to a conference in Canberra together."

Marvin opened his mouth to speak, looked at the men towering over him and decided to say nothing. Alex broke the awkwardness with some introductions.

"Gentlemen, this is Professor Marvin Lee from the Singapore National University. Marvin, these gentlemen are ..." he let his voice trail off so the cops could supply the rest.

"Wilkinson and Ward from the Australian Federal Police," the older one of the two answered. One of the cops stepped around Alex, flashed a badge with a seven-pointed star and asked the Singaporean to show him identification. Marvin showed him his passport.

"I hope nothing's wrong," he said.

"Nothing's wrong. We just want to ask Mr. Francisco here a few questions. I think you had better go on to Canberra without him. He may be delayed."

The cop's suggestion was more in the nature of a command, so Marvin bade a quick goodbye and hurried back the way he came.

"You don't mind walking to the office, do you? It's just a few blocks away," the older of the two cops told Alex. He had a florid, square face topped by male pattern baldness.

"Nope. I could use a walk."

The cops said nothing. They let him drag his suitcase behind him on its squeaky wheels and simply herded him along. The three continued a short distance down George Street, then turned left on Goulburn. In ten minutes, they reached a building that looked like a mirrored prison. It gave the impression of having no entrances or exits except for a pair of doors set into the ground floor of one of its shiny faces. They passed a security gate, deposited the luggage in a property bay and rode up an elevator – Alex made a mental note to call them "lifts" – that was the Australian word for them. They took him to a room with a single table. On it were an ashtray and a recording device.

"I'm Wilkinson," said the older of the two, "and this is my partner, Ward. I'll get to the point. We want to hold you here for a while to ask you some questions but we don't know the questions yet, so I can't say how long we want you to stay. The process can be easy or hard. If you stay voluntarily, you can save yourself the price of a hotel room in Sydney. If you don't want to stay, we'll have to charge you with something because otherwise we can't hold you. Once you're charged, it'll go on your record and follow you around the Interpol database like a bad penny. Now you're welcome to call a lawyer or your consulate, but I don't think you'll get much help from there."

"I don't think calling the consulate is such a hot idea either," Alex said. "So I think I'll save myself the price of a Sydney hotel room and cooperate. How's that, gentlemen?"

"You sound like a man of good sense, Professor Francisco."

"Glad you think so."

"Now what do you know about Mr. Johnny Fortunas?"

"That he was the governor of a province – which is between the size of a state and a county – in northern Luzon; that I knew him slightly in connection with a community forestry project I was working on; that he was a top adviser to the President of the Philippines. Anything else I got from the papers."

Alex had decided, after hanging up on Barcelon, that the only people he could trust were the Australian authorities. Despite an instinct never to trust cops of any kind, Alex was going to play it as straight as he could with the detectives.

"When did you speak to him last?"

"He came up to me in the pre-departure area in Manila."

"What did you talk about?"

"Oh, he told me it was better to take a plane up to Canberra than to drive. He recommended the food and wine here."

"What else?"

"Nothing else. The conversation was over in less than a minute. We boarded the plane, he was in First Class and I was in Economy. I was asleep back in the cattle car section when a flight attendant came up asking if I could help a sick passenger in First Class. She thought the Doctor in front of my name meant medical doctor. I told her to look for an M.D., not a Ph.D. She found somebody else who tried to help. I actually never left my seat to go forward."

36

The two cops were taking notes.

"So you never went near him on the plane?"

"Nope. And I'm sure you have ways to verify that. But it's a fact. I never came near him and simply learned from the rumors on the plane that a Filipino had died in First Class."

"Do you have your cell phone?"

Alex took it out and laid it on the center of the table. Ward took it wordlessly and stepped out the door. He came back fifteen minutes later without it.

"All right. We'll continue this interview later."

Alex guessed that they were analyzing his cell phone, running its calls through databases and looking through its memory. Maybe it would take a while. They escorted him to a slightly larger room with a smaller table and a hard brown sofa ranged along the wall. Five minutes later, a man with a fast-food meal and a drink arrived and laid them on the table. Wilkinson indicated a door leading to a toilet, "there's a gent's if you need it." Then, without waiting for an answer, he turned and went out the door to the corridor. It closed with an audible click. Alex had no doubt it was locked. He did not bother to try the handle.

He was alone. He got up and explored the toilet. It was windowless. A small ventilation grill in the ceiling exhaled a thin stream of cold air. He tried the taps. The left-hand faucet blasted out a torrent of extremely hot water. Alex, used to the anemic water systems in the Philippines, had to jump back until he could reduce the flow. He stripped to his shorts and wiped himself down with wet paper towels as best he could.

After putting his old clothes back on, Alex went out and methodically ate the hamburger and all of the French fries, including the ketchup that had been left on the table. He was remembering old habits, like the need to absorb all the calories on offer against eventualities. He threw the trash into a small plastic bin, but only after examining it for useful items like discarded metal forks or opened cans. There were none. He finished the fizzy drink that came with the meal, refilled the cup with cold water from the sink and drank two more glasses down. Now he was hydrated. After using his finger as a toothbrush, he gargled from the paper cup, then went back out to the sofa to sleep.

There was no light switch in the room so Alex faced the sofa backrest to block off the glare. He closed his eyes and focused on the hum of the air-conditioning as he tried to sleep. After some time, he seemed to hear a different air-conditioner, this time from a vibrating wall unit in a narrow, dark cell with a double-deck set of bunks to one side and a full-length wall of steel bars on the other. He was no longer on a sofa, but on an upper bunk with the low plywood ceiling only inches from his face. He could smell the dust and dirt wafting down from the plywood. His mind had drifted back more than thirty years to a far more fearsome cell, warded by jailors who didn't feed you hamburgers and didn't threaten you with prison.

Alex looked down at the man in the lower bunk, a dark wiry figure in his mid-40s. He was smoking a cigarette and reading a cheaply printed black and white pornographic magazine by the light that slanted through the bars. He set down the magazine and extended his hand to Alex, introducing himself as Mahmoud Medding and explained, as if Alex didn't know, that he was in for leading a half-dozen men in hijacking a domestic airline flight. Alex had read about it. Medding seized the aircraft and diverted it to Zamboanga City in Mindanao, hoping to barter the passengers in exchange for the release of a number of Muslim rebels held in Marcos jails. Medding returned to flipping through the pornographic magazine, appearing neither to hear nor mind the continuous succession of agonized screams that came through the wall across the narrow corridor beyond the bars. That was where "tactical interrogation" of prisoners was being conducted – with electric prods, wooden clubs, knives and heated pliers.

Alex thought about the hijacking. Marcos' security forces had riddled the jet while recapturing it and killed about a hundred passengers. By some ironic twist of fate, the dramatic Israeli commando raid on

Entebbe had recently taken place, giving the Marcos security establishment the unfortunate idea of trying to emulate the Israeli Defense Forces. The untrained troops rushed the airplane, firing from the hip on the assault, while Medding and his men poured out of the emergency exits to return fire from atop the wings and amid the landing gear. The result was carnage. Photographs of the airplane showed it burned from the window level to the cabin roof. No one except Medding and a few passengers survived. Alex lay back in the bunk and realized that if he was in the same cell as Medding then he was in "big-time" trouble. They had him pegged for a prize catch and were preparing to give him the treatment.

Alex knew the raid on his safe house had been no accident. He had just started organizing a new cell in the Quiapo district and was operating a mimeographing machine in a shack built in dead space between two buildings. To reach the shack required entering a rooming house on the opposite street and navigating a maze of stairs and corridors to reach the shack through a door in the back wall. It was completely concealed and should have been perfectly secure. Alex was changing a stencil when the door blew open and he was staring down the muzzle of two .45 caliber pistols.

Someone had tipped them off. That meant an informer in the new "Anna" circuit. As he lay in the upper bunk waiting for the cell door to open, Alex tried to think who the traitor might be, but the screams from across the corridor kept distracting him. He glanced down at Medding who appeared supremely unconcerned. He just kept flipping the pages of his magazine. Medding was as tough as they came, but Alex suspected another reason for his equanimity; the former hijacker had a lot of information to trade and maybe he had made up his mind to use it. Medding knew enough to turn what might otherwise be a very unpleasant experience into a lucrative deal. The good part about being the top man in a rebel organization was that you could sell a lot of people out. The small fry, on the other hand, had no one to sell down the river. Alex looked down at Medding reading his dirty book and wondered if there was a moral in there somewhere.

The cell door clanged open. Two men in short-sleeved khaki uniforms came in and took Alex down the corridor into Col. Bobadilla's office. The man behind the gray metal desk had a squat face and slanted eyes, looking for all the world like a Mongolian sadist from Central Casting. Bobadilla was in charge of M2, the premier counterintelligence force of the Marcos regime. The men pushed Alex into the brightly lit, air-conditioned room and pinioned his arms. The Colonel was reading Alex's dossier. A baseball bat studded with nails hung in a rack on the wall beside a picture of Bobadilla posing with President Marcos.

"Francisco," he said. "You are a reasonable man, an educated man. We've heard about you from other people we've interrogated and have been looking forward to meeting you. We know that you're not a Commie, in fact, the Commies rather hate you for reasons we don't completely understand. It would be a pity if we had to give you the Commie treatment when we might make common cause against people we mutually dislike. Throw in with us and tell us what you know." Bobadilla pushed his chair back until he was just under his spiky baseball bat. "We can be friends," he said.

They were offering him a deal. That's why he was in a cell with Medding. He was in with the dealers. It was an easy choice. Down one road lay the agony of electric prods and heated pliers. Down the other was a new identity, a steady income and eventual membership in an elite that could mete out life or death with impunity.

"You're right about my hating those Commies, Colonel. They're sanctimonious and slimy bastards. I hate them. There's only one problem."

Bobadilla looked at him slyly, waiting for the bargaining to start. He had heard all the requests: anonymity, money, a government position, drugs, maybe even a visa abroad. He was prepared, within reason, to accommodate them all.

"Tell me what the problem is so we can work it out."

"Problem is that I hate you more."

40

Bobadilla could hit like a truck. Alex barely saw the fist coming. The man sprang up like a Jack in the Box and gave him a right to the solar plexus. It doubled him over and dumped him on the floor. Bobadilla stood over him and barked out orders.

"Give him a medical examination and then take him to tactical interrogation. Give him the works. Francisco, I thought you were a smart man. But you are stupid, very stupid."

The two guards picked him up and dragged him down the hall to the military doctor's office. The doctor was part of the torture system. It was his job to certify that the prisoner was in good health before he entered the torture room and in good health after he left it. There were no medical instruments in his chambers, simply a rubber stamp, inkpad and a stack of forms which the doctor had already pre-filled except for the names, ages and descriptions of his patients.

The office was empty. The guards suddenly remembered it was the doctor's birthday, which meant he was standing free drinks at the cafeteria. Their faces cracked open in wide smiles. They let Francisco slump to the floor. They considered taking him back to the holding cell but decided there was no point. The whole building was a prison. They could just as well lock him in the doctor's office and come back for him later.

"Wouldn't want to miss the Doctor's birthday," one of the guards said. "We'll be back for you later so he can certify you're in good health. It's too bad you didn't take the Colonel's offer. But don't worry, you'll change your mind by the time we get to your middle fingers and you'll wonder why you bothered to hold back."

Alex heard the door click shut and the deadbolt thrust in place. He waited until the footsteps died away before moving, afraid that they were faking him out by pretending to leave. After some moments, he decided that they had really gone. He picked himself up from the floor and very silently rose to his feet. He did not try the door but pulled gently on the drawers of the steel desk, looking for a weapon – anything – that might help him escape. All the drawers were locked. Next, he examined the three steel filing cabinets against the wall. They

41

too were locked with a security bar across the front padlocked to a hasp welded to the top. Alex now looked for materials to improvise a weapon and die fighting. Even if they shot him dead, it would be better than the torture. He searched through the wastebasket, but it only contained a few papers. He upended the doctor's swivel chair, looking to pry out a length of stiff wire he could turn into an ice pick. The bottom of the chair had a big coil spring that buffered the backrest through a lever system, but it was too securely screwed in to pry out with his fingernails. In any case, the spring could never be straightened enough to make a weapon.

Alex leaned against the wall in despair. All he could do was hide behind the door and try to surprise the guards when they came back. He stood in the gloom of the doctor's office, listening to the wall air-conditioner hum as he racked his brain for ideas.

He stared at the air-conditioning unit vibrating in the wall.

He dashed up to it, ran his fingers around the edge and pulled off the front panel. With the cover off, he saw that the wall-mounted cooling unit was not welded to its frame, simply held in by screws with thumb-grips. Alex loosened them and pulled the unit inward. It shifted half an inch. If he could pull the air-conditioner all the way in, then he could exit through the hole it left in the wall. With his heart pounding, he gripped the inner edges of the air-conditioner and gave it a heave. A spray of rust flakes fell to the floor as it grated back. Alex continued to pull, hoping that a single continuous noise would be less noticeable than a series of screeching jerks.

The entire air-conditioner slid off the bracket and with the strength of youth augmented by adrenaline, Alex carried the still-running unit in his arms onto the doctor's upside-down swivel chair and laid it between the casters. He returned to the wall, half-afraid the unit's frame would have a grill welded around it, but it didn't. He pushed his head through the bottom of the bracket and looked out into the space behind the building.

Alex pulled himself head first through the opening and looked around. He was in a narrow, dark alley between the intelligence building and another structure. It was choked with leftover construction material that had never been cleared by the builders. The alley was closed over by overlapping roofs at an indeterminate height but the glow of a streetlamp at the end of the alley came down in a shaft of light at one end, silhouetting the barbed wire at the top of the ten-foot wall. That was the way out.

A pile of rubble at the base of the wall provided a perch from which to reach the bottom barbed-wire strand. He stepped back, took it at a run and leaped up, hardly feeling the barbs cut into his palms as he pulled himself over. With a quick glance to either side, he swung over the wire and dropped down on the other side. He was outside the M2 building but on one of the many roads which crossed the military base. He was clear of the inner jail; now for the outer one.

Putting his hands in his pockets to hide his bleeding palms, Alex walked with deliberate calm towards the eastern exit. If he could mix with the stream of civilian employees leaving the facility, he would be out on the city streets. As he got closer to the gate, he saw that a guard was checking the identification of civilian employees as they filed out. That was unusual. Was there some alert? Quickly abandoning his plan, he walked past the guardhouse and went along the road parallel to the perimeter wall. Alex knew it would not be long before Bobadilla's guards returned to the doctor's office and raised the alarm. He despaired of having come so far only to be recaptured.

Finally, he saw what he was looking for: a large mango tree growing reasonably close to the wall. He walked straight up to the tree and, without hesitation, used its lower branches to gain the fence. As he placed his feet on the wall, he heard a shout behind him. But Alex didn't look back, just dropped over into the civilian street. More shouts followed. Someone had seen him go over. By that time, he was walking as quickly as he could, without actually running, toward the streets of the surrounding Crame district.

"Hey, Francisco! Francisco!" The voice said his name over and over. Alex opened his eyes, turned and looked up at Wilkinson. He sat up and blinked at the two cops. They handed him his cell phone.

"You're free to go," Wilkinson said.

Alex was silent for a moment. Finally, he said, "What about all those questions you wanted to ask me?"

"The Philippine Consulate called and told us that after they got the coroner's preliminary report it became clear to them that Fortunas died from natural causes. They said they were sorry to have inconvenienced the Australian government."

"What time's the last train or bus to Canberra?" Alex asked.

The two cops smiled sardonically. "That left about four hours ago. It's the dead of night right now. There won't be a train leaving for Canberra till morning. Tell you what, we're driving up to Canberra. It's about three hours from here. How about we drop you off at your hotel? How lucky can you get? First a free night's stay in a famous Sydney address, then a free trip to Canberra in a cop car."

"Now if only you'd put me up in a Canberra jail cell, I could do the whole trip without spending a dime," Alex said.

"See," Ward said to Wilkinson, "I told you he's got no hard feelings."

Alex knew when a cop offered to let you go, you go while the going was good. As for the ride, it would save him the trouble of dragging his squeaky luggage through Sydney sidewalks until dawn, when the bus and train services restarted. He accepted the offer with genuine gratitude and, without realizing it, probably saved his own life. The two cops took him down the same elevator and pulled his bag from the property rack. It was in a slightly different position than he remembered and had probably been searched.

They went outside. He waited with Wilkinson out front while Ward went down to the basement parking garage and picked up a car, which turned out to be a four-door Holden. While they were waiting, Alex put in a call to the Rex Hotel. He told the front desk he had been delayed. Was his room still available? Yes it was, the hotel staff said. Very good then, Alex said, he would be in Canberra in four hours.

He put his luggage in the trunk, got in, and they drove southwestward for Canberra, the capital of Australia. There wasn't much to see along the way, just an endless ribbon of highway out the front and distant lights winking in the dark on both sides of the road. The Holden passed long-haul cargo trucks and a few automobiles on the road south. Occasionally they passed an island of brilliance, usually a rest stop with a fast-food outlet and rest rooms. The cops drove past them. It was two hours into the trip when Wilkinson looked back and spoke.

"We're going to get some *laksa*. We haven't had a proper feed and there's a place off the highway we can eat. You might want some too, because when we get to Canberra most of the cafes will still be closed." Alex nodded an OK. The Holden turned off past Lake George into a town called Beewong, a town settled by Chinese migrants attracted by the Victorian gold rush in the 1850s. More than a century later, a wave of Malaysian-Chinese migrants settled there, presumably because they felt more comfortable having Asian-looking neighbors. They brought with them the Straits cuisine and when some of them set up restaurants, they started selling the spicy soup called *laksa*.

In no time at all, Beewong became the *laksa* capital of Australia. The stew of vegetables, seafood and meat in a spicy coconut cream broth became extremely popular throughout New South Wales. Eventually, Beewong followed the time-honored Australian tradition of building a giant symbol of the town's main industry in the town square. Coff's Harbour had a 24-foot-long concrete banana on the town's main street. Tully in Queensland featured a giant concrete facsimile of a rubber boot. Nimbin, the hippie capital of Australia, prominently displayed a 33-foot-long marijuana joint. So Beewong had a 30-foot-high *laksa* bowl, complete with neon steam and a flashing soup spoon, marking the city limits.

The cops parked the car in front of an all-night *laksa* joint owned by a middle-aged Asian woman. Without looking at the menu they ordered the seafood *laksa*. Alex simply asked for the same. As he waited for the stew, Ward leaned back, put a toothpick in his mouth and checked his parked car through the window. The streets were empty as far as he could see.

"Where are you staying in Canberra?" Wilkinson asked.

"The Canberra Rex, I guess. I had a room reserved there."

"LBJ stayed in that hotel you know."

"Who?"

"Lyndon Baines Johnson. The American President back in the 1960s. He was in Canberra to talk about the Vietnam War with Prime Minister Harold Holt."

"Must be a pretty good place then."

"There's better now. But it's still a decent place. LBJ's room's on the fourth floor. There's a plaque in the corridor commemorating his stay."

"Betcha somewhere in Mexico there's a motel door with Oswald's name on it," Alex replied.

Ward looked at Wilkinson and said, "Say, this guy's got a strange sense of humor. I'm starting to wonder if it's okay to turn him loose."

Just then the bowls of *laksa* arrived, full of coconut-thickened broth, little yellow pieces of tofu, bits of seafood and assorted vegetables. The two detectives dug in. After a few minutes, Wilkinson burped and made an effort at small talk.

"Okay, Francisco, this is off the record. Do you think this Fortunas was bumped off?"

Alex knew that nothing was ever off the record with cops. But they were giving him a free ride after all, so he owed them a conversation.

"I guess he knew a lot of dangerous people," Alex said.

"So he wasn't a toff, you know, quality, being a governor and top adviser to the Philippine President?" Ward asked.

"The Philippines is a place where you bust out of jail and into the Presidential Palace to lead a life of crime," Alex said.

46

"Where do you fit in with all this?" Wilkinson asked.

"I don't. I'm small potatoes. A bystander in a game I don't know anything about and don't want to know anything about."

Wilkinson got up and motioned for the bill. They split the tab up three ways and headed out the door for the Holden. As he walked to the car, Alex felt a prickling along the hairs of his nape that made him glance over his shoulder, but the main street of Beewong seemed empty in the darkness, at least what he could see of it in the narrow pool of the street lighting. He dismissed his unease and told himself that he was with two cops and perfectly safe. Still, the disquiet remained.

"Come on, let's go," the older cop said as they reached the Holden. Alex got into the backseat and once they drove away the creepy feeling left him. In a short while, the car sped down a road with a dark plain to the left and the beginnings of hills to the right. The highway climbed into Canberra. A high tower above a tall hill blinked in the dark above the capital city as they cruised down Northbourne Street. The Holden drove up the entry ramp of a medium-sized hotel a mile shy of the city center. "Here's the Rex," Ward said. The two watched Alex pull his luggage out of the back and into the revolving doors of the Rex Canberra. They waited until the figure in the cheap suit jacket vanished into the lobby.

"Do you think he knows anything?" Ward asked.

"No. I think he's just as puzzled as we are. What bothers me about him is he's the kind that wants to find out what's going on."

SMALL WORLD

Bill Greer watched his display show the pressure building up in the conspiracy network. One of the lines on his wiretapping network diagram showed red. He clicked on the line and a window opened, showing the latest cell phone intercepts. Brillantes was panicking now that Fortunas was dead. He had stopped trusting the men assigned by the Senate Sergeant-at-Arms to guard him. He had replaced the official bodyguards with former soldiers who were personally loyal to him. Greer sighed. It was starting already. He moved his mouse to another red line and selected it. More bad news.

Other wiretaps showed Brillantes' former service academy classmates contacting high-ranking officers who were sympathetic to his cause. They were also convinced that President Licban would liquidate Brillantes next. Although none of this was surprising, the speed at which the sides were squaring off was alarming. Unless he could find a way to head it off, a showdown between the younger officers and the Philippine President was certainly in the works.

Greer finished the draft of a plan he hoped would avert the impending catastrophe. He saved the PowerPoint briefing, folded his laptop under his arm and went down two floors to the office of Col. David Maxwell, commander of the Joint Special Operations Task Force-Philippines. Maxwell had asked him for a plan and he was going to get it.

Greer put the laptop on Maxwell's desk, switched it on and walked him through the slides, bolstering each key point with verbal excerpts from intercepts. Maxwell sat through the briefing without saying anything except for the odd clarificatory question. Then came the final slide. Greer said nothing and let the graphic speak for itself. Maxwell looked at it carefully for nearly half a minute. Then he wrote on a pad. "Let's discuss this outside the building at ...". A time and address were provided. Greer nodded. Maxwell tore out the sheet as Greer headed for the door. The Colonel balled it up and put it in his pocket.

The two men arrived a few hours later at a small wooden dock on the South Harbor, four blocks from the American Embassy. From it a small
48

tour boat owned by a retired Navy Seal took sightseers out on the harbor in the evening cool, but now the little party had rented it for themselves. They hopped across the gangplank and the boat cast off. The ex-SEAL remained forward in the pilothouse and left the men undisturbed aft, where a small table had been set up. In minutes, they were chugging through the turbid water of Manila Bay.

The little boat made six knots on a north-south racetrack course between the Yacht Club basin and the Manila Hotel landing. The wind over the deck brought some relief from the heat. There was a Styrofoam cooler of bottled iced tea near the chairs. Each man grabbed one. Maxwell then nodded to Greer who started the ball rolling.

"The purpose of this plan is to prevent a confrontation between the Philippine Special Forces community, who we have trained for the purpose of fighting Islamic rebels, and the President of the Philippines, who the State Department will support no matter what. President Licban can't be allowed to derail the Senate investigation by killing off its witnesses. The question before us is how to do that without getting involved ourselves."

"Can't we just turn over our communications intercepts to the Senate? Can't we just tell them that we know Licban cheated?" Maxwell asked.

"No," Greer said, "we would be compromising our intelligence sources and methods. Moreover, wiretap info would be inadmissible in the Philippine Senate investigation. Finally, it would be an admission that we've been spying on President Licban all along, which we have. The fact that anyone with half a brain would watch that snake is self-evident but diplomatically incorrect. No, we can't tell them. What's left is to keep this guy Alex Francisco alive in the hope he can lead the Senate investigators to Fortunas' 'insurance policy' so they can discover the facts for themselves. But that won't be so simple."

Greer continued. "Let's examine how Licban plans to off Francisco. The special assistant to the President has been in contact with an agency in Paris we think is a front for contract killing. We intercepted signals from Paris to an IP – a computer address – in Australia which is assigned to a wireless broadband provider. They are sending messages to their hit man's laptop in Australia. We haven't decrypted the actual messages yet – we will, eventually – but we can guess from the context what it says."

"It says knock off Francisco, right?" Maxwell said.

"Yep. That's my guess."

"So, can your unofficial helper get to Francisco in time?" Maxwell asked.

"There's a chance, if we decide to bring him into the picture now. Francisco is in the temporary custody of the Australian Federal Police." Maxwell shook his head in disbelief. Greer spied on everyone, ally and enemy alike. Greer went on, "he'll be safe until they release him, which could be as early as tomorrow. But once he's out on the street, the bad guys will eventually get him."

"Who is this guy you want to bring in to help Francisco evade?" Maxwell asked.

Greer hesitated for a moment, as if trying to find the right words for a difficult subject.

"Ramon Delgato is a computer programmer in Sydney, Australia, but that as you would say is his 'day job'. He's mostly known as an author on the Internet, which is how I got to know him. He writes on information warfare, military history and current affairs – all based on open source, of course. But he's talented in that way. No intelligence connections or access to classified information, yet he writes well enough to attract an audience of about 10,000 readers a day. That's a lot of readers, as much as a small newspaper. He was in the Middle East recently for a series of workshops on the Hezbollah."

"A guy like that must have history. Computer programmers don't suddenly start writing about terror groups from nowhere."

"Oh, he has some history – and sort of the right kind of education. He went to Harvard for public policy and Case Western for applied math. But I think most of his intuitive understanding of – " Greer swept his
50

arm around to indicate everything around the table, "the universe we inhabit – comes from the time he spent in the anti-Marcos underground. Which brings us to the strongest reason for bringing him in. He knows Alex Francisco personally. That's crucial. Anyone else we might send would have to establish his bona fides. But Ramon Delgato already has his confidence. They were contemporaries in the anti-Marcos underground."

A brief smile crossed Maxwell's face, then he frowned. "It's good in one way but bad in another. It sounds like Delgato's been around the block. So we'll have to tell him something close to the truth. Then maybe he won't like the risks. What makes you so sure he'll agree once he knows the odds?"

"Because he's the type – the type that won't walk away when his friends are in danger because it goes against his own self-image. Personally, I would trust him," Greer said, "because he likes being trustworthy. We used to have a word for guys like that, but we don't use it any more. So we tell him the basic facts. He'll guess most of it anyway. Accounts of the election-stealing controversy and Fortunas' death are all over the papers. It'll be obvious why someone would be gunning for Alex Francisco. The main problem will be explaining who I'm working for and why we want to stop it."

Greer paused briefly, then continued.

"I think Delgato already knows I'm working in some capacity for US intelligence. At the conferences and workshops where we've met, we'd drink into the night. Everyone pretty much signals in broad terms who they work for. Keeps the boundaries marked. He's seen me with Embassy people and uniformed members of the military intelligence. So he's guessed."

"Would he have a problem working for the United States?" Maxwell asked.

"On the contrary," Greer answered, "he wouldn't do it otherwise."

"OK," said Maxwell, "that's all good. Still he's just a talented amateur. What realistic chance does he have of stopping professional killers? The diplomatic protection people and the Secret Service don't always succeed against them. How could this Ramon Delgato go up against the opposition?"

"For one, his job is simpler. He just needs to warn Francisco and get him to lie low until we can get him out and interviewed by the proper people. I think that's within reasonable expectation."

Maxwell looked at Greer. "OK. I think we should give it a try. There's no alternative right now. Make the approach. But honestly, if I were him, I wouldn't take the job."

That was the go-ahead Greer was waiting for. He fired up his laptop and connected via his secure wireless connection. "I'll raise him now by instant messaging. Delgato uses a secure IM client with a 192-bit AES encryption. He knows his stuff. There are benefits to being a computer programmer."

NIGHT RIDE

The eight-year-old boy was watching his father draw a cartoon tomcat. Ramon Delgato penciled in a couple of bent whiskers on either side of the pouchy upper lip and drew in a triangular nose.

"Daddy. Did you see any alley cats in Lebanon?"

"Not as many as I thought. But one night while I was walking back to my hotel in a drizzle, I saw this cat sitting in a windowsill just looking at me. And you wonder what they're thinking. Probably never the same thing for long; cats are always changing. Sometimes, they're angry or sleepy. At still other times, they're playful. They're like the face of the sea; never the same twice. But there's something about cats that's unchangeable. You know this when they sit on your lap."

"The cats you draw always look like they're thinking, but thinking in a cat way." The boy looked at the drawing.

"Well, what's the cat I'm drawing thinking now?"

"About alley-cat things, drinking from puddles, eating out of garbage cans. Running from scary strangers. Yet the cats in your drawings look hopeful, like they were expecting something wonderful to happen."

Just then, a beep sounded from one of the wireless computer speakers on the bookshelf.

"Excuse me, son, but somebody's calling me on the computer."

Delgato went down the narrow stairs leading from the living room to a small basement studio that served as a home office. Against one wall was a sofa-bed he used when working all-nighters. A 27-speed bicycle hung front-wheel up on brackets against the other wall. Shelves surrounded a computer work bay where a huge monitor sat in front of a rack full of humming equipment and peripherals. At one end of the room, a small door led to the outdoor parking lot.

A pop-up instant messaging window was blinking in the corner of the monitor accompanied by an insistent beep that came over the speaker. He saw from the ID that the message was from Bill Greer. Delgato accepted the connection and typed a greeting in the IM window.

Ramon: Hi, Bill. What's up?

Bill: Alex Francisco is in trouble. You know him from the old days. Can you help him out?

The words hit with the force of a hammer. Delgato sat up in his chair and pulled it closer to the monitor. It was the first time Greer had ever crossed the invisible line between civilian life and the secret world. They had always lived by the watchword of "ask me no questions and I'll tell you no lies". Now, by mentioning Alex Francisco and asking for operational help, Bill was breaking the cardinal rule. This wasn't Bill, the friend, calling. It was Bill the spook, telling Ramon that not only did he know about his past, but that he was proposing a mission. One that involved an old friend nobody was supposed to know about.

Ramon: I'm listening. Fill me in.

Bill: Alex Francisco's in Sydney, off the same plane Johnny Fortunas died in. I believe – trust me on this – that Fortunas was bumped off because he was going to prove Licban stole the election. But it's not over. The same people who knocked off Fortunas think he may have told Alex something before he died. They don't know what or even if Fortunas told him anything at all, but they are going to get him all the same, just to make sure. Is it OK to continue this conversation or should we end it here?

Ramon: Go on. I'm listening.

Bill: Here's the proposition. Can you warn him? Keep his head down. We want to help him, but can't right now. I hope at some point he can be brought in but for a couple of weeks at least he needs to disappear until we can organize the cavalry.

Ramon: Who's after him?

Bill: An undetermined number of contract killers, probably no more than three, from a European hit agency.

Delgato could hear his son upstairs talking to himself as he filled in the cartoon cat in pinks and grays. The ordinary domestic sounds seemed suddenly amplified. There was his wife talking to her sister on the phone upstairs. There was even the whir of the computer cooling fan. The sounds of the normal world where people worked weekdays, watched TV evenings and went to barbecues on weekends were talking to him, telling him something. And so was the IM window blinking in messages from another world. A place where it was normal to go without names, reasons or permanent addresses, where violence and conspiracy were commonplace. That blinking cursor was inviting him back to the other side. And all that separated the two worlds was a "yes" on the keyboard. Ramon needed to know more.

Ramon: Call in the Australian Federal Police.

Bill: We can't. Not even unofficially. Not until the guys in Washington make up their minds. You're Alex's only chance under the circumstances, but I wouldn't blame you if you refused. It's too much to ask of anyone.

Ramon laughed to himself. Bill Greer had him over a barrel and knew it. It was an impossible dilemma. If he got involved the danger could spread to his wife and son. But he couldn't walk away. Could he still face it? He wasn't twenty anymore, with a toothbrush in his pocket, a .38 in his waistband and the whole world to hide in. No. He was a middle-aged man whose son was upstairs coloring in a cartoon cat's nose in pink.

Ramon: Where did you get the intel on the 'old days'? You owe me that much. Because if you know, then someone else might know too and I would be the wrong man for the job.

Bill: After George Schultz convinced Ronald Reagan to warn Marcos off using force against the rising in February 1986, a contingency plan was put into effect to secure all the files of Marcos' secret police. Ronald Reagan was atoning for the sins of the past. So he deserved an absolution. That meant all the files which might connect US military assistance to the old regime had to disappear along with the Marcos government. The night Marcos flew out of Manila to Hawaii, a team was inserted into Manila to clean out every intel archive we knew about. They shipped it to Washington. So we're the only guys who can connect Alex and yourself. Your files are with us and nowhere else.

Ramon: My life's going to depend on that being absolutely true, Bill. And my family's too.

Bill: You have my word, Ramon.

Without meaning to, Ramon had fallen back into the dark like a drunk falling off the wagon.

Ramon: Okay. I'll do it. Where is he? What support can you provide?

Bill: Alex is currently being questioned by the Australian Federal Police. But we believe he will soon be released. Sit tight until we give you definite info on his whereabouts. But get ready to move. The article you sent to the Duodecagon Review will be overpaid. You'll get $5,000 for it. It'll help with expenses. Point of contact will be this IM.

Maxwell followed the IM exchange over Greer's shoulder. The Colonel looked down at the words on the laptop screen, shifting his balance as the little tour boat did another turn on its racetrack leg.

"I like him," Maxwell said.

Greer closed the exchange. "So do I. So let's work on convincing the powers that be to bring the professionals in. Because you're right, he's just an amateur and only the real cavalry can level the field."

Thousands of miles away in Sydney, Ramon ended the IM session and pushed the swivel chair away from the desk. He paused to consider the risks and knew the biggest risk was himself. He had to impose an uncompromising sense of reality on this task. There was no room for careless action or slipshod planning. Above all, he had to guard against the subconscious desire to turn this into a last hurrah, the final adventure of a middle-aged man, a parting adrenaline fix made the more intense by the knowledge that the adrenaline itself would soon be gone. That desire could cloud his judgment and end his life, his family's and Alex's too. There was no pity, no forgiveness in the world beyond the computer screen.

56

So, it was first things first. He went into the little basement bathroom and locked the door. He picked up the pot of plastic flowers in the bathroom corner. From the hollow bottom, he extracted a bundle wrapped in plastic. He put the fake potted plant back and took the heavy plastic bundle to his desk drawer and locked it. Then he went to his closet and pulled out a medium-sized dark-green nylon backpack.

Into it went his "poor man's Leica", a heavy, black metal digital camera about the size of a deck of cards with a high-quality, 5x zoom lens. Next went a pair of Nikon 8x25 binoculars and a small waterproof Global Positioning System unit. It was April, which in Australia meant fall, so atop the GPS went an extra pair of thermal underwear and a long-sleeved Polartec shirt. A toothbrush, small sponge, a pair of sunglasses and a six-inch folding knife went into the side pockets. He paused for a second to think and added a pocket-sized illustrated field guide to Australian birds he had on the bookshelf to the pack.

Opening the drawer, he took out the most important piece of equipment of all: a very thin laptop with an 11-inch screen. It had a black carbon fiber shell, a solid-state hard disk and a broadband device. It would run for 18 hours on the battery and a spare. With hardly any moving parts, it would survive anything short of a beating with a sledgehammer. The broadband device would connect to the Internet anywhere cell phone service was available. A small booster antenna, extra battery, and an AC charger went into a Ziploc sealed plastic envelope. He laid it in the backpack, so that the laptop would lie flat closest to the back.

Ramon ran up the stairs and sat down on the living room sofa for a few minutes to compose his wits before knocking on the bedroom door. His wife, Rina, had to be told.

He had proposed to her on the Peak in Hong Kong four years before the Chinese takeover. They met through mutual friends on one of her annual visits to her family in Manila. She had been an editor for a major international trade magazine based in Hong Kong and he a consultant to the peace negotiations between the Muslim rebels in

Mindanao and the post-Marcos government. They were as different as night and day.

Rina Pedrosa was the most honest and level-headed person Ramon had ever met. Clear-eyed and grounded, she kept Ramon focused on the things that mattered. When he regaled her with dramatic accounts of his adventures in Mindanao, she was unimpressed.

"The peace negotiations are a farce," she said. "You've said so yourself. And you're not achieving anything, just collecting one hair-raising story after another. If you were a journalist or maybe a politician, you could make something of it, but you're not even interested in any of these. One day you'll look back and find that real life has passed you by, that the years had run through your fingers like sand. Time to cut loose.

"Work is real, Ramon. Life is real, even if it's not dramatic. You just have to believe that it matters. What was it Cardinal Newman wrote? 'I have my mission. I may never know it in this life, but I shall be told it in the next. I am a link in a chain, a bond of connection between persons. Therefore, I will trust Him, whatever I am, I can never be thrown away.' Newman was a poet, you know, apart from being a cardinal."

He saw that she was right. The bravado that had kept him going through the underground days had degenerated into a form of blindness. The old days had really ended. They stopped when Marcos fled the palace. Now it was time to stop living in the past and get on with the present. When he finally proposed – which she accepted, much to his surprise – she urged him to get away and start a new life.

Now he was about to tell her that his bad old life was back. He rose from the sofa and knocked on the bedroom door before opening it. Rina had finished talking to her sister and had her back up on some pillows while reading a book. One look at him and she knew something serious was afoot. He took a deep breath and gave it to her straight. She listened without interrupting until he finished.

"Well, I knew this would happen," she said. "When you started writing on the Internet, and getting invitations to the Middle East, or getting requests to write all those articles about terrorism, I swear you began to bloom. You should have seen yourself. Deep in my heart, I knew it would never stop there. You see, I've known all along that while you love me and your son very much, there was a part of you that wanted to be someplace else."

He was struck by the bare-knuckled truth of it. There was nothing he could say in his defense. All he could say was, "I never went looking for trouble."

"You didn't go looking for trouble, but you always made sure that trouble knew where to find you," was Rina's riposte.

Suddenly, Rina changed her tack. "Go on, Ramon. I'm not so heartless as to let your friend die. Nor am I so stupid as to not realize that you're the best person to warn him. Go, darling, and do your best. But there's just one thing."

"What is it?" Ramon asked, suddenly nervous.

"Since it's the school holidays, I'm going with your son to visit my sister in Arizona. I want to be out of the way when you decide to waltz around with these killers. You can run whatever risks you want, but it's not a good idea to put our son in danger. Besides, if we're in Arizona, you will have less to worry about."

It made perfect sense. Ramon could think of nothing to say but thanks.

Rina called the travel agency and told Ramon to help their son pack some clothes into a travel bag. Mother and son were long asleep when the computer speakers beeped again. Ramon rose fully clothed from the sofa and saw the IM window winking in the dark. Greer was on again.

> **Bill:** The Philippine consulate has told the Australian Federal Police they have no further interest in Alex Francisco. Just now Alex has called the Rex Hotel saying he will be checking-in in about four hours. So he's released and somebody must be driving him up as there is no other way he can get there at this time of night. It's likely the police are giving him a lift or have

arranged for someone to do so. That's good news because it's unlikely anyone will make a move on him with the cops around.

Ramon: I'm heading off to Canberra now. Wish me luck.

He signed off on IM and unlocked the drawer, opened the plastic bundle and extracted from it two snub-nosed .38 Smith and Wesson revolvers and ammunition. He wiped off the protective grease and put both into the outer pocket of his green backpack. Finally, he put a pair of motorcycle pants and jacket over his street clothes, took a helmet off the rack and stepped out the back door. A dark blue 650 cc motorcycle was on its stand beneath the protection of the balcony overhang. The backpack went into the top box. Before mounting the motorcycle, he looked up at the darkened windows of his small apartment and wondered when or whether he would see it again. He switched on the electronic ignition and, noting the motor was running smoothly, pulled around into the street and set out on the 150-mile road to Canberra.

THE PERFECT COUPLE

The pair thought of themselves as surveillance professionals, not assassins. From a technical point of view, they were right. Pierre and Monique were a couple in their early 30s who specialized in setting up people for the kill. Most of the time they did nothing so crude as actually shoot or stab. As a rule, only those unfortunate enough to interrupt them at their work were killed and that hardly counted for enough to alter their job description.

From time immemorial, the trade in murder followed the same pattern. Watchers paved the way for the killers. Surveillance carefully examined a target's habits and vulnerabilities and once a chink in the victim's armor had been found, the actual hit men moved in with their lethal tools.

Finding vulnerabilities was the couple's job but, like all apprenticed tradesmen, they knew every aspect of the business. They were perfectly competent with firearms and unarmed combat as they were planting listening devices or torturing people for information. On very rare occasions, when an opportunity was too good to pass up, they even performed the wet-work themselves. Mostly they stayed unnoticed, waiting and watching. For this reason, they usually traveled unarmed though, when necessary, they could turn nearly anything into a lethal weapon – table knives, steel wire, ordinary tools, ashtrays, sculpture or jars, even bedsheets or bathroom toiletries. Once, an elderly security guard stumbled upon Monique as she was watching a target's country home from behind some bushes. The guard's eyes were still widening in surprise as she pushed the length of a ballpoint pen into his eyeball.

At the moment, Pierre and Monique were at the Westin Hotel in Sydney awaiting instructions. Their job had been to observe and verify the death of Fortunas. That had been completed and now they were looking forward to some time off.

Pierre was leafing through a pile of brochures of dive resorts in the Maldives. He loved brochures. They were practically all that he read.

61

He was an avid and discriminating consumer and would do extensive research first before he bought anything. For now, his attention was focused on resorts.

He looked at pictures of the enticingly named "water villa suites". These were resorts built out into a lagoon, the priciest of which were like palaces rising magically out of the tropical ocean, each with a series of pools, sea grottos, rooms and balconies, all connected by elevated pathways, and serviced by staff trained to be almost invisible. There were also beach-front villas with private docks from which dive boats went out to sea. The daily room rates began at a thousand dollars but this did not seem to bother Pierre in the least.

He drew three columns on the pad in front of him and meticulously listed out the features of each resort, comparing them point-by-point. There were check marks and crosses along each row.

"I am comparing the beach-front ones with the water villa suites," he said to Monique. "The beach-front ones have a lower rate but aren't really a bargain because they overcharge on the dive facilities. They make the room seem cheap, but actually make it back on the boat. If you add everything up, it actually costs five dollars more than the water villa."

"What's five dollars, more or less, when you are talking about a resort charging more than a thousand dollars a day?" said Monique.

"I don't like to be cheated," Pierre said, "it's the principle of the thing. Building up wealth is a matter of watching the little things. Which reminds me, when we get back to France, let's look at the possibility of installing a solar water-heating system on the east roof. The real-estate broker said we can increase the resale value of the house by adding eco-amenities."

Pierre and Monique traveled as journalists for Ultimaventura Europe, an online magazine for extreme sports aficionados such as rock-climbers, hang gliders or wingsuit flyers. Their "work" gave them the perfect excuse to nose around, take photographs and ask questions. Anyone who checked would find Ultimaventura to be a fully functional online magazine with a respectable amount of Internet traffic. But only an accountant with access to its advertising revenues would realize that the little magazine could hardly support their extensive travels.

Sports journalism was not the real business of Ultimaventura. Murder was. It was owned through cut-outs by an Uzbek entrepreneur named Nuriddin who had connections to Russian intelligence. Nuriddin's early career consisted of match-fixing and crooked gambling, including once fixing an event at the Summer Olympic Games. Then he moved on to bigger business. Although nominally a citizen of France, the Uzbek maintained close links to Russia, particularly its organized crime and state security agencies. Ultimaventura was the front for his latest business venture: high-end contract killing, usually for clients in Asia and Africa.

Monique thought back to the flight with Fortunas. She sat one row diagonally behind him in First Class, watching him eating everything on offer and swilling one glass of wine after the other. About six hours into the flight, Fortunas began to wheeze. At first, he attempted to wipe the mucus that trickled down his nostrils with a tissue. Then, increasingly distressed, he began to slump back in his seat. In a minute, he vomited up his dinner on his shirt. Monique called the stewardess, then turned to Pierre and whispered, "The greasy pig is starting to die. I just hope it isn't too disgusting."

Fortunas began to convulse, losing control of his bowels. A fecal odor permeated the cabin. The crew realized the gravity of the situation and began to search for a doctor. A muscular man with a buzz cut Monique intuitively sensed was military came to the First Class section with the stewardess. She shrank back in her seat to avoid notice. The stewardess brought up what looked like a small suitcase. While the medic stripped off Fortunas' jacket and laid him out on the aisle, the stewardess opened the case and took out an electronic device with a green and orange button on it. The man detached two pads from it, placed one pad on the upper right chest of Fortunas and the second pad on his left ribcage. After checking Fortunas' airway to see that it was clear, the medic pushed the orange button and sent a powerful electric shock through the victim's heart. To no avail. The medic tried again, and again, and again. Finally, he gave up. Monique watched while the medic, with the assistance of the crew, carried Fortunas' corpse into the galley area and covered him with a blanket. Pierre and Monique took note: Johnny Fortunas – politician, tycoon, racketeer, beauty contest judge, and election fraudster – was dead.

Monique mentally noted the time and details for her report. Not for the first time she congratulated herself on her career choice. Like all killers, she worked in a manner of speaking for a very ancient and special client. Being a minister of death was the last cool priestly vocation of a secular age, she thought. A Europe that had lost its belief in God had not yet lost its awe of Death.

Right after leaving the security area at Sydney's Kingsford Smith International Airport, Pierre sent a prearranged signal of mission completion over his cell phone to a Paris telephone number. It was relayed almost immediately to the Office of the Special Assistant to the President of the Philippines. Normally that would have been the end of it, but not this time. Subsequent analysis of the security camera footage at Manila's international airport showed the victim talked to one Alex Francisco long enough to constitute a potential problem. But the couple were as yet unaware of these developments and took a taxi directly to the Westin where they had booked a room in case they had to support a follow-up attempt that now seemed unnecessary. The job seemed over, the case closed.

Pierre was halfway down his checklist of dive resorts when his cell phone beeped. A text message from Paris instructed them to initiate encrypted communication on their laptop. He turned on the laptop and the words running across the bottom of the IM window ended any hope of a dive holiday. Something had come up.

> **Base:** The client believes the target may have passed unspecified information to economy passenger Alex Francisco before take-off. You will eliminate Francisco in place of the contingent follow-up. Current rates apply.

Pierre was surprised. Paris must think it urgent if they had been switched from the surveillance role to hitmen. He typed back.

P: What weapons will be provided?

Base: No weapons will be required. Target is about fifty-two years of age, a civilian with no known military training. Improvised weapons should be adequate. Dossier follows with whereabouts.

P: Acknowledged.

Pierre showed the IM message to Monique. "I think our holiday will have to wait a few days. Paris thinks Fortunas might have told someone his secret before dying. Some passenger on the plane."

"Fifty-two years old? Academic? Piece of cake," she said.

"A middle-aged soft target. You can have fun with this one. His dossier is downloading now."

The dossier was disappointingly vague. The photographs showed a middle-aged man in fairly good physical condition standing in front of a blackboard. Another photo showed him wearing a short-sleeved shirt and dark pants at what looked like a Christmas party. He was described as "a professor of management" at the Business Institute of Manila with a Ph.D. from Cornell University. "Currently Francisco is booked at the Rex Hotel in Canberra and scheduled to attend a conference on forestry."

Under "Other Background" was written: "Believed to have been active in the anti-Marcos underground between 1972 and 1986, but details are unknown." This last entry bothered Pierre. What did Francisco do in the underground? Maybe he was not as "soft" a target as they thought. He would send an email to Paris asking for more details. The target's current whereabouts is the Sydney headquarters of the Australian Federal Police, 110 Goulburn Street, Sydney. "He is being questioned pursuant to a request by the Philippine Government to pin him down. They will withdraw their request tonight after which the police are expected to let him go."

Monique, who was looking over Pierre's shoulder, spoke up.

"Well, let's get moving. All we have to do is watch the Federal Police headquarters and wait for him to come out."

Pierre nodded in agreement. He sent an email formally accepting the job and shut down his laptop. The pair grabbed their equipment and went downstairs. Both knew Sydney well. It would be far easier to walk to Goulburn than to look for a taxi in the city. As they walked, the pair checked if their cell phones worked over the local network. In fifteen minutes, they were at the Australian Federal Police building on Goulburn Street.

Monique took up position at a café with a view of the building entrance. She had a wireless headset for her phone over which she said to Pierre. "I'm in position to watch the entrance. Now go rent a car and set up the mobile base. We'll be ready for him if he leaves tonight as expected." She ordered a coffee and settled in for the long wait.

LYNDON JOHNSON SLEPT HERE

The Suzuki was peppy at low speeds, but at 60 mph the torque of its small 650 cc engine began to run out. But the little machine would get him to Canberra quickly enough. It joined the traffic south from Sydney and settled in beside long-distance truckers and commuters whose bored drivers knew every inch of the well-traveled, almost manicured highway. Ramon kept just under the legal speed limit and passed only when the vehicle ahead of him was clearly a road hog. He would get to Canberra long before the sun rose. The problem was what to do when he got there.

Ramon had already decided against trying to make contact at the hotel. All hotels were traps. They were designed both to keep out thieves and prevent people from skipping out on their bills. That meant if Alex was being watched by a hit team at the Rex he would probably run into them. As he up-shifted past a small sedan whose driver sat trancelike at the wheel, Ramon reflected that once the killers became aware of him then he – and his family – would become the next problem to be solved. His opponents went by the rule that Dead Men Tell No Tales. The hotel was out.

Ramon laughed at how absurd this middle-aged escapade now seemed. Long ago, he lived the life of a fugitive. That was no burden at 20. With neither a wife nor a son to consider, the dangers were mere entertainment; now they were intolerable worries. He had to protect people who could never understand the awful finality of mortal combat – an understanding that came only with facing it. There were no timeouts, no pauses for injury, no room for second place. Survival requirements changed the way you lived, slept and ate. It changed the future – in fact abolished it – leaving the participant with only an uncertain present. He looked at the dark highway stretching ahead and wondered where it would eventually take him.

He was up against an enemy probably far tougher than any he had met before. With the first rush of excitement now past, Ramon went over the situation again more objectively. The odds were bad, but how bad?

Maybe he should turn off at the next rest stop and tell Greer that he couldn't do it. But that was impossible. He just couldn't let Alex die and come home the same man.

The real cost to turning tail was the psychological penalty of trashing the self-esteem you built up all your life. As you got older, the secret medal of memory in the drawer was all you really kept. The trouble came from hanging on to it long after you could afford to. Maybe old-time Western gunfighters lost the last one because they didn't know when to quit. Then hell, so be it. Ramon either had to come back through the apartment door the same man who drew the cartoon cats for his son or not come back at all.

So he pressed on, muttering to himself, "professional killers, here I come". He leaned forward and twisted the accelerator up just a little more.

The Suzuki growled past the Rex Hotel at just after 4:00 in the morning. It was still dark and Ramon turned the bike left 300 meters down the road into an all-night café on Mort Street. Canberra, the capital of Australia, was designed by a committee and looked it. Since the site was chosen to offend none of the competing states, it was constructed in the middle of nowhere. Being both inland and 2,000 feet above sea level, it was much colder than Sydney. A gust of icy wind swept down from man-made Lake Burley Griffin, ruffling tree branches in the parking lot. Ramon looked up past the swaying branches and saw the stars just beginning to fade. He sat the Suzuki on its kickstand, took the backpack out of the top box, stowed the helmet and walked into the coffee shop.

The door closed out the cold. A look around showed an espresso machine puffing out a cloud of steam. The *barista* looked from the dark wooden counter and his gleaming coffee apparatus. There were two couples in serious conversation at widely separated tables and two middle-aged men who stared blankly at nothing in particular. He ordered a coffee and asked the way to the rest room.

The *barista* indicated a pair of doors in the alcove beside the counter. "What part of America are you from?"

68

"Massachusetts," Ramon answered automatically. It wasn't remotely true and he sounded nothing like Massachusetts but it stopped having to make explanations about the origin of his American accent.

He went into the men's room, took a leak, took the folding knife out of the backpack and clipped it inside his waistband. He stepped out in time to claim a steaming mug of espresso mellowed out by an equal quantity of hot water.

He found a corner table, set up the laptop and considered his position. His major advantage over the unknown hit team was that they did not suspect his existence. He had the element of surprise. In every other department, the enemy had the edge. If they ID'd him before he made them they would catch and destroy him. It was that simple.

He had two other possible advantages. As a professional software developer, he was probably better at using computers and online resources than they were. This plus the intel support from Bill Greer was what he had to even things up. He decided to plan around the principle of avoiding detection and pit invisibility and information dominance against physical strength and professional skill. Would it be enough? He would be the first to know.

His first problem was to anticipate where the hit team would close their net around Alex. Being professionals they would probably surveil first and spend a little time deciding where best to strike. Would they start the watch at the hotel? Maybe, but they couldn't hang around a hotel for too long because hotels were hard to hide in. They'd surveil some other place. And that was where he would start his own counter-surveillance, where he could spread his net *around them*.

Ramon started up Google Earth and set the mapping program's coordinates to Canberra. The display zoomed in on Australia where he focused it first on the Rex Hotel on Northbourne and then the National Convention Center on Constitution Avenue. The hotel and the convention site were the two places Alex would be. He examined both sites in detail, tilting the display to show the contours and reveal lines of sight to find the places where a surveillance team might establish observation posts. The Rex was unsuitable so he turned his attention

69

to the Convention Center. It was a bigger, more public location that offered better opportunities to blend in.

The satellite display showed a roughly rectangular convention building with a large park to its rear and a smaller green area across the street in front of it. There were only two ways in and out: a front and a back door. The streets all around the center were lined with benches and outdoor cafes. A casino next door ensured a steady flow of people through the sidewalks. That created plenty of crowd in which to watch the building without arousing suspicion. Ramon was sure the Convention Center was where the killers would set up their watch. But if the crowd could hide them, it could hide him too.

Where would the enemy watch the entrances? The obvious places were from the park in front and the park behind. They would have Alex in a box. Now, Ramon imagined a larger box enclosing the smaller box; all he had to do in principle was enclose the enemy team of watchers in his own bigger surveillance box. Could he do that alone? Yes, by using the photographic reconnaissance technique. He would use his "poor man's Leica" to capture a photographic mosaic of the surroundings the way recon airplanes took strip images. By interpreting the resulting photos, he might pick out the enemy surveillance team from the crowd.

But what would he do when he found them? Nothing came to mind. He would cross that bridge when he came to it. The immediate problem was finding the enemy and delivering the warning. He took a long pull on the coffee and looked at the satellite images of the Convention Center again. There were too many unknowns to think too far beyond the first move. He looked at his watch, then walked up to the coffee bar and ordered another coffee and a Danish.

70

SHADOWS

Monique was on her third cup of coffee when Pierre's voice came over the Bluetooth headset.

"I've got the car," Pierre said. "Are you still at the coffee-house?"

"Not for much longer. It's closing." When it did, they would lose the vantage point. The Australian Federal Police building had been sited so there were no parks, all-night cafes or places of concealment from which someone might observe its doors. Like cops the world over, the Australian Federal Police liked to watch but hated being watched themselves.

"OK," said Pierre. "I'll have the remote cameras up in just a few minutes. I'll let you know when they're deployed."

Pierre stepped out of a Toyota Tarago, an 11-seat minivan, carrying a small satchel. In it were two wireless webcams, devices about the size and shape of a pack of cigarettes with a lens in the center and a small antenna protruding from the top. Each was powered by 9-volt batteries and capable of transmitting video to a laptop over a wireless signal. Pierre had packed the cameras in foam containers with holes cut for the lenses. Each package was wrapped in a brown paper bag bearing the logo of McDonald's. The bag had been glued to the containers so that the webcam peered out of the hole punched in the central "o" of the McDonald's logo. Ketchup-stained napkins and balled-up food wrappers layered atop the cameras deterred anyone from looking closely. The paper bags concealed small, portable surveillance stations able to transmit video images to a laptop up to 250 meters away.

With a practiced eye for line of sight, Pierre carefully positioned the paper bags below a bus bench and behind a rail screening a row of potted plants about a hundred meters from the entrance to the Australian Federal Police headquarters. From there, the cameras could cover the front entrance even if the other was obstructed. Then Pierre returned to the car and booted up the laptop to check the feed was working. He loaded his web browser and typed in the IP address of webcam number one. A video of the police entryway came on clearly. He checked webcam number two. Another sparkling clear image from slightly further was displayed. He resized the windows until both feeds were displayed side by side on his screen. Satisfied the entrance was fully covered, he told Monique she could go get the other car.

"The remotes are up. Join me north on Wentworth near the corner of Liverpool Street. I'm in a gray Toyota Tarago near Hyde Park."

The pair normally used two vehicles for surveillance. With two cars they could alternately follow behind a target vehicle without being obvious. After Monique left the café, she quickly found a car rental agency and 45 minutes later parked a Minicooper S a short distance from the Tarago. She took a screwdriver from her bag and disabled the interior lights so she could leave and enter the vehicle in the dark without giving herself away.

Then she got out and transferred to the Tarago. Pierre had folded down the back seats to create a rest area. A plastic bucket in one corner did duty as a toilet. There was packaged food and bottled water. Monique booted her laptop and tuned into the webcam signal. From now on, the pair would keep a double watch at all times except when one took short bathroom and rest breaks. With both standing watch, there was less chance they could miss Alex Francisco coming out of the building due to fatigue or inattention.

The long nocturnal watches reminded Monique of her old job as a gang lookout in the *cites* of Paris. She had joined the gangs at twelve. While most muscle jobs went to the boys, the girls made better spotters. She kept an eye out for the police and rival gangs. When a major drug syndicate muscled into her neighborhood, the male gangsters were demoted as worthless muscle but her brains were even more in demand. Gradually, she moved up from neighborhood watching to working with the gang enforcers.

At first, her role was limited to keeping other drug syndicate snoops out, to watch for infiltrators. She quickly learned to maintain lists and watch from static posts, usually the apartments of a family which had been forced into cooperating. She mastered stakeouts using binoculars, cameras and recording devices. She learned how to conduct surveillance from a motor vehicle. She learned everything there was to know about watching for watchers.

Eventually, she moved up to offensive operations. Her first big job was to set up a hit on a rival gang leader. He lived in a secure housing complex that he rarely left without heavy security. But Monique patiently plotted his movement patterns using a series of observers linked up by radio. They studied the gang leader's habits until they found a chink in his armor: he liked the bouillabaisse at a certain bistro and ate there Wednesdays when the catch was at its freshest.

Monique's team visited the restaurant to probe for weaknesses and found it. There was only one men's room – a cubicle with one toilet – whose wall adjoined an alley in the back. The rest of the operation was simple. One member of the team followed the gang leader into the restaurant with an electronic signaling device whose clacker was hidden in his sleeve. The rest of the team waited in the alley behind the bistro with MP5 submachine guns hidden under their jackets. When the rival gang leader went to use the urinal, the spotter simply waited until the victim entered the bathroom and pushed the signal button in his sleeve. The hit team opposite the toilet wall sent 90 rounds zipping through the cubicle. The man who sent the electronic signal had been Pierre. That's how the couple met.

Pierre and Monique had come a long way since that first romantic day; the *cites* were far behind them now. Staring at a video screen, intent and focused, neither allowed any distractions into their thoughts. The dive holiday could come later.

The hours passed. The video feed showed a number of people coming in and out of the police building, mostly cops and civilian police employees working shifts. None of them was Alex Francisco. As the night wore on, the two watchers saw the character of the street crowd change. Office workers gave way to late diners and theater-goers, themselves replaced later by maintenance personnel heading for work in rubber-soled shoes and uniform clothes. As the night deepened, the red flashing lights of emergency vehicles seemed to multiply. But Pierre and Monique knew this was an illusion – they only seemed more numerous because of dwindling ordinary traffic. The pace of death and human misery remained constant through the day. It was life that ebbed in the darkness.

Pierre couldn't help feeling at home in the night. In a way he was just another kind of emergency responder. The paramedics pulled people up while he put people down. He was the other side of the equation, balancing things out.

When growing up in the northern suburbs of Paris, Pierre would sit in the vacant lots around his housing estate. On summer nights, he'd watch the rows of windows in the tenements light up like a galaxy of shabby stars. His favorite hangout was a derelict car that had lain undisturbed for many years in a field of high grass. It was where his gang – the only family he really ever had – met to discuss the day's events.

In later years, he would occasionally look north from the balcony of his expensive Paris apartment and wonder if the car was still rusting there. That derelict had been his home, school and start in life. But that was past. Reality was the gray video screen in front of him.

Five more years of this, he thought, and he would have enough to retire to Spain, enough comfort and sunshine to distract him from the darkness he both craved and feared, especially that one that would one day come calling for payment plus interest.

He looked down at the video display and saw Alex Francisco step out the door with a police officer, pulling luggage that he set on the curb. Monique saw them at the same time.

"They're moving. I'll pick up the video remotes. Follow them in the Mini and keep me posted."

"Right," she said. She picked up her laptop and walked to the little car. Pierre reached the first webcam just as an unmarked four-door Holden pulled up. The cop got in front and Francisco climbed into the rear passenger seat. As the police car got to the end of the street the Mini flashed past Pierre in trail position.

Monique kept well back from the Holden. When she had settled on its tail, Monique called Pierre and described her position, heading, and the Holden's taillight pattern. Twenty minutes later, she saw the Tarago closing up behind her. From this point onward, the two cars would alternate behind the cop car to avoid alerting the driver they were being followed.

Skilled as they were, Pierre and Monique didn't like following cops. Cops were suspicious by nature and, if they guessed they were being tailed, had a nasty tendency to call in backup units and turn the tables on their shadows. The two had too much surveillance equipment aboard to look completely innocent. Pierre decided that since the Holden was probably bound for Canberra, a continuous tail was unnecessary. After they hit the highway, he told Monique to go on ahead and await the cops at the Canberra city limits. In the meantime, he would maintain intermittent contact, closing only periodically to keep touch.

He dropped back and inched forward until he saw the taillights of the Holden, then fell back again. But two thirds of the way to Canberra, Pierre accelerated forward to find the cop car gone. He pushed down hard on the gas and topped a hill only to find a long black stretch of empty highway before him. The Holden was nowhere to be seen. Where had it gone? He pulled over to the shoulder and consulted a road map with a flashlight. He saw that the cops could only have turned off on Beewong. He reversed directions across the median and headed for the Beewong turnoff. What was in Beewong? Probably a restaurant.

His hunch proved right. Soon, the Tarago was speeding past a giant concrete bowl of noodles and into the small town center. Pierre looked up at the giant neon-edged bowl. "Why not donuts?" he yelled out the window. Then he shrugged and decided that people had strange customs in Australia.

He found the Holden parked beside an all-night restaurant. Pierre drove past and parked the van in a dark side street. He doubled back toward the restaurant, taking care to walk in the deep shadows cast by the streetlights. He found a watching position in a parking lot some distance away and kept an eye on the restaurant entrance.

Half an hour later, two very hefty men and a smaller, middle-aged Asian man emerged from the café and walked toward the Holden. The Asian stopped for a second on the sidewalk and looked back in the direction of the parking lot. Although Pierre knew he was invisible, Alex Francisco was behaving as though he sensed him. But that was impossible. Then the cops called to the smaller man and all three got in the car for the last leg to Canberra.

THE ROAD SOUTH

Alex lay on the quilted hotel bedspread listening to the tub fill with hot water. Before going to his room he had passed the fourth floor and sure enough, the Lyndon Johnson room was there. By the doorway was a plaque commemorating the stay of the 36th President of the United States. He looked at it and wondered who was sleeping in there now. Not Lyndon Johnson anyway.

A change in the sound of the hot water running into the tub told Alex it was full enough. He shuffled to the toilet and found himself face to face with a middle-aged man in the mirror. The old smile was still there but there was no jauntiness left in it, only a slowly increasing decrepitude. The dark eyes though still held traces of their youthful intensity. He turned away abruptly from the mirror and turned off the hot water, mixing cold water into the tub until the temperature was tolerable.

He dumped his clothes on the bathroom floor and lowered himself into the water. Alex closed his eyes. The hotel was silent in those early morning hours, so quiet he thought he could hear the pipes thrumming like a tuning fork in low key. As he lay back, the soft rocking of the water took him back to the days he spent on the beach as a child, lying on his back in the sunny, shallow water. It was exactly as he remembered it: the rise on the wave, the brief bounce on the sandy bottom before rolling onto a beach. Then the surf would leave you on your back with a salty taste in your mouth and give you a glimpse of the dazzling blue sky.

The water lulled him back, as he knew it would, to the first day he arrived in Zamboanga City after his long and circuitous escape from Manila. That was more than 30 years ago. He remembered her laugh drifting from under the palm tree where she sat watching him wade in the shallow water looking past him at Santa Cruz Island in the distance.

"Was it hard getting out of Manila with Bobadilla after you?" she asked.

"I had to go the long way round," he answered as he picked himself out of the surf. "I made sure never to change rides at bus terminals and changed rides between towns at little stops where no one was watching. It took me two weeks to get to the end of Luzon where I hid out for a time. And it took nearly another two weeks to get here."

Alex unhooked his shirt from a tree branch, shook out the sand and put it on. He thought of the parish in the shadow of Mount Mayon, a huge volcano in Albay province, where he hid out for almost seven days. It was run by a kindly but absent-minded priest who was a secret supporter of the underground. The priest introduced him as a seminarian seconded to the parish to straighten out the records. That gave him the excuse to hole up in the registry and pretend to fix the files. It was a small basement room under the parish hall where a rain of termite dust sifted down like a tropical snowfall 24 hours a day. When he got up each morning, he left an outline on the floor where he had slept. When the priest had gathered up enough clothes and money to equip him for the next stage of his journey, he bade goodbye to the good Father and left in the dead of the night.

That was nearly 14 days ago. After escaping from M2, Alex decided against returning to his old underground network. The informer was still at large. Instead he made for the southernmost tip of Mindanao where his friend, Dante Arevalo, ran a labor union. They had spoken together at public rallies in the years before Martial Law. Alex, the student leader and Arevalo, the honest labor leader. Now, Alex the fugitive, was counting on his help to assume a new identity in Mindanao.

Alex had no inclination to join the Communist or Islamic guerilla armies, so his only alternative was to create his own clandestine network from scratch. He would raise funds, build cells, cultivate alliances – make his own way. The odds of failure were high, but the time for regrets was long past.

Dante Arevalo agreed to help him out and offered Alex cover as a union organizer until he could make a start. Justine, Arevalo's wife, would show him the lay of the land in Zamboanga City. The fifteen-minute detour to the beach was part of the traditional welcome given to new recruits. After that, it would be all business. Alex looked up at the green hills to the north and wondered what it would be like to spend the rest of his life in them but Justine's voice brought him back to the present.

"What's the most useful thing to know when you're on the run?" Justine asked.

"Make sure to take along a long-sleeved shirt," Alex said.

She laughed. "A long-sleeved shirt?"

"Sure. When you're sleeping in a culvert or under some trees, a long-sleeved shirt and a bandana over your face are great for keeping away the mosquitoes."

Alex thought of all the odd and arcane bits of knowledge he picked up in the underground: the utility of long-sleeved shirts, spotting surveillance in store-window reflections or making an ice pick out of stiff wire. They were the skills of lives wrenched in the wrong direction.

He often wondered how different things might have been if Ferdinand Marcos had not declared Martial Law on September 21, 1972. That day he gave up all the vestiges of a normal life, like so many thousands of others, by the simple act of dropping out of school. His parents, who had spent all their savings to give him a university education, were inconsolable. As he got older, he often regretted the pain he caused his family. But youth was often callous in its idealism.

With the end of college went the job that should have come afterward, and the family it would have supported. On and on the effects cascaded. A whole future trajectory died that September day, closing off some roads and putting him on a path to this spot by the warm waters of the Basilan Strait.

"I guess we'd better start back now," Justine said.

They walked back to the main road past ramshackle homes from which the smoke of cooking fires wafted. Barefooted children ran from the shacks and onto the road only to disappear down some footpath with unseen voices calling after them. A man carrying a sheaf of green bamboo poles on his shoulder trudged past them in the opposite direction. Alex gave them little notice. They lived in a subsistence world. He was lost in his clandestine one, rehearsing his cover repeatedly until he was convinced he could assume his alias naturally. New identities were always shaky at the start because they lacked the foundation of real memory.

In contrast, Justine and Dante still lived their own lives, under a cloud of suspicion it was true, but with their own names and addresses, and professions that grew in stature over time. He, on the other hand, would always be a ghost. In a few months, he might shed his alias the way a snake shed its skin to make way for a new one. His life would be a series of discarded inventions. The trouble was that secret lives, carried on long enough, eventually became non-lives. Any existence sufficiently secret to achieve invisibility effectively became a nonexistence.

They reached the house a half-hour later. Justine, clad in jeans, a white blouse and a straw hat, led Alex through a wooden gate into an acre lot. It was bordered by large trees and dotted with small ponds, some no larger than mud puddles. A tethered goat grazed on a grassy mound that rose like a little island from a pond of rainwater. The main house was constructed entirely of bamboo and thatch and looked less like a city house than a gigantic tribal chieftain's hut. They stepped across a small footbridge that led via the vestibule into Dante's office. He was just finishing a meeting with five union members down from Kabasalan town.

"How do you like Zamboanga?" he boomed. Turning to the group, he said, "here's our new organizer. Alex, I'd like you to meet the officers of the Zambito Wood Company Employees Union."

"I'm pleased to meet you. Sorry if my Cebuano isn't very fluent. I'm just in from Luzon."

"Oh, that's all right," one of them said. "We all understand Tagalog here so if you run out of Cebuano just switch languages and we'll continue just fine."

And so it proved. Alex listened with rapt interest to their stories. It was small talk and all the more instructive for that. He welcomed not only the opportunity to learn the language but to understand the ordinary concerns of life in Zamboanga. They pooled a few pesos to buy a bottle of rum and moved as a group to the combination dormitory and warehouse behind the main house to continue yarning until dinner was ready.

Alex and the union officers would stay the night in bunks built along the storeroom walls. The center of the storeroom was piled high with bags of rice, all of it marked with the words "A gift from the American people." How Dante Arevalo got hold of USAID disaster relief supplies was one mystery Alex never solved.

Alex knew Dante was taking a considerable risk in harboring him and resolved to cut loose as soon as he could. As soon as his Cebuano was better, he would distance himself and begin building his own organization. Alex's plans were hopelessly vague but in the underground, improvisation was unavoidable.

There was a knock on the door. Justine, her hair pulled back in a bun and wearing a *malong* – a tube of batik cloth widely worn as a wraparound dress in Mindanao – asked them to the dining room for the evening meal. They filed into a large room with a thatched roof in which a bamboo table was set with hot food. Dante sat at the head of the table. To his left was a small, balding man a few years short of middle age wearing a fixed grin. Alex wondered who he was as he took his place furthest down from the table. They ate a simple meal of rice, fried fish and a vegetable stew seasoned with fermented shrimp paste. Alex kept his counsel during the meal and watched the group's interaction.

After dinner, Justine introduced Alex to the small balding man. His name was Romeo Vallarte. He liaised with all the Arevalo-affiliated unions throughout the Zamboanga peninsula, something between a troubleshooter and a traveling postbox. He wore a fixed but disquieting grin that was not quite humorous yet stopped short of being sardonic.

The smile, Alex discovered, was an accurate reflection of the little man's character. Vallarte had a dim view of human nature and his natural cynicism expressed itself in his maddening smile. Yet he was clearly a formidable and practical individual, the Sancho Panza to Arevalo's Don Quixote. His usefulness may have stemmed precisely from a lack of illusion, making him the ideal brake on Arevalo's idealistic impulses. His innate pragmatism allowed Arevalo to play the role of a visionary. Vallarte himself traveled up and down the peninsula carrying messages for the whole organization, making the decisions on the ground: what to do, what to say, who to trust.

But Vallarte did not seem to be either a Communist or government agent, the Scylla and Charybdis of the underground representing two different but equally fatal dangers. Alex let his eye range around the dinner table, judging and weighing. He felt sure that Dante was not a secret Party member, but he was not so sure about Justine. She had oddly philosophical questions for him on their tour of the city, the answers to which he had finessed by humor or reference to common friends. But it was clear she was sounding him out, for what he did not know.

The process of sounding out was a continuous one in the underground. It was going on all the time, though people outside the Life might never pick the endless round of challenge and countersign, the 'who goes there' followed by the reply. It all took place in code. And if you didn't have the key you never heard it.

His friendship with Dante bought him admission to the general circle. But Alex knew that later that evening, when people broke up into smaller circles, they would sort themselves out according to their deepest loyalties, whatever that might be. It was a horrible, exhausting process. In time it made you paranoid. The best thing about being among ordinary union members was the momentary chance to get out of the circles of suspicion and rejoin the human race.

The sounding-out process had begun even when Justine and Alex began a circuit of the city from the airport district; it continued as they moved clockwise through the broad residential boulevards and leafy campuses that led to the Cawa-cawa seashore. There in the most beautiful part of the city, its streets still sleeping under the broad acacias, they found a spot on the seawall beside a small beach. While tossing pebbles at the waves, Justine extracted the story of his life and told him somewhat of hers. They passed a half-hour trading guarded stories and half-truths.

She had fewer falsehoods to tell and he envied her that; hers was a simpler world of *avante garde* films, ideas, theology, art and literature. In the underground that was always a bad sign and, sure enough, many of her college friends and classmates were Party members. Alex recognized their names. In that sense she was of a piece. Did that make her one of the True Believers? Not necessarily. You could belong to the Party and yet not be part of that hard core of operators.

Alex looked out at the dark shape of Basilan Island in the distance, whose jungled interior had been a pirate and slaver's lair for centuries, and tossed another pebble in the water. Wheels within wheels, he said to himself, and decided to suspend judgment.

Afterward they went along the docks and watched the longshoremen load small coasters, then walked up the short road to the old Spanish stronghold of Fort Pilar, whose garrison had survived the pirates of Basilan until the US Army relieved them of the job at the turn of the 20th century. Behind the old Fort, Justine pointed out the slum of Rio Hondo, a warren of dingy shacks. It was another world into which they did not venture further. From Rio Hondo, they walked back to the docks and headed home.

The homely character of the dinner conversation at the bamboo castle, as Alex thought of the Arevalos' home, convinced him that the Party had not yet established a cell within the federation. The union officers, though by no means simpletons were still in the natural state. They were self-educated men with callused hands who felt better walking without shoes than with. A pall of cigarette smoke hung between the ceiling and the dinner table, stirred every now and again by a sluggish ceiling fan. The men spoke of wages, commodity prices, guns and knives. They spoke of war, games of chance, and of births and deaths.

The character of their conversation was completely different from the debating-society atmosphere of Manila's underground where young men who lacked the knowledge to change a light bulb spoke confidently about changing the world. Alex decided that if Justine was a member of the Party she had not been seriously tasked, at least not yet. The Party worked that way, sometimes. They left you in place for a long time until they decided to switch you on.

Dante took Alex aside and asked if he could start with Vallarte in two days for the field. The little man was headed for the timber and mining camps of the northern peninsula.

"That sounds great. The sooner I hit the field, the better," Alex said.

"Well, you could have used a few days' rest after that long trip getting here," Dante offered.

"We can't always get what we want. If we're lucky, we'll get what we need," Alex said in a mock ironic manner that surprised even himself, but Dante didn't get the Rolling Stones reference.

Alex went back into the bunkroom after the dinner party broke up and put everything he owned into a small gray canvas backpack. He was ready to go. He was always ready to go. All he had to do now was wait 72 hours. He was turning toward the bunk when he heard the door open, and Justine beckoned him out into the corridor. They stood by the doorway and could hear the union leaders still trading stories on the balcony.

"You never told me how you got away from Bobadilla's prison."

"The guards locked me in the doctor's office while they went out to get a drink. I found a way to pry the wall air-conditioner from its bracket. It's a trick worth remembering. It might come in useful someday."

He gave her an abbreviated account of a short dash through the streets outside the military camp and how he clambered onto a passing cargo truck that had slowed to take a curve.

"I jumped down again a few hundred yards away and zigged through some alleys. Then I was home free."

"But where did you get the money you needed to travel?" she asked.

"I spent that night at a funeral parlor, one of the bigger ones with dozens of chapels. They are good places to hide during curfew; mourners turn up and nobody asks where they are from. They just hand out the coffee and assume you knew the deceased. I got down on my knees and prayed – partly to mask the cuts in my palms, but I really prayed – for myself as much as anyone else.

"Then as soon as curfew ended, I walked a long way out of town to somewhere I know and got some money and changes of clothes. I taped up the cuts and left the way I came. The rest is pretty much the way I told it: by stages to Southern Luzon, then a ferry across the strait to Samar and down the chain of Visayan islands until I could get a boat to northern Mindanao and overland to Zamboanga. So here I am."

"A piece of cake, huh?" she laughed. "You make it sound like fun."

"It gets old after a while."

"Dante says you're leaving the day after tomorrow."

"Well, Vallarte's due out and it's best I leave with him so he can show me the ropes."

"I'm sorry you have to leave so soon. There aren't very many people here who I can talk to about books and things – except for Dante – and he's so busy. The union officers are great hearts, but their intellectual interests are a little narrow. I was wondering if you'd like to join us tomorrow at a scripture reading at the church next door. Sendoffs should involve some kind of gathering. This is the best I can do. I'm afraid we're a little short of champagne."

"I'd be glad to go. What time will it be?" Alex asked.

"Early evening, after supper."

"Do you go to church much?"

"I did, as a child," Justine replied. "Still do, but not in the religious sense as much as a therapeutic one. Being in church gives me a sense of peace, like being in a garden. Maybe it's a holdover from my girlhood."

"A lot of things change as we get older," Alex said, "and we assume it's for the better. But we lose as well as gain with the years. Who knows if therapy is better than religion?" He paused, then said, "I'll see you tomorrow."

"Goodnight, Alex," she said.

He pushed open the door into the bunkhouse, lay down in an upper bunk and fell into a dreamless sleep.

The next evening, Justine and Alex crossed the garden to the little church down the street. The night was dark and the fireflies were out, making little circles of light among the tree branches. Somewhere, a goat bleated. The two went through a small gate in the fence to the little evangelical church run by Pastor Rudy Velasco. Alex had warmed to the idea of attending the prayer meeting as a sendoff. Tomorrow he would be in the hills facing a new future. The church would be as good a point of departure as any.

Pastor Velasco was a small, wiry man in the long-sleeved shirt, dark pants and cheap leather shoes favored by Protestant ministers found throughout Mindanao. Two-dozen parishioners, mostly teachers from local schools, professional men and mid-level employees, were in attendance. The church itself was furnished with a few rough wooden benches arranged in a circle. Velasco sat opposite the door. After the greetings, he took out his Bible. The rest followed suit.

"We'll follow the usual procedure," Velasco said. "A reading from Scripture followed by reflections from the congregation. The reading for today is from 1 Corinthians 13. Would you care to read the passage, Justine?"

She began to read the familiar verses in English with just a hint of singsong Cebuano in her voice. Now that he could look at Justine carefully without being impolite, Alex noted a hint of north Indian or perhaps something of the Arab in her ancestry. Her face was small, narrow and brown, and her features were far sharper than the Malayan. She spoke clearly, but the words of Paul echoed slightly off the galvanized iron roofing of the dimly lit church, slurring them with a slight echo. It didn't matter; everyone knew them by heart.

> Though I speak with the tongues of men and of angels and have not love, I am become as sounding brass or a tinkling cymbal. And though I have the gift of prophecy and understand all mysteries and all knowledge, and though I have all faith so that I could remove mountains and have not love, I am nothing.
>
> And though I bestow all my goods to feed the poor, and though I give my body to be burned and have not love, it profits me nothing.
>
> Love suffereth long and is kind. Love envies not. Love vaunts not itself, is not puffed up, doth not behave itself unseemly. Seeks not her own, is not easily provoked, thinketh no evil, rejoices not in inequity, but rejoices in the truth. It bears all things, believes all things, hopes all things, endures all things.
>
> Love never fails.
>
> When I was a child I spoke as a child, I understood as a child, I fought as a child, but when I became a man I put away childish things. For now we see through a glass darkly, but then we shall meet face to face. Now I know in part, but one day I shall know even as I am known.

Justine put away her Bible and Velasco turned to Alex and said, "I am sure these words are familiar to all of us and we have often thought upon their meaning. But since we have a guest here with us today, someone who is working with Dante Arevalo's labor federation and leaving for the field tomorrow, maybe we should listen to what he believes this passage says to him."

The congregation looked at him and Alex had no choice but to return their honest gaze and lie to them. He had introduced himself by his alias; a man on the run didn't have much choice. But though he had begun with a lie, at least he would keep the falsehoods to the minimum and be as true to the text as he could.

"Pastor Velasco and friends," he began as he rose. "We all know that 1 Corinthians 13 is a discourse on love, about how it endures and its greatness. But we sometimes forget the passage is also about knowledge and how we obtain it. There are different kinds of knowledge, the sort we get from books or the sort imparted by revelation. But there is knowledge that even prophecy cannot bestow, and that is the knowledge gained from love. For it is only with the eye of love that we can truly see."

He paused and then continued.

"Today marks the beginning of my life in Mindanao. I have come to take up a job – a challenging one in distant places – and with it, start a new life. My old home, family and everything familiar is now far away in Luzon. With normal sight, I might see only strangers around me. But here you are wishing me Godspeed on my journey! Only with the eyes of love can I see you as you truly are, not strangers, but my real brothers and sisters, or at any rate the only ones I have.

"I hope to visit Luzon again someday. But for now unless I can see with the eyes of love, then I would be utterly alone. Yet I am not, for as the apostle Paul says, 'love never fails'. Whether I return or not is of little importance if I have seen, and seen truly. I go in your love and whatever happens, I will never truly fail."

Pastor Velasco led a closing prayer after Alex's reflection. The little group broke up and they left the church. The fireflies lit their way back. On that last night, Justine made Alex promise that he would write from the field. Alex promised, meaning to laugh lightly at the request, but found himself in some strange way nodding seriously, as if it were the most important promise he could make.

Shortly before sunup the next day, Vallarte and Alex sat at a crossroad on the outskirts of Zamboanga waiting for a ride on a cargo truck while sipping instant coffee bought from an old woman's variety store. The truck they were waiting for belonged to a transport company whose workers were affiliated with Arevalo's labor federation. Vallarte had arranged for the truck to stop and take them aboard as unauthorized passengers.

The cargo truck pulled up at 6:15 am. Alex and Vallarte clambered atop the boxes of dry goods piled on the open-topped high-sided truck. The driver's assistant swung down with a practiced movement and bought smokes from the variety store. He looked up at Alex and Vallarte and signaled the driver to start.

Bumming rides atop trucks or buses was a practice called "topload", the Mindanao equivalent of Depression Era hobos riding the rails. Although company drivers were not supposed to take passengers, they often did to augment their income. As it bumped its way north up the 200-mile winding length of the mountainous peninsula, the truck would eventually transport dozens of passengers – soldiers returning to garrison, off-duty policemen, small-town clergymen, practically anyone – much as if it were a regular bus.

The truck left the relatively safe Zamboanga City area and entered the stretch of highway north of it that was still a war zone. Just a few years before, a young Tausug firebrand named Nur Misuari had started a Muslim insurrection in southern Mindanao. The uprising had been beaten back by the Philippine Armed Forces, but not completely. The country roads were still plagued with ambushes and sudden raids.

The cargo truck droned through a 10-kilometer section of dusty road between the towns of Curuan and Vitali, which now had been emptied by fear. Nothing dared move on the highway until daylight, when trucks such as the one Alex was riding risked a crossing. He looked down from his perch into the open windows of deserted homes where prosperous farmers and tradesmen once lived. The homes were still in the same condition in which they had been abandoned. Pots were racked against the walls, cushions strewn on the sofas and newspaper cuttings used as decorative posters flapped on the walls. The people had gone but the fear remained. Even looters seemed to have been kept away by the invisible barrier of menace.

The Misuari insurrection had come close to reviving a Moro nation that had been nearly extinguished seventy years before by the US Army. By the 1960s and early 1970s, a chance for it to rise again had come. Misuari figured if Ho Chi Minh could take on the US Army then he could take on the Armed Forces of the Philippines – of course with help from his contacts in the Arab world and Soviet intelligence. When Misuari sensed that President Ferdinand Marcos' seizure of power in Manila had weakened the legitimacy of the government and tied down the army to keeping order in Luzon, he saw a chance to retake the old Muslim capital of Jolo and fly the Moro flag over it. He hoped the Libyans would recognize Jolo as the capital of a newly independent nation. Then, with the US occupied in Vietnam and Marcos preoccupied with Luzon, the Moro nation might rise again.

It almost worked. Thousands of Misuari's men launched a surprise attack on the town in February 1974, setting off the largest land engagement on Philippine soil since World War II. The rebels quickly overran the army brigade headquarters and overpowered its garrison. All that stood between Misuari and victory was a Philippine Marine battalion holding a last, desperate perimeter on Sibalu Hill. The Moro commanders reckoned they could destroy it before Manila could send seaborne reinforcements, but they had not reckoned on the Philippine Air Force.

In fact, no one had reckoned on the Philippine Air Force, not even Marcos. After declaring himself dictator in 1972, Marcos had focused his energies on corrupting the Army and the Police. The Navy, to which the Marines belonged, and the Air Force had remained intact as a fighting force from the days of President Ramon Magsaysay. As frantic calls for help from the trapped Marines began filtering into the Air Force headquarters at Villamor Airbase in Manila, they responded quickly. The air staff decided to move everything that would fly from Luzon to an airbase within range of Zamboanga in Mactan, Cebu. If the Marines could survive the night, the Air Force would make an all-out attempt to keep the Marines from being overrun by the rebels.

The next day, the Philippine Air Force had 60 aircraft on the flight line at a former US installation in Mactan. They sortied at dawn. It looked like a vintage air show. C-47 Dakotas, crammed with troops, lumbered into the air, followed by F-86s and T-33 trainers armed for close air support. Old as the armada was, it was better than anything Misuari had. The F-86s and T-33s plastered the area around Sibalu Hill with their .50 caliber machine guns while the C-47s landed their infantry loads onto the grass fields.

At sea a single destroyer escort of the Philippine Navy, already obsolete when it joined the US Pacific Fleet in 1943 and hopeless for anything when it was transferred as surplus, wheezed up the coast to fire its 3-inch gun in support of the Marines. Although the original Mark 52 gun director had long rusted into uselessness, the gunnery officer proceeded to control fire with the "Mark 1 eyeball". The first 3-inch shots went wild, landing among the packs of feral dogs nosing around the corpses strewn on the beach. But eventually the little warship got its shells close enough to be effective. The naval popgun began picking the Moro attacks apart. Slowly the combined efforts of the naval and air force antiques beat back the attackers on Sibalu Hill.

For two days, Jolo writhed in smoke and flames. Misuari's men finally fell back into the jungle. But Jolo was retaken at the price of its destruction. Many of its Christian inhabitants fled the ruined town forever, too traumatized to return. Their places were silently taken by Muslims from the island's interior. Jolo became, as Misuari intended, the Moro capital, in fact if not in name. But the insurgency didn't end with the battle of Jolo. All over Mindanao, copycat uprisings sprang up. The provinces of Zamboanga, Cotabato, Lanao and Basilan blazed in conflict.

Now Alex's cargo truck moved over that conflict's embers, its wheels rolling over a battlefield whose fires still smoldered. The cargo truck labored north into the dead zone, the tense stillness broken only by the whine of the engine. Alex looked back at the armed passengers. Logging camp security men angled their M-1 Garands outward and adjusted their bandoliers for easy access. Two Army infantrymen on their way back from leave to garrison checked the seating of their magazines in the wells of their M16s. Both groups were staring intently into the vegetation on either side.

Alex knew these preparations would be of little avail if Muslim rebels staged one of their well-crafted ambushes. The machine guns would sweep them off the roof before they knew what hit them. It was unlikely the rebels would waste their fire on a single cargo truck carrying crates of dried fish. Still, ambush teams occasionally picked off a minor target to keep the army guessing. In war, chance counted for a great deal and Alex knew this could be his unlucky day. Suddenly the terrain changed and Alex knew that if anything would happen, it would happen here, along this length of road.

The truck straightened out of a climbing curve onto a long stretch cut into the side of the mountain. To one side was a sheer drop, on the other, a solid rock wall. It was a perfect setup for an ambush and someone had used it to do just that. Three hundred meters down the road, Alex saw the bullet-riddled wreck of a fifty-seater bus leaning at angle against the rock wall. The logging company security guards saw it too and quickly gave a yell of warning. The air was punctuated by the sound of M-1 Garands and M16s being chambered. The soldiers and guards looked hard at the surrounding heights. Alex looked up to the hill at the head of the road, where a machine gun would ideally be positioned to fire down upon the length of the highway.

But there was no hail of supersonic 7.62 mm rounds. No flight of deadly, singing bees, nor the terrible slap of .50 caliber. The ambush was over, and probably had been for a half-hour, since they had not heard the firing. The truck driver floored the accelerator, squeezing the truck past the pitiful wreck of the bus. As they sped past, Alex could see bodies sprawled in groups, some obviously missing their heads. One corpse had kept his head but was missing both arms and legs, which had been chopped off to either side of him. Packages and bags were strewn randomly around the vehicle where they had been rifled in search of valuables. In the dim interior, Alex saw a number of women and children in various attitudes of death.

"Don't stop!" yelled the Army troopers. "Don't stop for anything!" The driver had no intention of doing so. For a moment, Alex felt the impulse to leap from the cargo truck and help anyone left alive. He felt Vallarte grip his arm. The incongruous smile was still there.

"They're all dead. Perhaps some of the young women had survived. But they too will be dead before tonight."

And then they were past. Alex looked back. His last glimpse was of a child's corpse in a striped shirt, his little arms outstretched, holding a yellow plastic toy his parents probably got for him in Zamboanga City.

The truck stopped at the first Army detachment they reached to report the attack. An Army captain in flip-flops, dirty T-shirt and a belly that hung like a bag of jelly six inches over his belt came out of the gate to hear the breathless report of the ambush. From the expression on his face, it was nothing new. The captain went back inside the perimeter and came out ten minutes later with a company of truck-borne infantry and a V-150 armored reconnaissance vehicle as if it were the most natural thing in the world. They would clear the road and recover what was left of the dead.

The ambushers probably staged from the outlying islands on fast, motorized outriggers. Landing by night and force-marching themselves into a pre-selected position to attack by dawn, they could hit the highway at many points. The Zamboanga peninsula was vulnerable to seaborne attack on both flanks and had a long mountainous spine along which raiders could hide and strike to either side.

The raids had transformed many small Zamboanga towns into armed camps. Vallarte described how the rebels had raided his village and showed about as much mercy as the ambushers had shown the bus passengers.

But "armed camps" didn't capture the effect of the raids. The real walls had gone up in people's hearts. Survivors armed themselves with bolos, weapons left over from World War II, and, if they could afford it, modern assault rifles sold on the black market. They patrolled their towns, suspicious of strangers and inclined to shoot first and ask questions later. Once, Vallarte said, a busload of ordinary Muslim travelers made the fatal mistake of turning into his village. Everyone was killed and dumped in a ravine. Alex wondered whether Vallarte had been one of the militiamen. Vallarte was silent for a few minutes after the cargo truck left the Army base. Then he spoke.

"Next time, we'll do the ambushing."

Alex said nothing.

"Anyway, welcome to Zamboanga," Vallarte said. "Most days, it's a very nice place."

Thirty miles later, they parted ways. Alex hopped off the truck at a small road junction and waved goodbye to the small, balding man who continued north to Siraway.

Vallarte gave him instructions on how to reach his union contact. From the junction, he was to walk west along the gravel road that wound under the shade of the rubber trees until he came to a cluster of houses with a small open-air chapel. There he would ask after the pastor and give him a letter of introduction from Vallarte. The pastor would guide him to the logging camp where the union had a large local branch. As he left the highway, Alex looked back through the tunnel of gray and green trees at the white concrete ribbon of highway. Then he turned and plunged into the gloom of the rubber plantation. He was on his own.

CONFLUENCE

It was nearly six o'clock when Alex awoke in his bathroom at the Rex. He had fallen asleep in the tub. The water had turned cold around him. At least he got an hour's worth of sleep. He pulled out the drain plug, toweled off and shaved at the sink. He gathered up the limp clothes he had worn since his departure from Manila and put them on a shelf in the hotel room closet. He walked over to the sideboard and filled an electric hot water kettle a third full with water and switched it on. Alex was starting to put on a fresh shirt when the kettle gurgled and switched itself off automatically. The sideboard had a pile of instant coffee sachets. He ripped one open and tipped the powder into the hotel cup, pouring boiling water after it.

He put on the rest of his clothes and pulled a gray blazer from his garment bag, then took a small sip of the instant coffee. It wasn't great but the hot liquid had enough caffeine to get him going. Cup still in hand, he walked to the window and looked out between the curtains. The fall sunshine was just banishing the nighttime grays from the street below; the eucalyptus trees on the sidewalks were regaining their colors. An elderly man and his wife walked a dog down a side street, their Labrador pausing to sniff at a Minicooper S parked beneath some trees. A few pedestrians were walking briskly to work. Canberra was waking up. A thin stream of cars, interspersed with cyclists in Lycra outfits, moved south on Northbourne Avenue toward the city center.

There was a knock on the door. Alex put the security chain in its slot and cautiously opened the door. The cheerful face of Prof. Marvin Lee looked back at him.

"The front desk said you came in this morning."

"I made it in about two and a half hours ago."

"Are you finished helping the police?"

95

"I think so," Alex said, "I was just having some coffee." He pulled the security chain out of the slot and let Marvin in.

"Oh, we can get better coffee downstairs," Marvin said. There's a breakfast buffet in the dining room. We should eat something substantial because it's going to be a long session this morning."

His colleague's simple optimism was contagious. By his normalcy, he brought the morning back into the room and made Alex laugh. He put on the blazer, made sure his passport, wallet and cell phone were in his pockets and then followed Marvin down to the lobby restaurant. The Rex had laid out brewed coffee, tea, cereal, eggs cooked in several styles, fruit and a variety of sausages on a long table. The two academics were nearly halfway through their breakfast before Marvin asked him about the intriguing "police business" that had delayed him the day before.

"Oh, that? A very prominent Filipino politician had died on the airplane coming over. The Philippine Consulate wanted to make sure all possible information connected with the incident had been collected. I just told everything I knew to the Federal Police and they drove me up here afterward."

"That sounds pretty exciting. My wife would kill me if she found out I was taken to a police headquarters," the Singaporean joked. "Or maybe she'd be delighted at the change because my life has become totally boring."

"Take it from me, you don't know how lucky you are."

"I'm not so sure, but I guess you're right. You could do worse than be married to a good woman." Marvin took out a picture of a cute little girl from his wallet. "Here's my daughter. She wants a toy koala bear from Australia," he said.

"You're going to get her one, aren't you?"

"There may be some koalas for sale at the Convention Center," Marvin said. They paid their bill and started for the sessions. They passed a young couple eating near the restaurant entrance. The pair suddenly lost interest in their meal and hurried after the two academics, leaving a sum of money at the cashier's as they left. Alex and Marvin crossed the lobby crowded with arrivals from a tour bus and headed down into the busy parking basement.

As Alex strapped on his seatbelt, he noticed the breakfast couple emerge from the stairwell and walk quickly out into the street. He thought it odd they would follow them down to the basement only to go right back out. In the next instant, Marvin put the rental Hyundai in gear. The little car pulled out of the garage and onto the short road to the Convention Center. Ordinarily Alex would have liked to walk to the conference hall. But after two days without sleep, he was glad of the ride.

Not far away, Ramon Delgato was preparing his own stakeout. He had parked the motorcycle in a garage and headed for the Convention Center, taking the field guide to Australian birds and digital camera with him. He attached the wide-angle pancake lens, set the focus at infinity and set the shutter release to continuous. With the camera's onboard processor choosing the right lens opening and shutter speed it would snap three images a second for as long as he kept the release button depressed.

Holding the camera one-handed, he began a circuit around the Convention Center from the west clockwise along Binara Street, right on Glebe Park behind the Convention Center parking lot, then back again along the front. In this way, he circled the whole building. Without raising the viewfinder to his eyes, he shot the camera one-handed to cover the areas of interest. Ramon would occasionally pretend to consult the bird-watching guide while surreptitiously angling the camera to capture multiple interlocking images of the places the enemy surveillance team might lurk. The huge memory card stored the hundreds of pictures the camera captured as he held down the shutter release. After making the first circuit, Ramon began walking in the opposite direction and repeated the process, acquiring more pictures as he strolled along.

Satisfied that he had blanketed everything, he walked away from the Convention Center area and found a café half a mile away. He ordered a coffee and got a table where he could put his back against a wall. He took the laptop from his backpack and inserted the camera memory card in the computer's reader slot. He transferred over 1,000 images onto its solid-state hard disk. The laptop's powerful processor let him scan through the images quickly. The pictures showing nothing were moved into a discard folder. He focused on the scenes that contained people.

Now where were the watchers? The trick to spotting them was to look for individuals who did not fit the scene. It was more art than science. The mind, through some process, built a model of how a scene should naturally look. Each situation – a crowd, a group of people, a collection of objects – had a characteristic pattern and whatever didn't belong stood out. By paging through the images quickly, he created an animation effect akin to flipping through drawings to create the illusion of motion. Years before in the anti-Marcos underground, he had honed an instinct for spotting the anomalous to a fine edge. All he could do was hope that some of those cognitive skills still remained.

He divided the images into sequence groups and focused on sequences where something, or someone, didn't quite fit. One scene with a middle-aged man and a younger woman looked suspicious. But on closer inspection he could see the two were quietly quarreling. That went into the discard folder.

The next sequence, taken near the front of the Convention Center, showed a fit-looking man in his late 20s or early 30s in a gray soft-shell jacket carrying a McDonald's fast-food paper bag in his hand. The picture, snapped one third of a second later, showed the same man with his face angled slightly more to the left. The third picture captured his head still swiveling further left. There was something wrong with him and Ramon asked himself what it was. Then he knew: the McDonald's fast-food paper bag. There weren't any McDonald's outlets within a half mile of the Convention Center and the picture was taken at a time slightly too late for breakfast and way too early for lunch.

He clicked through the sequence of images again, this time faster to get a better sense of motion. At the faster rate, the man's head movement stood out more clearly. He was swiveling his head as he scanned the front of the Convention Center.

Nothing else stood out until he came to images taken on the return circuit. In the middle of the second sequence, he found the man in the gray jacket again. But this time he was in apparent conversation with a woman of similar age and looking equally fit and strong. These pictures were taken from further away, about 50 meters from where the two sat on a park bench. He magnified the image. The woman was a hard-faced brunette, nails cut short, with expensive running shoes on her feet. Gray Jacket sat next to her, without the McDonald's paper bag this time. He speeded up the images again and noticed that while they sat close enough together to be a couple, neither seemed focused on the other; their head movements were oriented outward. Their heads were swiveling, covering specific arcs. Again, they could only be scanning the back entrance to the Convention Center.

Ramon re-examined the first sequence of pictures with Gray Jacket and zoomed in on the McDonald's paper bag. The enlarged digital image showed a slight reflection behind the "O" in the McDonald's lettering. He zoomed in on other images of the paper bag. The changing light angles clearly indicated a shadow instead of solid paper where the "O" should be. There had been a hole cut in the paper bag. The shine was a lens. Gray Jacket was carrying some sort of surveillance device.

The hairs stood on the back of Ramon's arms. Until that moment, despite everything Bill Greer had said, despite his intellectual acceptance of the facts, he had remained emotionally unengaged. Now something in the pitiless faces set off alarms in his limbic system, that part of the brain formed when men still lived like animals. Ramon felt as his prehistoric ancestor might at the sight of a carnivorous reptile plodding relentlessly forward. His hands shook slightly and then steadied. Let them come, he thought. Let them come.

He drank a little more coffee and found the clearest image of Gray Jacket and his female companion on the park bench. He cropped it to isolate the couple and copied the cropped image back onto the memory card. Now he knew he was up against at least two people. How could he deal with them? He was certain that one watcher would remain on foot to follow Alex if he left the building in the pedestrian mode. The other would remain in a vehicle in case Alex shifted to a car. They would be in constant phone or radio contact to coordinate with each other. That was standard procedure: one shadow for each mode, pedestrian and vehicular. Ramon instantly realized that split mode was the weak point in the enemy deployment.

He used Google Earth to re-examine the area around the Convention Center, but this time he measured the distance to the adjacent Casino building from the Center's entrance with the Google Earth Ruler Tool. A courtyard ran right through the Casino building from the front to the back. The back entrance opened on a short connecting alley to a pedestrian-only shopping mall called the City Walk. Along that route, only the pedestrian watcher could follow. The other would be pinned down in the vehicle. Lose the pedestrian watcher and you lose them both.

He sketched the layout of the Casino and noted the distances from the Convention Center on a paper napkin. He then shut down the laptop, re-stowed his gear and left the cafe. His plan looked good on the map, but the only way to be sure was to walk the ground. Ramon entered the front door of the Casino building next to the Convention Center. Just as Google Earth showed, it opened on an internal court that ran the length of the building. The court ended in a swinging glass door with push bars on both sides. Beyond the glass doors was the alley to the City Walk pedestrian mall. He examined the push bar handles carefully and knew it could be done.

Ramon went through the doors into City Walk. Using the sketch from Google Earth as reference, he explored the maze of interconnected malls until he found the route he was looking for. Then he proceeded to buy a string of items in untraceable cash. The first were three cheap, prepaid cell phones, each belonging to different networks, of the kind

100

that did not require subscription to a plan to use. These were often used by teenagers or children who had no ID or credit references. At another store he picked up a cheap motorcycle helmet and a bicycle cable lock, the kind that wrapped around fences or street posts. The next item was a black nylon zip-up jacket and knock-off Ray Bans obtained from a small store run by a Chinese merchant who issued no receipts. Lastly, he took his camera memory card to a self-service photo print shop and ran off a 4x6-inch print of Gray Jacket and his female companion.

On a piece of paper, Ramon wrote precise instructions to Alex, referring occasionally to the sketch on the paper napkin. He double- and triple-checked the instructions before putting it and the photo into an envelope. Then he walked back to the parking garage and stored everything except for one disposable cell phone in the top box of his motorcycle. He took the prepaid cell phone out of its packaging, inserted the SIM card and confirmed that it worked.

It was too risky to speak to Alex openly in case someone was watching. But he had a plan to transfer the message nearly invisibly. In an hour, the conference participants would be breaking for lunch. The lunch bustle would give him a chance of contacting Alex by brush pass, a technique by which a note could be passed to another while "brushing" past.

He put on the imitation Ray Bans and walked to the Convention Center, staying with the crowd on the sidewalk. He reached the Convention Center lobby at five minutes past twelve. A locator board in the lobby showed the dining halls assigned to each of the ongoing conferences. Ramon climbed the stairs to the second-floor dining area, where the community forestry group was at a buffet.

He held the envelope and disposable cell phone in his hand and removed the sunglasses so that Alex would have no trouble recognizing him. Then he walked through the lunchroom and found Alex, looking much older than he remembered, engaged in conversation with several conference participants. He feigned interest in the academic books being sold near the dining room entrance until

Alex's group broke toward the buffet line. Ramon angled his approach to come up behind him. This was the riskiest part of the entire maneuver because Alex, who was not expecting a brush pass, might react unpredictably. He drew level and in a soft voice said, "Alex, don't say a word. It's a letter from Smokey Mountain," and handed him the envelope and disposable cell phone as if it were the most natural thing in the world. Then Ramon left the dining room, replaced the sunglasses on his face and walked out the front door again into the bright sunlight. The message was delivered and the plan was in motion. In three hours, he would see if it worked.

BREAKAWAY

For the next 15 minutes, Alex suppressed a desire to open the envelope in his jacket pocket. Seeing an older Ramon Delgato suddenly execute a brush pass in a Canberra dining room was as startling as finding a T-rex wading in Lake Burley Griffin. But somehow the events of the past few days had prepared Alex for something extraordinary to happen. Ever since Fortunas died, he had the feeling of landing in the middle of an ongoing drama – and now maybe he would begin to find out what it was. The answer would be in the envelope he had stuffed next to his passport. But he did not dare look at it yet. The brush pass meant that he might be under observation, so it would be wise to assume it.

Alex walked down the buffet line and put a roll, potato salad, vegetable casserole and a slice of pot roast from the steam table onto his plate. Then he joined Marvin and a lady from Cornell at a corner table. He carefully looked around the room. No one seemed out of place. Everyone, except for the food service staff, was part of the conference. If he was being observed, the watchers were either very good or outside the room, maybe outside the building.

He could see Marvin laughing and sharing a joke with the professor from Cornell but somehow couldn't make out the words. Though every item in the room stood out clearly and every sound was preternaturally distinct the conversations registered only as shapeless sounds. The man next to him, an elderly Australian academic with a very long and bony face in a dark suit with a regimental tie, mumbled something. Alex nodded back automatically. Someone approached him on the left. He looked up to see a pretty waitress offering him red wine. Her guileless smile warmed the room. He accepted a glass and looked around him as if he were an outsider staring in on a fishbowl. The people, the banter, the food seemed separated from him by an enormous distance. Then he turned and gazed out the window and felt, even through the bright sunlight, that the dark old Life was waiting for him. Alex pulled himself together, excused himself, rose and walked to the rest room.

The rest room was empty except for an elderly man who was washing his hands at a sink with excruciating deliberation. Alex went into an empty toilet stall at the end of the row. He closed the door and straddled the bowl, leaning back until supported by the wall. Anyone glancing under the doors would think the toilet was in normal use. He pulled the envelope from his pocket. It contained a high-quality photograph of a man in a gray jacket sitting beside a woman on a bench. Their faces were vaguely familiar but he couldn't remember where he saw them. Suddenly, it clicked: the couple in the breakfast room. He read Ramon's letter.

> These are professionals hired to kidnap or kill you. I'll explain the reason later.
>
> First, we have to get you out of there.
>
> At 14:30 today call 0415 833 942 on the cell phone I gave you. Hang up immediately after it rings. You'll get a confirmation text message that I am in position to meet you. Go out the front entrance of the Convention Center at 14:40 with no bag or baggage to slow you down – abandon everything you can't fit in your pockets or give it to someone else – and walk as quickly as possible without attracting attention into the building on your right, the Canberra Casino. Go through the front doors to the long inner courtyard. See the sketch below. On the last bench in the courtyard you'll find a bicycle cable lock looped over the armrest. Unlock it with code number 276. Take it <u>unlocked</u> to the glass door at the exit with the push bar handles. Once past the exit and out in the street, lock the doors behind you from the <u>street side</u> with the cable lock. Leave no slack for anyone to squeeze through. Then walk fast one block to Akuna Street and walk into the doorway of the Capitolo Shopping Center. I'll be there. Don't hesitate. Your life may depend on it. It'll be just like old times. Good luck.

Alex re-read the simple instructions, looked at the photo again and returned the note and phone to his pockets. He flushed the toilet and stepped out of the stall. Walking out into the dining room, he found to his amazement that he could hear everything again. He sat down beside the Australian academic and began to converse, in the highest spirits since he boarded the plane to Sydney. He even drank his glass of wine and listened with interest to the banter between Marvin Lee and the lady from upstate New York. Then he glanced at his watch. It was 12:30 p.m. In two hours, he would make his move. He dug into his lunch with gusto and went back to the steam table for seconds.

Meanwhile, Pierre and Monique were going ahead with their own plans. Monique had used a valve core extractor tool to deflate the tire on Marvin Lee's rental Hyundai parked in the back lot. She positioned one of the mobile webcams to monitor the rear exit of the Convention Center. Through the remote, she kept watch over the back entrance from the Minicooper. Pierre covered the front exit on Constitution Avenue from a bench across the street, getting up to walk every so often to avoid being too obvious.

The two assassins had not only covered both entrances, but each of the modes by which the target might escape. As Ramon had anticipated, they had split their forces to cover the vehicle and pedestrian modes of egress. If Alex left on foot or by car, whether through the back or out the front, they could follow. Their idea was to stay on him until he could be trapped, like a fly in a glass tube. And then the spiders would go to work.

Both carried ice picks bought from a kitchen supply store. It was all the weaponry they needed. Just a few seconds alone with Alex and either of them could deliver a sequence of rapid thrusts to the heart area. The ice picks were ideal because they could do irreparable damage without creating much external bleeding.

Pierre and Monique had enough confidence in their skills to try for a quick kill at the earliest opportunity. But while a fast hit reduced the chances of getting caught, it also robbed them of the chance to bring artistry to the kill. Part of their job satisfaction was the joy of predation. Hit men and serial killers always left what the police called "an organized crime scene". Unlike unplanned crimes of passion, the pros displayed a meticulous control over everything, from the selection of the victim, to the exquisite execution. It was choreographed violence, the modern equivalent of the ritual of the hunt.

105

Monique was particularly disappointed because she would have no time to watch Alex die. Monique was fascinated with human faces and planned to take up portrait painting in retirement. Indeed much of her professional success was due to her skill at reading faces. Surprise, hope, fear, pain and despair registered as plainly to her as a word upon the printed page. But the rarest of expressions was the mysterious, fleeting and evanescent look at the moment of death. It roused in her the same fascination some felt at the sight of game collapsing into a heap: the feeling that came on the heels of the rifle-jolt. It was the feeling of godlike power. Her storage closet in Paris was full of sketches of the faces of people as she remembered them at the point of death.

But Pierre was adamant. Business before pleasure. He did not expect any real action until the conference ended at 5:00 p.m. The most likely scenario was for Alex Francisco and Marvin Lee to walk to the parking lot and find the Hyundai's tire flat. The Singaporean would probably try to change the tire himself. Monique would call him around to the other side just as Pierre approached from the opposite direction. Together they would offer help just as darkness was falling. Passers-by would think nothing of people writhing on the ground beside a jack and tire iron. The dusk would provide more than enough cover to finish both. Marvin Lee was acceptable collateral damage. "Who cares about one more dead Chinaman? There are enough of them in the world," was how Pierre put it. Alternatively, Alex Francisco might leave Marvin Lee to the car and walk to the hotel. In that case, they could intercept him in the park between the Convention Center and the Rex Hotel. Either way, Alex Francisco would be over quickly.

The least likely possibility was that Francisco would walk out the front. But that eventuality was covered too. Pierre could follow on foot, remaining in contact with Monique in the car, who could trail at a distance if they needed a vehicle. One way or the other their chance would come. The quarry would leave an opening and their ice picks would finish the job. Then it was off to the Maldives for that dive holiday.

Neither assassin knew Alex was at that moment staring intently at their photographs inside a toilet stall. What he saw was an athletic couple on a park bench, their professional intensity burning through their casual clothes. Staring at their faces, he realized that he could only see the shell of what really lay inside. And the real core – whatever it was -- lay completely out of reach in a far, far place. But not so far, Alex thought to himself, that he hadn't heard the rumor of it.

Two hours later, Alex mentally rehearsed what he would do until he had it down pat in his mind. Then he taped a note to Marvin on his laptop case, explaining he had been called away on an emergency and could he please take his laptop back to the hotel. He enclosed two hundred dollars with the note, with instructions to settle any outstanding charges and to leave his luggage with the front desk where he would collect it later. That would stall a search for him and prevent a missing person investigation by the police. He patted his pockets and checked he had everything; he would take nothing but his passport, his old cell phone and the new one, a charger, and his wallet.

At 2:25 p.m. Alex left his laptop case with Marvin and told him to hang on to it. The Singaporean looked surprised, but accepted the bag. Alex left the room for the last time and went out into the lobby. He made the call to the number Ramon gave him. No one answered but half a minute later he received an SMS message: "all ready". He looked down at his watch and saw it was 2:39 p.m. It was time to go. He stepped out the front door of the Convention Center and skipped down the steps.

It took Pierre a half-second to realize that something odd was afoot. The conference sessions hadn't ended and there was the target descending alone onto the sidewalk. Pierre considered the possibility that he was simply making a trip to the convenience store for batteries or aspirin. But his instincts suggested otherwise. He rose from his bench to follow.

He saw the target turn right on the sidewalk. Without hesitation, Pierre told Monique over his headset the target was heading northwest on Constitution Avenue and to bring the car around. Pierre's greatest fear now was that Alex Francisco would board a vehicle before the Minicooper could loop around to Constitution Avenue. But he wasn't even looking for transportation, just walking at a brisk pace northwest.

"Where is he going?" Pierre had no answers yet, but knew he had to get closer in case the target made any sudden moves. He shadowed Alex from the opposite side of eight lanes of road matching him step for step and slightly behind. Turning to look, Pierre saw the Minicooper waiting to turn into the Constitution Avenue traffic. He refocused on Alex who was nearly level with the next building, the Canberra Casino. Pierre sped up, going as fast as he could without attracting attention, but still staying on the opposite side of the road. An instinct told him something was going down.

Suddenly, Alex turned right again and hurried from the sidewalk up the steps of the Canberra Casino. He was nearly through the doors before Pierre began to cross the street. The cars honked their horns as he ran across the roadway, dodging vehicles to close with the target who had disappeared through a doorway. Pierre accelerated as he took the steps in bounds toward the Canberra Casino's entrance. Then he checked himself before he actually reached the doors so he wouldn't barge in and provoke a confrontation with a Casino security man. Pierre slowed to a walk and told Monique over his Bluetooth headset to wait for him at the side entrance as he calmly entered the Casino building. He saw his quarry walking to the far end of the open court that ran through the building. Pierre quickened his pace.

Alex could feel the panic rising in him despite his best efforts to remain calm. His pulse pounded as he walked through the interior courtyard. It was open to the sky and decorated with a row of plants along its center. At intervals, there were metal benches where people could sit in the open air to have a sandwich. At that hour of the afternoon, they were deserted, but the last bench had a bicycle cable lock fastened to the metal backrest. Behind him, he heard someone push open the front doors vigorously. He resisted the impulse to look back. For a second he wondered whether he had enough time to work the bicycle cable lock. But it was too late for second thoughts. It was now or never, do or die.

Alex's pulse quickened as he heard footsteps begin to clatter some distance behind him. He fumbled with the tumblers of the lock. The combination had been set to one short of the correct one at 275. Gripping the lock with both hands to steady his grip, he turned the last tumbler to "6" and pulled. His fingers were slippery but he yanked the cable joint apart and with one smooth motion uncoiled it from the bench. The push bar doors were just steps away, but he could hear the footsteps behind him gaining rapidly. They were close, but he forced himself not to look. Now the steps behind him broke into a frank sprint. Alex threw caution to the winds and raced for the door with everything his middle-aged legs would give.

He heard a low shout behind him, but he was now through the glass door which swung open under his impetus. That was a mistake; it had driven out so far the pneumatic closer slowed the door's return cycle into the frame. He used the split second to effect by looping the bicycle cable lock around the push bar of the closed half of the door, leaving only a little of the loop in play. The voice was yelling now, trying to gain his attention. He ignored it and with his left knee hurried the closing door homeward toward its strike. He slipped one end of the cable lock under the push bar lever and joined it to the other end. With one vigorous push, he snapped the lock shut and spun the combination tumbler.

It clicked home just as Alex was staggered by the sudden impact of a man hurling himself sideways against the narrow gap. The door sprang back on its hinges and the frame squeaked under the force. But the plastic-sheathed quarter-inch braided steel cable held. Alex looked up through the thick safety glass at the staring eyes of Gray Jacket – the man in the photograph – but with the mask of control gone. It had been replaced by a look of pure rage. There was spittle against the glass. He stepped back from the door just in time to evade a forearm pushed through the gap brandishing an ice pick.

With cold deliberation, Alex put his foot against the door and shoved the door edges against the trapped arm. He heard a sharp yelp as the corners of the aluminum door frame bit sharply. The hand reflexively opened and the ice pick clattered to the floor. Then the arm withdrew as quickly as it had come, like a cobra retracting into its hole. Alex did not wait to see what happened next. Turning his back on the locked door, he jogged as fast as he could toward Akuna Street.

Pierre pulled his arm out of the door vise and angrily glanced at the welt on his left forearm. He watched Alex turn and head toward the pedestrian promenade northwest, where he knew there was a mall that sprawled over a two-block area. He was furious with himself, but there was no help for it now. Alex Francisco had an unbeatable head start to a labyrinth that could emerge anywhere. Pierre headed for the nearest exit west. A Casino security guard who was attracted by the commotion attempted to stop Pierre at the door with an outstretched hand, but the Frenchman simply pulled the man's wrist forward with his left hand and broke the guard's elbow joint with his right palm in one fluid move. The guard went down on the floor. Pierre heard more voices calling after him, but ignored them. He stepped out of the building and got into the Minicooper, which had pulled up on the sidewalk. He told Monique where to drive, but knew it would be too late.

PARRY AND THRUST

After the brush pass, Ramon returned to the parking garage and moved the motorcycle to a pre-selected site near the shopping mall. At 14:15, he put on the knock-off Ray Bans, stuck the cheap nylon windbreaker and a tabloid under his arm and went into the courtyard of the Casino where he sat on the last bench and pretended to read the news. When Alex's phone call came, he looped the bicycle cable over the armrest and locked it. Then he sent back the "all ready" message. He waited a couple of minutes more, folded up the paper, made sure that no security staff was watching him and went out the back. He crossed the City Walk and waited in the shadow of the shopping mall entrance. At 14:45, a flustered Alex jogged out of the promenade, slightly out of breath but full of confidence and control.

"Put on the jacket and keep twenty feet behind me," Ramon said. He turned and quickly led Alex through a maze of changes in levels, interconnected walkways and tunnels until they came to a street exit. A little ways down the street was the Suzuki motorcycle. Ramon mounted and began donning a helmet and riding jacket. He gave the spare helmet to Alex. Both lowered their visors and the motorcycle pulled gently away in order to attract the least attention. His parting check in the rearview mirror as he leaned into a turn showed no pursuit. They were clear.

The pair rode north and then east in a silence broken only by the rumble of the twin cylinders. They looped south around Canberra city center through the suburb of Queanbeyan. Once over the river, they stopped off Nimrod Road, where Ramon pulled over behind a copse of trees. Cars zoomed past as the two men dismounted the motorcycle in a depression behind some bushes.

"Howdy, pardner," Ramon said.

"Oh-ho!" Alex laughed. "Man, do you look the worse for wear!"

"You should see yourself."

The two middle-aged men shook hands till their arms hurt. They laughed and skipped in circles like schoolboys.

"Well, I'm on the run again," said Alex. "This time I don't even know who from." That was the signal for things to turn serious.

"I'll explain later," Ramon said. "We seem to be in the clear now. But first, let's secure our comms, in case we're suddenly forced to separate."

He handed Alex a new disposable cell phone. He took back the disposable which Alex had used only moments earlier to signal his readiness, removed the phone battery and SIM and tossed it all into the river. He took the SIM from Alex's regular phone but handed the mechanism back to him.

"Don't use your old cell phone under any circumstances. Use the new disposable one instead. Keep the battery removed. Remember that even if it's turned off, there's the chance it can be remotely activated through a backdoor utility from the phone company. Disconnect the battery and the network can't mess with it."

"Gotcha."

"These phones are our link, your lifeline. They can be our best friends or our worst enemies. If we use them right they can keep us alive. Wrongly used and they can lead the enemy straight to us. Remember that as long as cell phones are powered and within range of a network, whether we use them or not, the phone company tower can keep tabs on us. The system can track a phone to whichever cell it is in. In a city there are lots of little cells and we can be tracked to within a very small area. In the country the cells are much larger because the phone densities are smaller so we can be tracked less precisely. We don't know what resources the bad guys have but we've got to assume they can get into the cell phone company databases. That's why I disabled your old cell phone and dumped the old disposable into the river. From now, we're going to use two completely unknown phones instead. Clean, with no known associations with either of us. We'll communicate by SMS and through a set of prearranged phrases."

112

Alex nodded. "OK. I understand. I will only use the phone you gave me. Right now it's off and the battery is removed. Safed. Now, who are the bad guys?"

"Well, let's go somewhere we can talk at length." Both men remounted the Suzuki, donned their helmets and sped southwest into the suburb of Oxley.

About 11 kilometers from where Alex and Ramon were zipping along on the highway, Pierre was struggling to put his anger under control.

"It was a clean breakaway. He made a fool of me! Paris told us he was an easy target, a middle-aged civilian. Well, there's more to this *civilian* than meets the eye. Alex Francisco walks into a building and breaks contact just as smoothly as you please. Somebody helped him – planned the route, left the lock for the glass door, probably met him at the rendezvous too. It means there's an opposition team out there that knows who we are. The question is: who are 'they'?"

"What does Paris think?" Monique asked.

"Does Paris think at all?" Pierre asked bitterly. "What could they do but blubber and say they are asking the client for more information?"

"If you ask me, they won't come up with any," Monique said.

"Why do you say that?" Pierre asked.

"Because whoever did this isn't working for a national intelligence force, the police or another criminal syndicate. No, Pierre. Ask yourself the real question: why are we still here? Why aren't we in some jail cell? Or, if we were up against another syndicate, why aren't we dead? Why did Francisco use that cheap-ass bicycle lock trick instead of heavies? It's a mystery, Pierre. And that's why I don't think Paris will get any information that will be useful. Paris can find out about spies, policemen and criminals. I don't think we're facing any of those."

Pierre thought about it briefly and drew a blank. "What then?"

"I don't know, Pierre," Monique said, "but I do know that either we find out or we get out of here."

"What possible way of finding out, if Paris can't?"

"Have you forgotten? Known associates: Prof. Marvin Lee from the Singapore National University. His tires are still flat. The conference hasn't ended for the day. We're not out of moves yet, Pierre. But warn Paris. Tell Paris we've stumbled onto something we don't understand."

He recognized the force of the argument. Without a word, Pierre booted up the laptop and began composing a memo to headquarters. When he had sent it, he looked at Monique and said, "Good thinking."

THE MAN FROM SINGAPORE

At the Convention Center, Marvin Lee was saying goodbye to the lady professor from Cornell. "Where's Alex?" she asked.

"He had to go suddenly. He left a note explaining that a sudden emergency had come up."

"Oh dear, I hope it's nothing serious!"

"Alex always lands on his feet. He'll be all right."

"Are you coming to the dinner at Manuka tonight?" she asked. One of the Australian professors was hosting a pizza party at a local restaurant.

"I will," he said, "I'm looking forward to having a glass of wine." With that he said goodbye and left the room.

Marvin Lee went into the parking lot, carrying a stuffed koala bear he had bought in the souvenir shop of the Convention Center under his arm. From a distance, Pierre watched him cross the darkening lot to his rental car.

Marvin unlocked the door and was halfway inside when he noticed that his left front tire was flat. He got out and inspected the damage, his glasses nearly slipping off his nose as he bent down for a closer look. Through the Leica 8x52s binoculars, Pierre judged that the moment had come. He gave Monique the signal over his headset and started the Tarago slowly toward the Hyundai.

Monique walked from her Minicooper to where Marvin was hunched over the tire, trying to figure out the cause of the flat with the help of a small flashlight. Suddenly, he became aware of a young woman standing behind him. He looked up a long pair of muscular legs ending in a short skirt.

"I saw you were having trouble," she said in a helpful voice. "Can I help you?"

He rose with instinctive gallantry to tell the nice lady that as a reserve officer in the Singapore defense forces, having been trained to replace truck tires, brake linings and even straighten out minor suspension damage, he needed no help. But he never got a word out. He had just straightened his body when it doubled again as Monique drove a set of brass knuckles, with the considerable twisting force of her body behind it, into his midsection. As he sank down, she sharply raised her knee to strike the point of his chin. There was a sharp click as his jawbone transmitted the shock to his skull and he fell to the ground stunned.

Pierre came to a stop a few feet from them, blocking the view of any inquisitive strangers. Anyone who might catch an unlikely glimpse of the commotion would have assumed that two Good Samaritans were helping someone into a car. In reality, Pierre pulled Marvin Lee's arms back and snapped a pair of handcuffs around his wrists. Then they half-carried him, as one would a drunk, into the passenger seat of the Tarago. In the meantime, Monique had collected his briefcase and Alex's laptop. Thinking there might be something hidden inside, she also took the toy koala. She checked to see that nothing had been accidentally dropped. After reclosing the rental Hyundai's door, she went back to the Minicooper.

The two assassins drove in a column of vehicles west along Cotter's Road to the Murrumbidgee River. The road was dark and deserted. From a topographical map, Monique had picked a spot along the river that was ideal for their purposes. It was an isolated picnic site at the end of a short dirt road. When they reached their destination, the pair switched off the engines, listened in the silence to make certain they were alone, and had a look around. There was nothing but the sound of the wind in the trees. Satisfied the coast was clear, they gagged Marvin and dragged him to a rocky shelf by the river's edge. A rope went round both his ankles and the handcuffs so that he was curved backward in a bow.

They left him snuffling in the dark and went through his things in the Tarago. They ripped up the toy koala and powered up his laptop from an adapter connected to the cigarette lighter of the car. Pierre took a pair of pruning shears from the trunk. He returned to Marvin and without a word cut both his thumbs off just to demonstrate his seriousness. The Singaporean arched in agony, but could neither scream nor escape with his gag and bonds.

Pierre bent over the man's sweating face and said, "I'll ask you once, what is the password of your computer – and Francisco's? Tell me or I'll cut the rest of your fingers off."

He took off the gag and Marvin stammered out his password. "User ID 'Mayfly6', password, 'happyluck'. But I don't … I can't know Alex's password. He left his laptop with me just today. Look at the note in my jacket pocket!"

Pierre knew this already. They had found the note Alex had written to throw off the pursuit in his pockets. It was probably true that Marvin Lee had no knowledge of Alex's password. Pierre grew increasingly doubtful that he would learn anything from interrogating the Singaporean but having gone so far as to kidnap the guy, he thought they would interrogate him anyway.

Pierre replaced the gag and went back to the car. He logged into Marvin's laptop. A customized desktop, with Marvin and his family forming a background to the icons, appeared. He browsed through the directory structure. Nothing. Then his offline email files. Nothing. He uploaded a special search utility and used it to hunt for keywords among all the files on the hard disk. Nothing. Finally, having spent two fruitless hours searching, Pierre shut off the computer. They could examine it further, but he doubted they would find anything of value. He looked at Alex's computer. Although he had not logged into it yet, the mere fact that it had been abandoned told him what he would find in it. Nothing.

He went back to Marvin and tortured him for Alex's password. Finally, when he had snipped off all the man's fingers, he became convinced that his denials were genuine. "Prof. Marvin Lee," Pierre said, looking down at the bleeding stumps, "I truly believe that you don't know Alex Francisco's password. Now I will ask you to tell me something about his life. What do you know about Alex Francisco's past?"

"That he went to Cornell University and taught at the Business Institute. Beyond that, nothing!"

Pierre kicked his bleeding hands. The man screamed.

"Does he know how to shoot?" Pierre persisted.

"I've never seen him with a weapon of any sort."

Pierre kicked him again.

"Did he mention what he did during the Marcos years?

"He never talked about anything but forestry. Please believe me."

Pierre repeated the blow. Again came the agonized answer. There was nothing new. Eventually, Marvin Lee began to repeat himself. The answers grew weaker as the suffering and fatigue took their toll. Pierre realized he was not going to get much more from the man.

"I have no reason to continue this interview further," Pierre said.

Somewhere in the depths of his pain, Marvin Lee realized that the end of torture meant he was going to die; that he was never going to see his daughter and wife again. A steely resolution rose inside him and he became determined to hurt his captors in any way he could.

As Pierre and Monique approached him, Marvin whispered as if he were trying to say something without being able to. The pair bent down to hear him. Then Marvin tried to bite Pierre's ear off. But the assassin was too quick for him. Pierre sprang back effortlessly and struck a savage backhand blow with a closed fist. Marvin slumped, his nose broken, his body bleeding in one more place.

"The Chinaman bites. Well, he's all yours now," Pierre said.

Monique had made a garrote from a piece of wood about 12 inches long, through which a thick cotton cord had been strongly secured in a groove at one end. The free end of the rope had been knotted at intervals so they could be slipped into a notch at the other end of the stick. In this way, the strangler might adjust the tightness of the rope around the victim's neck to the precision of an inch. Monique jerked the trembling man upright and secured the garrote with moderate tightness around his neck. He was now curved backward and, with Monique's knee in the small of his back, was involuntarily staring up at Pierre bending over him. Then the pair switched places. Monique bent down and played a flashlight on Marvin's trembling face. She gave a nod.

Pierre pulled on the loop until the cords cut into Marvin's neck, the knot slotting into the last notch. She watched as he died.

"Interesting," was all she said.

"This Chinaman had more fight in him than I suspected," Pierre said. "But he didn't tell us anything about Francisco. I don't like it, but I think you're right. Whatever he did in the past, he wasn't in intelligence, the police or crime."

"Do you know what I think?" Monique said.

"What?"

"I think he was some kind of revolutionary. And those kinds of cells are the hardest to penetrate."

THE PLAN

Twenty kilometers to the southeast, Alex and Ramon shivered in the dark along another dirt road. What they had to discuss was too sensitive for the environs of a café, and the risk of being caught on some CCTV was too great. So supplied with some take-out and soft drinks they found an empty rural park with a clean wooden table where they could talk through the night. Nobody bothered them.

"Licban is playing for keeps," Ramon said. "He'll do anything to stay in power. You remember him from back in the day. Cold as a snake. When Brillantes walked into the Senate, he lit a fuse that would lead straight to a powder keg under the President. So he tried to cut it short at Fortunas and now with you."

"Is there any chance he'll figure that you're helping me?" Alex said.

"No. Licban never met you in the underground. In any case, there is nothing to connect you with me. The Marcos files are gone."

"What!" Alex exclaimed. "How do you know?"

Ramon explained. "US intelligence grabbed the files the night Marcos left for exile. Came in and cleaned them out. I have this unofficially from someone I trust, in fact the same person who warned me about the plot to kill you. After all this, I'd say my info was good."

"Good God, who are you involved with, Ramon? The CIA? The NSA?"

"None of the above. And maybe all of the above for all that I know. I've probably met people from all those agencies unofficially," Ramon laughed. "For the last five years I've been writing on the Internet. I've been invited to speak at international conferences on information warfare and how it all ties into terrorism and chaos. But the main thing is I've come in contact with a lot of people who work for intel agencies on an informal basis.

"Now for some reason US intelligence, or some part of it, has tumbled on to Licban's plan to spike the election-cheating investigation in the
120

Philippine Senate. They want the investigation to continue and to do that they have to keep you alive. For political reasons they can't help you directly. From the Marcos files, they know about our mutual history in the underground. So they want me to help you unofficially. The end result is I'm working with US intel – but not for them. I intend to keep you alive until the pros come to help.

"It would be dangerous if Licban could connect us. With the Marcos files under wraps, there's only one other person who knows we knew each other in the underground. You know who it is."

Alex's expression became thoughtful. "No, I don't think she'll give me away. Not even after all these years. But that's no help," Alex said. "Fortunas didn't tell me anything before he died. There's no secret to bury or protect. Even if US intel gets me out of here, it will have been for nothing."

"Don't write yourself off," Ramon said. "There may be something he said you haven't remembered, some association you haven't made. In any case, since you cannot convince the killers you're ignorant, you shouldn't convince my friends there's no percentage to helping you. Without their intel support, it will be hard to keep you alive for the next two weeks. Give yourself a chance to remember, at least until then."

Alex sighed and said, "OK. Then it really is just like old times, where we make it up as we go along. What's your plan?"

Ramon laid it out. "The basic problem any fugitive faces is where to hole up. The safe house problem. You can't stay in a hotel, motel or hostel of any kind. But you have to stay under cover, otherwise sooner or later some camera, electronic transaction, or person on the street will pick you up. You have to stay out of databases and stay out of sight. But where can you do that?"

"Yes, where can I do that?" Alex asked, knowing Ramon already had a plan.

Ramon was in full expository mode now. "Have you ever asked yourself where the most successful fugitives in history had hidden out? Hiroo Onoda, the Japanese straggler, hid out in Lubang Island for 29 years despite the efforts by the locals, who knew the place like the back of their hand, to find him. Eric Rudolf, the Atlanta Olympic Park bomber, hid on the Appalachian Trail for five years despite being on the FBI's Most Wanted List. How did they evade capture so long? They found a place away from databases and people. They lived in the great outdoors, in God's safe house, which doesn't have a registration book or take American Express, Mastercard or Visa. We are going to hide you out on a bushwalking trail."

Alex couldn't think of a better idea.

They walked around to keep warm, working out the fine points of the plan until dawn was breaking. Then Ramon left Alex to hunker down in the bushes while he went off to get some coffee and breakfast rolls from the nearest town center. When he came back, the men sat in the morning sunshine poring over the maps.

"Well, what do you think?" Ramon asked.

"It's doable."

The northern end of the 655-kilometer Australian Alps Walking Track began in the small town of Tharwa, just 30 kilometers from the park where Ramon and Alex sat talking. From Tharwa, the trail went steadily southwest, past upland lakes through high passes which would be covered with snow in winter, but were usually clear in early fall. It ended in a small town in Victoria, only 40 kilometers from Melbourne. A strong hiker could go from Tharwa to Melbourne in about eight weeks. Alex didn't have to go that far, just remain undetected on the trail for two or three weeks.

Alex and Ramon knew from past experience that a man could carry about a week's food supply in a rucksack. The only way to extend endurance out to two or three weeks was to resupply from caches left along the roads that cut through the wilderness. Using Google Earth, Ramon had marked out the GPS coordinates for drops where he could leave food and other supplies in fox-proof containers. The drops would bear from local landmarks to make them easier to find. The caches would allow Alex to range over more than a hundred kilometers, moving from cache to cache if necessary, traveling steadily southwards. It would give him a measure of mobility across the vast landscape, an area so sparsely populated he might not meet another person along the route at all.

The main problem was the weather. It was autumn in the Southern Hemisphere. Soon, the snow would fall on the lower reaches of the trail and make the entire track dangerous and difficult. But danger was relative. The natural hazards of the mountains could be met by equipment, experience and caution; contract killers were harder to defend against. On balance, it was far safer for Alex to head for the hills.

The greatest advantage of hiding in the outdoors was that it would deny the enemy any information. On the trail, there was nothing to buy, no one to meet, no camera to encounter. He would even be out of cell phone range except when he approached a road or settlement. The enemy could have all the databases in the world at their disposal and find nothing, because there would be nothing to find. He would be lost in the blank spaces of the Australian wilderness which were emptier than any other place on earth, with the possible exception of the Canadian north.

The more Alex thought about the plan, the more he was drawn to it. Everything about it – the renewed purpose, the challenge of the mountains, the fascination of operational detail – brought him back to a world he had long forgotten but which Ramon, through his writings and contacts, had somehow retained a tenuous connection with. Even the danger could not completely dampen his spirits. Most people had very little to look forward to at fifty-two except an impending old age. Alex at least had this one last mission – a great cause against daunting odds: the last chance to live the Life. With the planning well in hand, it was time for Alex to ask.

"Ramon, how is Justine? You're the guy with all the news at your fingertips. Is she still in New York?"

"Her eldest is getting married in a couple of months, I think. I can't remember where I saw the notice. With any luck she'll soon be a grandmother."

It was hard to think of Justine as a grandmother.

"I never saw her since that day," said Alex.

"Oddly, I never did either, even after Marcos fell. Not even when I went to New York. There wouldn't be much to talk about really. When we finally got rid of Marcos, it broke the glue that held so many things together. In a way, Martial Law made our world as much as shattered it."

"I felt the same way," Alex said. "I was lost after Marcos fell, unprepared for it. Maybe deep down I never believed we would really succeed. When we did the only home many of us had ever known vanished with it. But I can see you have found another."

"Two homes," Ramon answered. "A family and the Internet. I drifted away from the old circles and decided I'd do something completely different. So I became a computer programmer and stayed in the business until about five years ago when I began writing over the Internet. It was like I'd gone around in a big circle." Ramon paused before asking, "Justine was six years older than you, wasn't she?"

"Yes. It seemed a major, major difference at the time. Her husband, Dante Arevalo, was about thirteen years older than me and that made him seem like an old man. Is he still a labor lawyer?"

"He's the grand old labor lawyer now."

"He was a good guy and tough in a way I never could be," Alex said. "He had the kind of endurance that keeps a tree rooted in one place, defying every storm, never giving in. Dante Arevalo lived one good life under one good name. We had so many names and so many lives it was hard to keep track. I had as many lives as names. By the end, I wasn't sure who I was at all."

Ramon laughed. "Nonsense, Alex. It was you who stayed in one place. And it was Dante who knew how to move on. A tree that has put down roots never stays the same. It changes with the terrain. But with us it was different. Underneath the constant, superficial changes it was always the one life. I know why it was so hard to live in the present. Because so much that we loved was in the past. We were corrupted by the memory of the best years of our lives. The trick to having a future is to let go of the past. That's why I became a programmer, Alex. I needed to drive a stake right through the heart of yesteryear. And despite that it didn't stay dead."

"So enough of old times," Alex said. Let's focus on the plan. It may work with a certain amount of luck. We'll need it."

RACE FOR THE KEY

Bill Greer looked down twenty floors at the maze of traffic below him. From his vantage, the red taillights clogging the small streets of Baclaran in Manila looked like a procession of glowing ants. They were a river of countless vehicles heading south over the Coastal Road toward the dubious haven of bedroom suburbs already overtaken by Manila's urban sprawl before they even had a chance to develop.

His computer display showed the transcripts of every telephone call Johnny Fortunas made in the last sixty days. He made or received an average of 43.1 telephone calls each day, totaling more than 2,500 separate connections. Getting the transcripts had taken about 48 hours. It took so long because transcriptions had to be done by humans. Getting the conversations themselves was a real-time process. A wiretap operation scooped them off the Philippine communications networks through secret software loaded into the telephone switches of the major phone providers. The software had been inserted by company employees Greer had bribed. They subverted the switches while running as background processes: only a detailed audit would reveal them. What they did was send the conversations of interest to Greer.

Greer's software exploited the fact that every modern telephone system was designed to be "wire-tap ready" in order to implement court-ordered surveillance. Every modern telephone system came ready to pick up signals in the switch where the signals were completely in the "clear" or unencrypted. Those signals were cloned and sent to a *shadow phone* where a court-ordered recording device was hooked up. All Greer's rogue software did was to illegally activate the built-in wiretap utilities and transmit the signal to him.

The Fortunas calls had been tapped for months. The hard part in the last 48 hours had been to get authorization to pay contractors to transcribe the calls. It would be a while before software could completely comprehend natural language. But with the US military and the State Department desperate to predict the trajectory of the

Licban-Senate clash, Greer got the money to hire the extra translators. A log of conversations, amounting to nearly 500 pages in total covering the last 60 days of Fortunas' life, was on Greer's computer screen.

Col. Maxwell pulled up a chair next to Greer and said, "Well, Bill, what do you make of it?"

"We can guess some things," Greer said, "though we're still in the dark about others." He typed some commands into the computer and a complicated table appeared. "This is a crosstab of his baseline pattern of calls: who he called on a regular basis and for what purpose. Calls to his mistresses, political associates and what we might call his tradesmen – his barber, tailor, etc. Now look at how his communications habits changed after Brillantes walked into the Senate claiming he witnessed the election theft."

Greer typed some more commands and a markedly different table of numbers appeared on the screen. Maxwell squinted at the numbers as Greer highlighted a cell with his mouse pointer. "Lots of changes. Fortunas starts communicating with people he had never talked to before. But look at this one in particular." Greer double-clicked on a cell in the table of numbers. A new window appeared with a transcript of conversation.

"On the day Brillantes walked into the Senate, Fortunas got a text message from a cell phone in Sydney that had never called him before. He replied to it. The text message asked 'will you take delivery?' and the reply was 'as soon as possible'. We looked up the cell phone number and – surprise, surprise – it was part of a block of pre-paid cell phone SIM cards: a throwaway number. A check showed it came through a downtown Sydney cell tower. So it's safe to infer someone in Australia was asking Fortunas about putting a pre-arranged contingency plan into motion."

Maxwell interjected. "OK. What do you think the message meant?"

"I figure they were asking Fortunas if he was going to Australia. And he said 'yup'. That was the signal to contact other people. Maybe make arrangements for a press conference," Greer said.

"Why couldn't he denounce Licban from Manila?" Maxwell asked.

"Because Licban could shut him down in Manila or at any rate put a bullet through his head. Fortunas needed an expat base. But why Australia? Most Filipinos like to plot out of the US and Honolulu's only about two hours further than Sydney. Something about Australia made it a better base of operations. On a hunch I told my analysts to examine the calls made from pre-paid SIMs from that cell tower at around that time. And bingo, there was one call from a SIM which had never been used since. Another throwaway."

"And who was the call to?"

"The call was to the chairman of the Communist Party of the Philippines in exile in Brussels, Antonio Moran Singson. The reason Fortunas was going to Sydney is because Singson is on the US terrorist watchlist. Fortunas couldn't play footsie with him from the US without ruining his visa and all."

"Is Singson still active?" Greer was asking about the septuagenarian leader of the 1960s Communist insurgency in the Philippines who had been designated a terrorist by the US State Department, not in the least for his nasty connections with North Korea and Islamic extremists.

"Alive, bitter and gnawing at the ends of old plots. He still can't get over his failure to anticipate that Cory Aquino could challenge Ferdinand Marcos. As you recall, he was so sure she would fail that he ordered his Party to sit the uprising out. I guess he didn't count on Ronald Reagan. He missed his chance. Now the old coot's sitting in Europe praying – I know there's irony there – for a second chance. So the way I read it, Fortunas was going to lie low in Australia, then call a press conference and then get Singson to get his mobs rampaging."

Maxwell followed the logic where it led. "But that still brings us to the most interesting question. Who placed the two telephone calls from Sydney? Fortunas didn't have any documents or data devices on him when he died which means his unknown partner in Australia must have the hard evidence showing Licban cheated."

"Yup," Greer nodded.

"Then why hasn't this silent partner in Australia called a press conference denouncing Licban? Why not release the video or whatever to Al Jazeera? With Fortunas gone why not just take over the whole plot from where it left off and tell Singson to start his riots?" Maxwell asked.

Greer was coming to the central point of his deductions. "Because they can't read the evidence without a decryption password from Fortunas," he said. "Fortunas wasn't stupid. He didn't want that evidence used without his say-so. So we think he encrypted it. About a week after Licban was re-elected, Fortunas bought a commercial file-encryption product called **Sure Vault** for $300 over the Internet. It's a Windows-based product that allows you to encrypt video files and burn them on a DVD. Fortunas fixed it so his partner in Australia couldn't start the ball rolling without him. And without the video evidence to create outrage, Singson can't start the riots."

"Then it's useless to us too. Since the password was lost with Fortunas the DVD is unreadable," said Maxwell.

"Not quite. It's only unreadable if you can't break the encryption," answered Greer. "**Sure Vault** only protects to a level of 128-bit encryption – the equivalent of a 16 character alphanumeric password – and we can break it. We don't need the key. We can pick the lock. Our problem is to find the guy who has the DVD. Let's just hope Alex Francisco remembers something that will lead us to it."

THE ROOF OF AUSTRALIA

Ramon left Alex to wait while he shopped for gear and supplies. The Australian Alps in late fall would be cold and pitiless, hard-going for men in their 50s. To traverse it, Alex would need gear that was light yet able to protect him from the icy mountain conditions: a rucksack with enough capacity to hold supplies to last between resupplies and reliable GPS gear that could lead him to the food drops. Fortunately, the Canberra area had many outfitters that catered to the outdoor crowd. Ramon and Alex were nearly the same size so that made buying clothing simple. They exchanged shoes briefly to compare shoe sizes and decided that a boot one size larger than Ramon's would be ideal for Alex.

Ramon stashed the motorcycle in a parking garage and rented a cheap, compact car. Then he bought the necessary gear in a dozen stores, distributing his purchases and paying cash for each item. The first item was a single-person, 22-square-foot tent built around shock-corded aluminum poles that weighed less than three pounds. A good tent was the difference between life and death in wet or extremely cold weather. Next came a thermal pad and a goose down sleeping bag rated down to -20 degrees Fahrenheit which totaled four pounds. The seven pounds of tent, sleeping bag and thermal pad were all the shelter Alex would get.

Next up was a camp stove with an integrated cup and pot, along with two micro-canisters of fuel, each with enough rated energy to boil 12 liters of water, along with weatherproof matches. Two large bicycle squeeze bottles would serve as water canteens and an aluminum spoon would do duty as cutlery. A small package of 3M scouring pads would keep it all clean. Ramon looked at the growing pile of gear. That would be all, apart from consumables, that he dared risk for cooking equipment.

Now for clothing: a pair of Gore-Tex lined hiking boots added three pounds; then came four sets of warm socks, 2 pairs of polyprop tops and bottoms, a Polartec stretch top and sturdy hiking pants. This would be the basic outfit for the march, when body heat made heavy outer clothing unnecessary. Next came a Patagonia R4 windproof fleece jacket, thermal pants and finally, a Gore-Tex XCR parka with zip-in lining with a matching set of overpants to serve as a shell in heavy weather. While this meant only one suit of clothes and a single change of underwear to wear over the trek, Alex could clean his clothes when lying up till his clothes dried enough to put on again. Against the accidents of the trail, he procured a needle, thread, adhesive and repair patches for the shell and the under-layer. With the clothes included, the load stood at about twenty pounds total.

Now for the navigation gear. The entire enterprise depended on finding the resupply points, so good reliable equipment was paramount. Ramon selected two handheld Global Positioning receivers from rival manufacturers to protect against the possibility of failure. Both were well-tested and reputable models, waterproofed down to 3 feet and powered by two AA batteries. Both units had nonvolatile memory which would retain the coordinates of the planned drops. Each unit displayed an artificial compass with heading and distance indicators and a track that stored their movements while the unit was turned on. To provide a frame of reference for the satellite equipment, Ramon purchased a set of 1:250,000 scale maps of the Australian Alps and a waterproof plastic folder to store them in. Twenty high-capacity AA batteries went into the cart. Now, with two GPS receivers and a backup map and compass, he had provided vital redundancy against breakage, malfunction or misadventure. Nearly as an afterthought, he picked up a pair of waterproofed Pentax 8x32 compact binoculars. Finally, he purchased a Suunto mirror compass and a folding nine-inch knife.

With the load now at an estimated 23 pounds, he chose a 5,500 cubic-inch internal frame pack weighing six pounds to store it in. To check that everything would fit he returned to the rental car and removed every piece of packaging from his purchases and stuffed or lashed every piece of equipment into the pack except the hiking clothes that Alex would start in. It looked like there was enough remaining internal volume to pack the food. He stored the gear in the trunk and made a careful list of the medical and food supplies he would need.

Ramon went into one of the several doctor's clinics housed in the mall whose GPs directly billed Medicare for an examination. A receptionist ushered him into the doctor's office. Ramon insistently complained of a toothache in a molar. After poking around with a flashlight and tongue depressor, the GP advised Ramon to see a dentist and gave him a prescription for the antibiotic amoxicillin to suppress the infection in the meantime. He thanked the doc and signed the government billing form.

With the prescription in hand, Ramon went to a drugstore and bought the amoxicillin along with over-the-counter disinfectant and dressing for cuts and bruises. Then he picked up a sponge, toothbrush and a small roll of dental floss for hygiene. Finally he bought some paracetamol against aches and pains. He put these into Ziploc plastic bags. That was the medical kit.

Then he turned to the all-important question of food. From a large supermarket he bought instant oatmeal, noodles, dried fruit, hard cheese, dried sausage, granola and candy until the totals from adding the calorie counts on the packaging reached 27,000. Since a hiker needed 3,000 calories a day to power himself over the hills this was nine days of food: a week plus safety margin.

He now returned to the car. By discarding every bit of excess packaging and strapping the tent, sleeping bag and thermal mat to the outside of the pack, he managed to jam all the food in and cinch it closed. That was it. The equipment was ready. Excluding the clothes on his back, Alex would have to start over the hills with a load weighing nearly fifty pounds.

It was nearing noon but Ramon had one vital task left. Consulting Google Earth on his computer, he chose a number of food drops near identifiable landmarks, like highway bridges, ponds and lakes. He gave them code names and wrote down their coordinates on a piece of paper. He verified the coordinates against the paper map to make sure he didn't get them wrong, then enclosed the drop coordinates in the map case.

He returned to Alex and they spent a couple of hours eating Chinese take-away at a wooden picnic table and going over the equipment, maps and coordinates. Then, having inspected and repacked everything to Alex's satisfaction, they both got in the car and drove to the trailhead in Tharwa. There the track into the mountains began. They went over the drop-points again and reviewed their communications procedures. They devised a number of code phrases to represent prearranged actions. Ramon wanted to keep the comms to an absolute minimum.

"You'll be out of cell phone tower range for the most part. But once you get near the roads the service will start up again. There'll be a cell tower near the first food drop at Kiama. Don't power up unless you have to, as for example if you can't find the drop or if you suddenly figure out the significance of the Fortunas conversation."

"If I do figure out the secret then the agreed phrase is 'see you at the Blinking Bottle'. After the old *Boteng Umiilaw*," Alex said.

"Exactly. Send the message 'see you at the Blinking Bottle'."

By the time they got to the trailhead it was late afternoon. Alex had already changed to trail clothes and emerged from the car fully dressed. But there was one item of equipment remaining. Ramon took a .38 out from underneath the seat and handed it to Alex. "Just like old times," he said. Out of reflex, Alex popped out the cylinder to check the alignment and the general condition of the revolver, then replaced it in the holster. Both the holster and spare ammo went into the hip pocket of his hiking trousers. "It's the same one," Alex said.

"The very same," Ramon answered.

They took the backpack out of the trunk. There was nothing left to say so they shook hands and Ramon drove off. Now Alex was alone. He knew it was too late in the day to start on the trail itself. Besides, he was exhausted from the escape and the long vigil the night before. He decided to sleep nearby and start early the next day. He hiked until he was well away from the Visitor Center. There he found a tiny clearing amid some trees far from the beaten path. He unrolled the thermal mat and lay down in the waning light. The weather was clear and warm. He was still in the low hills. There was no need for a tent yet. He took off his boots and half-slipped into the sleeping bag, leaving the zipper open for ventilation. When he awoke two hours later, it was fully dark.

The stars were out in force. He wriggled the rest of the way into the bag. The stars and constellations of the southern hemisphere looked unfamiliar, but having nothing else to do he searched until at last he found *Crux*, the Southern Cross, and from it identified the other emblems of the night. Beside *Crux* was the constellation Centaurus. He worked his gaze across the celestial dome to locate the other stellar landmarks until he grew sleepy with the effort. The night was so quiet you could hear the occasional swish of wind on the grasses. In the distance, a dog barked from somewhere near the Visitor Center.

It seemed to Alex that nothing could be as quiet as sleeping under the Australian sky. There was no booming of the ocean from a far shore, no ceaseless chatter of insects or the far off rumor of the world of men. On the islands of his youth, human presence was never far – even when bivouacked on mountain sides there might be the distant clatter of a passing vehicle or a pinpoint of light from a hut on a distant hill, some little oil or gas flame lighting a family's way to sleep – always some sign of human existence. But here, far inland on the vast southern continent, among the ruins of ancient mountains that ran through New South Wales and Victoria, one might have been on an uninhabited planet, cold under these strange stars. Alex knew that once on the trail he might go for days without seeing another person. That was good; that was the plan.

LOOKING FOR GAPS

When Ramon got back from Canberra he found his home deserted. His wife's suitcases were gone as were many of his son's summer clothes. All the perishable food in the refrigerator had either been consumed, frozen or thrown away. Rina had well and truly gone to Arizona.

Suddenly, the living room lamps came on, activated by timers Rina had set up to simulate occupancy in the house. Ramon stepped away from the window, the old caution returning reflexively. He went down to the basement office, shutting the upstairs door behind him. It was dark but he knew the way. He switched on the computer and began to order his online affairs to be ready for whatever happened in the next few weeks.

After a couple of hours he left the keyboard and clumped back up the stairs. From the pantry he pulled a jeroboam of Chateau Kefraya, a red wine grown in the Bekaa Valley that had been a gift from a Druze chieftain. He filled an ordinary plastic tumbler with the red, replaced the bottle on the shelf and went back downstairs.

He hoped to drink himself to sleep but it would not come. He put the cup down and returned to the problem at hand. He and Alex had examined their shared past step by step the night before he hit the trail, seeking some flaw in their security arrangements that the enemy could turn to advantage.

Anyone could theoretically connect Alex to himself if they invested enough time and resources. But it would be very hard even in the best of circumstances to reconstruct a vanished clandestine network from 35 years ago. The sheer gulf that separated them from those events was protection from immediate discovery.

But all the same, Ramon couldn't shake the feeling of danger. Licban was a wily one. He called up the most recent pictures of Licban on the Internet to remind himself what that strange face looked like. "You son of a gun," he said, looking at the President's picture. "Singson thought he owned you back then, but you were leading him on from the start."

Ramon thought back to that last night before Alex started on the trail. He asked him to retell the story of how he and Justine started back for Manila.

"What got you running again?" Ramon asked. Alex had pulled on the hood of his jacket to keep out the wind. Nothing of his face could be seen in the dark.

"I was up at the Southern Timber sawmill," he said. "Timber was a boom industry then – before the logging companies cut everything down, when nobody believed the forests could ever be exhausted. The worker's pay was good, especially for the heavy-equipment operators. Even unskilled workers earned so much they didn't bother to cook meals for themselves. Just ate at the canteen. Fresh fish trucked in from the coast and up into those hills, if that means anything. I worked as a storekeeper at a contractor's for cover. We had secret union meetings at night which really didn't amount to much. But I didn't care. I was just learning the ropes, looking around.

"I was never up there, what were the camps like?"

"They were once-in-history things, the kind of place that comes up once and disappears forever. Like a boomtown. The sawmill buildings were made of unpainted scrap timber nailed together and piled one on top of the other in a crazy way. Structures leaned against each other linked with passageways, walkways, even bridges that led from one upper storey to another.

"The whole camp was stacked on a hill. As you drove up to it the first thing you saw was a palisade topped with wire and a gatehouse like a miniature wooden castle. Past the gate you were in an open square with alleys going in every direction. A main road led straight ahead to the sawmill but there were a half-dozen smaller alleys branching off across a 180 degree arc. Some led to streets with honky-tonks, others to lanes of stores and dormitories and warehouses. There were about 10 acres of this crazy wooden camp surrounded by a wall and watchtowers for security. It looked like the pencil sketches of those mad artists who imagined ancient cities on distant planets. If there were three moons in the sky it would not have been out of place.

136

"All day the trucks carried huge logs five-feet-in-diameter to the mill. When night fell the main generator started up and added the thump of that big diesel to the whine of the saw. Then the two-stroke gasoline generators would open up. People sold electric power to each other and electric wires delivering the juice crisscrossed the streets at different heights. Nothing was painted. Everything was built from newly sawn timber.

"I was somewhere in that maze at a union meeting – really a drinking session – when someone poked a stick through a gap in the boards I was leaning on. It was Vallarte. He whispered to me to come outside. There he was nervous as a cat in the alley and he explained that a special team from the Military Intelligence Security Group – Bobadilla's boys – had arrested Arevalo while he was at a meeting at the nearby Peninsular Lumber. They had no warrant; they said they didn't need one.

"Vallarte was worried they were going after the whole union and that it might only be minutes before MISG came through the compound gates. He had been on his way to Peninsular Lumber earlier to join Arevalo for the union contract negotiations. But a cousin who was in the local police force tipped him off and warned him not to go in. So Vallarte turned around and came up to Southern Timber hidden under the tarp of another truck to warn us.

"Nobody knew how far behind him the MISG was. We decided to warn the local union officers, figuring that the rank and file were too insignificant to be in danger of arrest. In any case there was no time to warn more than a few because we wanted to be clear of the sawmill in twenty minutes.

"I went back to the union meeting hall and gave the officers the news straight. You could see the alcohol drain from their faces. Most had families right in the compound. Anyone who walked out with us into the night would be leaving their families, jobs, everything – for the unknown. Yet if they stayed, who knew whether it would be the electric shock treatment or the heated pliers pulling out their nails? Or maybe they would be let off with a warning. If they knew what their

137

fates would be the decision would be easy. But that's the problem with dealing with a dictator: you never knew what to expect. That was part of the terror. In the end, only the union president decided to go with us. The rest decided to keep drinking. As for me, the backpack was already over my shoulder. I stepped out of Peninsular Timber and never came back again.

"We waited at the end of an alley near the perimeter fence while the union president got his things and said his goodbyes to his family. We were straining our ears for signs that the raiding team had reached the camp. But it was just nerves. Fifteen minutes later, the union president showed up with a little bag under his arm. We went through the perimeter wire at a place where the security guard was the union president's brother. There was a steep, narrow track down to a stream at the bottom of the hill which served as the camp drain. We crossed over the wet stones by the light from the camp watchtowers.

"Once across, we followed the stream down to a rubber plantation. It extended for miles like a big dark sea, served by roads that trucks collecting latex used. We found one of the roads without trouble – it ended by the stream – and now at least we could walk on a road instead of having to struggle over roots and tussocks. Those plantation roads are deserted at night. Have you ever walked under rubber trees at night?"

"Can't say I have," said Ramon.

"There's no light in under that thick canopy," Alex continued. "The leaves cut off most of the sunlight by day and all starlight and moonglow by night. You can't see the hand in front of your face. Our little group groped along like blind men, keeping to the road only by feeling for its edge with our feet. We stayed together by holding on to the belt of the man in front of us. Every now and again, the road would go straight on and we could make good time despite the total darkness. I knew from previous visits to that plantation that everyone stayed buttoned up in their camps at night – the workers in their housing and the guards patrolling near the equipment sheds – because everyone was terrified of the Muslim bandits that prowled in the dark.

It was like those Jim Corbett stories where nothing moves in the countryside except the man-eating tigers except in this case the tigers had automatic rifles. We were acutely aware that anything we attracted would be something we didn't want to meet.

"We would hear danger long before we saw it. We kept an ear open to get the half minute's warning to scatter between the rows of rubber trees where the headlights couldn't reach us. We stopped every now and again on the leader so we could hear the approach of anything in the silence of the gaps. But nothing ever came: not Bobadilla's men, not the rebels nor the company guards. By the time the sun came up we were close to the highway.

"We hid in the bushes just off the road. Behind us you could hear the rubber tapper's camps stirring and in front of us was a blacktop asphalt curve that would soon be carrying the day's traffic. None of us had thought much beyond getting out of the logging camp the night before. But now with the highway in front of us we were forced to make further plans. Vallarte was first to figure out his move. He told us he would make his way somewhere he could lie low. He had lots of contacts and relatives on the peninsula. He could wait out the heat or square his beef with the military through his contacts. If necessary he could negotiate surrender to a relatively friendly set of authorities. The union president, on the other hand, had fewer resources. He sat there like a frightened rabbit, unable to go back to the camp and unable to think of anywhere else to go. Eventually, Vallarte offered to take him along. The union president grabbed the chance gratefully, and both of them waited until Vallarte saw someone he recognized driving a truck – he seemed to know a lot of people. The two of them ran out onto the road, flagged down the vehicle and hitched a ride. It rumbled off and I never saw either of them again."

"And you?"

"Me? I was strangely glad to be rid of Vallarte. That smile of his creeped me out. He helped me in his own way, but there was something unpredictable about him and I felt better alone.

"I saw that the key to survival lay in going where nobody in the blown networks knew about. Somewhere the poor victims of Bobadilla could never give up, no matter how bad the torture. That meant going back to the Program, which was my deepest secret. I sat by that road for a time thinking about the road north and maybe a way over the strait to the Visayas. If I could get off Mindanao Island, there was a chance of making my way to Cebu and from there ... and then it occurred to me that MISG would be looking for Justine too. Where would she go? Maybe they had already gotten her, but I didn't know that. It took me till about noon to make up my mind to go back to Zamboanga first."

"It must have been a long way back to Z city. What did you do? Hitch another ride on a truck?"

"Oh, that was too dangerous. So I decided to cycle back," Alex said.

"You did what?" Ramon laughed.

"I didn't know I was going to do that at first. My first thought was simply to get back to the little chapel where I stayed my first night out from the bus ambush. It was only about 30 miles down the road from the plantation. That little chapel was served by a rubber tapper who was a part-time preacher on Sundays. It took me almost 24 hours of steady, careful walking to get there, moving just inside the plantation boundary with the road. I drank from streams, hand pumps and picked fruit off trees to keep me going. Slept in some bushes and then walked again when morning came. When I got to the preacher, he gave me a meal. Opened a small can of sardines, which must have been the family Sunday lunch. Then I saw the bicycle.

"It was a piece of junk with a grindstone fixed to the front handlebars, the kind itinerant knife-sharpeners use. It was sitting in the yard and we found some waste crankcase oil to grease the moving parts, tightened up the nuts and wired up everything else. The grindstone worked by raising a back wheel stand so it turned freely and hooking a fan belt to a spindle that ran off the wheel. You pedaled and it turned the grindstone. I knew it was just the thing and bought it together with a T-shirt and a pair of old trousers all thrown in a burlap bag."

140

"That was a smart move. Nobody notices the itinerant peddlers."

"On the bicycle, I was just another bum scrounging a buck. I pedaled it down the road past all the vehicle checkpoints and sharpened some knives along the way. I made a little money too, which was good, since I had paid well for the bike. It took five days to pedal back to Zamboanga City."

"Were you really worried that Justine was in trouble or did you just want to see her?"

"Maybe in the back of my mind I just wanted to see her, though I wouldn't have wanted to recognize it as a motive. She was the first real woman I could talk to about politics, God and literature. We wrote each other a lot in the preceding months. I had promised to write. Every now and again, she'd send me a book through a union official. Or put it in a package on one of the bus lines which they'd hold at the store in Ipil for me. Good books: Ignazio Silone, Albert Camus and once, I think, Milovan Djilas."

"No George Orwell?" Ramon asked.

"I think she was afraid of Orwell. He was a threat to her beliefs. People on the Left feared him like religious people fear eloquent atheists. Funny that self-proclaimed atheists should worry about losing their unfaith but they probably dread losing trust in the Party even more than religious people fear losing faith in God. Once you lose your faith in the historical imperative, then all the horrible things you do in its name would be just that: horrible. Even today a lot of people are afraid of Orwell. Interesting how a writer can still carry the taint of fire and brimstone with him more than decades after his death.

"But mostly we wrote to each other about life and death. It sounds preposterous to say that people in their twenties should worry about old age, but no one is more preoccupied with youth than the young."

Ramon took up the theme. "I knew the feeling, that same secret nightmare. It took different forms but it was always the same bad dream – that one day you would wake up and find that everyone had moved on and left you an old loser clinging to forgotten causes."

"That was the subtext of our correspondence, at least from my end," Alex said, "the *certainty* that one day the letters would stop and the books would no longer come. Sooner or later Justine would move on, have a baby, or maybe leave Dante and meet a rich, leftist European or someone on one of her conferences abroad and finally decide she had no time to answer letters from a yokel in the Zamboanga Peninsula who described the same old coconuts growing on the same old trees. It's the old story."

Yes, it was the old story. Ramon remembered how Alex's story petered out at that point and how the stars began to fade from the sky as the dawn approached. Although they didn't know it, somewhere Marvin Lee lay strangled in the dirt, with the same stars looking down on his body. Alex and Ramon got up from the side of the ditch and walked in circles to keep warm. Ramon finally broke the silence.

"The underground was the best and worst thing that ever happened to some people. Which it was depended on what they were in it for. Those who wanted to overthrow Marcos and go on with their lives found themselves either changed or consumed by it. But those who were in it to *replace Marcos* never had to change at all. For them the underground was simply a continuation of power politics."

"You're referring to Ulysses Licban," Alex said.

"Sure, Licban and Antonio Moran Singson of the Communist Party. Not many people knew Licban was in the underground. But Singson did."

"Do you still think there's a connection now?" Alex asked.

"No. Licban wouldn't bother with him now. Singson's washed up, an old terrorist giving speeches to crazy academics in Europe and collecting drug money from his leftist minions in the Philippines. A glorified thug but strictly small-time now compared to Licban. That is why Fortunas could use him. He could prey on his sense of humiliation and offer him one last chance at power."

142

Suddenly Alex pulled down his hood and said quietly, "Why don't you leave this to me, Ramon? You've got a family now. Don't get mixed up with these people again. I can handle this myself. You just get me some supplies and equipment, drive me to the trailhead and let me take care of it. I'm not stupid and I've got nothing to go back to but a leaky apartment in Manila that isn't worth a damn. But you – you're a family man now – you can't do this anymore."

"I appreciate your concern, Alex. And maybe I can't handle it any more but the hard fact is you wouldn't survive out there without continuous logistical and intelligence support, with the low temperatures, with the hit team hunting you. I'm as condemned as you are to seeing this through, though for a different reason. I don't have to explain it to you because you know why. People start down a road sometime in their lives and it sweeps them along till years later it's become so much a part of them that there's nowhere else to go except to the end."

What lay at the end of the road? That was the problem that nagged them. They were two middle-aged men sitting in the Australian bush worrying about debts of honor and ideals that people had long ago forgotten.

Forgotten. Yes it had been too long.

At least Ramon was sure now that there would be no leak from the past simply because there was nobody left who cared about it. The schism between Licban and Singson meant that neither would have a chance to delve deep into a history which still held dangers for both of them. For the moment at least, Ramon and Alex were safe in the shadow.

Ramon rose from the couch in his office, went upstairs for another shot of Lebanese red, then went back down. He looked at the silent IM window on the computer and hoped it would leave him in peace for the night.

JUSTINE

In the hour before dawn, Alex pulled the hood of the sleeping bag tight around his face and looked up at the sky. It was still dark in Tharwa and a white dusting of stars rolled slowly overhead. In three hours, he would be on the trail. Mentally he glanced back along the road he had come and continued the story of his flight from Zamboanga from where he had left it with Ramon.

He was back in the third-class compartment of a small passenger ship, a single-funnel vessel of just under a thousand tons, every weld shaking with the rumble of the diesel engines. He lay in the upper berth of a row of steel framed bunks, each furnished with an orange plastic-covered cushion, in an open-plan cabin that ran the whole width of the ship. There were two hatchways: one on the forward bulkhead led to a crowded dining room where the passengers were fed in shifts and the one heading aft opened on to the poop deck.

He sprang off the bunk and walked aft to the poop deck, an open-air space stacked with wooden crates lashed to brackets on the deck by steel cable. A number of passengers lounged there, glad to be in the open despite the diesel exhaust which occasionally sent its greasy coils down to them. Air and spray mingled with cigarette smoke and conversation as men drank beer despite the early hour. The men watched islands pass to port and starboard, occasionally pitching empty bottles and crumpled cigarette packs out into the white wake.

Justine was nowhere to be seen. She hadn't been in the open row of ladies' bunks. The dining room was still closed. And she wasn't aft and he wasn't going to knock on the ladies' room. Alex went around the side rail to the bow and found her sitting by a large coil of rope forward watching the forepeak rise and fall between the sea and sky. He sat down beside her. She said nothing.

After making his way back to Zamboanga City, he had scouted the Arevalo home for danger by pedaling past when the morning traffic was at its busiest to hide in the rush of people heading off to work. Although he knew what he was likely to find, he did the recon anyway.
144

The house was deserted; the balcony where labor union leaders normally sat smoking their evening cigarettes was totally forlorn. Even the goat was gone from his island.

Alex did a circuit of the lanes which went around the sprawling lot. A gap in the fence along one street provided a glimpse of the bunkhouse in the back where the Arevalos had kept the USAID relief goods. The back door stood ajar and two jowly men with gun butts poking from their waistbands sat on the steps reading newspapers. Alex knew that wherever Justine was, she wasn't there.

He chained the bike to a fence railing in an alley and took a jeep to a city bazaar where he bought a pair of dark trousers and a long-sleeved cotton shirt. With a new suit of clothes under his arm, Alex paid a few pesos to a lodging house innkeeper for the use of an outdoor washroom to clean up and shave. That evening, suitably attired, bathed and barbered, he waited until the congregation that gathered nightly at Pastor Velasco's chapel began to leave. When the last parishioner had gone, Alex went into the chapel, knelt quietly in a back pew and bowed his head in prayer.

Although Pastor Velasco knew Alex at sight, he gave no sign of recognition. Instead, the pastor swept the aisles and as he walked past Alex's pew slipped a note into his hand. Alex pocketed the note, made the sign of the Cross and left. He read the note by a streetlight some distance away. They contained Velasco's instructions to meet at a café in Pasonanca Park the next morning.

The café had once been a private residence. It was screened from the main street by a verge of orchids, ornamental shrubs and frangipani. The former family living spaces were now a large dining area dotted with small tables. Velasco and Alex sat in a corner table in a room empty except for a mother and a small child having cakes and lemonade. Alex gave Velasco a short version of events so far.

"I'll be leaving for Luzon in a very short while. But I didn't know how Justine was and came back to check."

"She's okay. She was away from the house when the raiding team arrived. We saw them from the church and suspended the service. Some of the parishioners went out to warn her and someone found her in the market," Velasco said.

"I'm glad she's okay," Alex said.

"She's been looking for a way to get to Manila because she thinks there's a way to get Dante out of jail. Can you help her get there?" the pastor said. Alex was surprised anyone would even consider getting someone out of prison, but readily agreed.

"It will be a long trip north," Alex said.

"I think she'll accept your offer. She wants to go badly. When can you start?"

"As soon as she's ready."

"OK. Meet me tomorrow at Cawa-cawa," Velasco said. He took a slip of paper out of his pocket with a hand-drawn sketch of the meeting place.

The rendezvous turned out to be a park bench along the seashore. Velasco gave him detailed directions to Justine's hideout. As soon as it was dark, Alex left the shed where he had been staying. He unchained his knife-sharpening bicycle from the tree and left the key in the lock. Whoever wanted it could have it.

He walked southwest towards the sea. He turned off the road at a billboard advertising a local soft drink. The track led to a small slum. Alex threaded his way past a group of shacks, passing unnoticed among the shanties until he came to a grove of scraggly coconut trees, the last remnant of a plantation that once covered the area for miles. A small hut stood in the middle of the grove. Smoke from a small cooking fire curled up from the hut into the moonlight.

He rapped on the door, which opened quickly. He slipped in and by the light of a small oil lamp saw an old lady in a shapeless dress and battered sandals.

146

"I will be your guide," she said in Visayan. They went out the back door on to a path that led after a couple of kilometers over a footbridge spanning a small creek. Across the bridge a dirt road continued to a checkerboard of salt beds. Beyond them was the sea.

The old woman took him to the front door of a house near the salt beds. She knocked and whispered something through a crack in the door. Alex caught a glimpse of a small living room before it closed. Then it opened again, letting out a woman wearing a bandana and clutching a small bag.

"Hello Pietro," she said. It was Justine.

"Never a rose without a thorn," said Alex, giving the countersign from the Ignazio Silone novel in which "Pietro" was a character. The old lady who guided Alex said a quiet goodbye and disappeared back across the bridge. Justine led him to the beach. It stretched a long white way under the moonlight and ended in a small outrigger canoe in the middle distance.

Justine had rented a motorized outrigger to take them across the inner arm of the Moro Gulf to the northern Mindanao port city of Pagadian. From there, they went overland to the seaport of Cagayan de Oro. Now they were on a ship bound for the Visayas. There Justine's contacts ended and Alex's began.

The coil of rope on the foc'sle provided a convenient seat from which to watch the bow rise and dip. The ship's prow dug up spray every time it punched its nose into the waves. Alex came back with a small cellophane-wrapped package of crackers and a bottle of warm Coca-Cola that he handed to Justine.

She took them without comment and asked, "I know what to do when I get to Manila, but what about you?"

"Oh, I'll make it up as I go along. The main thing is to get under cover as soon as we can. We can join a cell run by a friend of mine."

"Isn't it odd to be going back to Luzon after heading south?" Justine asked.

"Distance in the underground isn't measured in miles," Alex said, "but in the gaps in the enemy's knowledge. Zamboanga was safe while nobody knew I was there. There's a cell in Manila that Bobadilla doesn't know about so it is further from him in the measure that matters."

Alex saw land in the distance, a sign that sometime in the next few hours, the little ship would make port in teeming Cebu City, the shipping hub of the Visayas. From there, they would go by land and ferry up the Visayan chain of islands until they could cross to southern Luzon. From there they would go to Manila.

The shadow in the distance soon resolved itself into a large island. On its slopes, a great city sprawled down to the sea. By late that afternoon, the small passenger ship was chugging up the Mactan Channel to Cebu City.

Alex and Justine positioned themselves in widely separated parts of the debarkation queue in case the intelligence agents who watched every major port recognized one of them. Separated, there was a chance one of them could get away even if the other was identified.

They slipped past without incident. Alex walked straight off the dock to the Cathedral of the Holy Child near the flower market. He took a pew by the side entrance, just another traveler giving thanks for a safe sea-passage. Ten minutes later, Justine entered the church and sat three rows in front of him. After a time Alex rose, made the sign of the Cross and stood. He lighted a votive candle in one of the alcoves, scanning the dark interior of the church for signs of a tail. There was none.

They left at two-minute intervals from the side entrance of the Cathedral and rendezvoused two blocks away. From there, they went to a small lodging house off Colon Street where they booked separate rooms. Later that night, they celebrated the first leg of their escape at a restaurant around the corner: two bottles of beer to accompany a meal of rice, fried fish, soup, and tomato and coriander salad.

The next day, Alex woke to find a heavy rain beating against the wooden jalousies of the boarding-house window. He pushed aside the mosquito net, jumped into his clothes, went into the corridor and knocked on Justine's door to let her know it was time to go. It was still dark as they walked through the heavy downpour to the bus terminal.

The bus went as far as the sleepy coastal port of Bogo from which a cargo ferry left for the little port of Biliran in Leyte on the next island. Biliran was a little quay sticking out into a channel surrounded by high hills. It seemed less a port than a fishing pier on an inlet.

A small bus took passengers disembarking from the ferry to the town of Tacloban. The rain had stopped by the time they got to the Tacloban town center, a place crowded with stores that sold farm supplies, automotive parts, dry goods and general merchandise. Justine and Alex wandered around the muddy streets of town for a while looking for a ride onward. No more buses were leaving that day for the San Bernardino Strait, the last body of water separating the Visayan island chain from the southernmost tip of Luzon. The leg north to Luzon would have to wait for morning.

Alex proposed sitting out the night under some benches, but Justine was tired and would not hear of it. Asking around, they found a small beach resort on San Pedro Bay, about two kilometers away. They took a little motorized rickshaw there. The manager who lived in a nearby house rented them two huts built on wooden piles right next to the resort lavatories.

"They're conveniently close to the toilets," he said, apparently regarding the proximity of sanitary facilities as an attraction, "and they've just been cleaned."

Alex looked at the huts and said they would do.

The little cottages were unfurnished apart from a central plank table and little bamboo benches along the sides. But the scenery from the front doors made up for everything. The resort had a panoramic view of San Pedro Bay, which rapidly narrowed until it formed part of the San Juanico Channel to the north. In the fading light, the channel resembled an immense river as it flowed in the gap between Leyte and Samar.

Alex gave the caretaker some money to cook hot rice and sauté some canned sardines for their dinner. The caretaker took the money and walked up the street to buy the ingredients at a small store. Alex sat down at one of the beach picnic tables and watched a few palms shudder in the strong breeze as the waves, still agitated by the recent squall, threw a dirty surf up on the shore. Suddenly the rain in the distance stopped. Alex noticed a clear band of sky moving westward above the mountains of the huge island of Samar just across the channel.

Justine came out to the picnic tables, having changed from her jeans and shirt into a *malong*. Alex guessed that a real lady could manage to look good even in reduced circumstances. And Justine was a real lady.

"Here comes dinner," Alex said.

The caretaker had returned with a large platter of rice, a dish of sardines in tomato sauce sautéed with onions, four small bananas and two bottles of 7-Up. He laid it with great ceremony on the beach table. Alex gave him a small tip, asking him to come back in about an hour to retrieve the dishes. Justine took a small battery-powered cassette tape recorder from her bag.

"Let's have music with our meal," she said.

The tape was of Nikolai Rimsky-Korsakov's *Scheherazade*. The woodwinds and the violins musically representing Sinbad's ship made it easy to imagine a sail beating up against the darkness of San Pedro Bay. Alex could barely make out Justine's profile in the dusk. The band of light over the hills now disappeared entirely as the sun sank and the space beyond the shore became a sounding blackness, punctuated only by the distant flicker of gas lanterns from fishing boats venturing out into the strait.

Alex was only vaguely familiar with the back story of *Scheherazade*. He knew it was about a Persian princess who kept the cruel Sultan from killing her as he did all his past wives by beguiling him with successive tales for 1001 nights.

"Did Scheherazade ever escape the Sultan's sentence of death?" he asked.

"Yes," Justine said. "After 1001 stories the Sultan fell in love with her. Her stories worked a subtle magic that changed him from a monster into man who could love. The tales brought him to life, a sorcery greater than any described in her tale."

The music changed to the slow rhythms of Prince Kalendar's theme as they ate. After a time, Alex heard the caretaker's footsteps return in the darkness. He turned to thank the man and helped him heap the empty dishes on a tray. The caretaker padded back up the road and disappeared into his dimly lit doorway. A little boy opened the door for his father and his face in the brief illumination was one of innocent expectation and happiness.

"Maybe our little dinner here made it possible for a boy to get some candy," Alex said.

"It's nice to know we've done some good. How I wish we could make the boy's joy last forever." She swept her slim arm out across the sky. "Every night we live out is like a story when you think about it but is there magic in our stories? And will it be enough to convince the sultan of fate to spare us?"

"He doesn't need to spare us for the magic to happen. If something we do in our 1001 days lasts forever, it's sorcery enough," answered Alex.

"Forever?" Justine laughed. "How can you say that anything we do lasts more than a moment? People go to all lengths to avoid oblivion. They start families, religions, even empires so some part of them may go on. And in the end it all comes to nothing. Dante told me he was 21 before the possibility occurred to him that God might not exist."

Alex felt slightly uneasy listening to this beautiful woman talk about the secret places in her married life, the confidences between husband and wife. His reading had been desultory compared to hers, composed largely of pulp science fiction, Irish poets, military history, the lives of saints, joke books and historical romances. He could quote the *Prisoner of Zenda* or the *Four Feathers* while Justine could invoke Dietrich Bonhoeffer. But he answered as best he could.

"I think Jefferson said that all we could see were the 'external facts', but that the real magic which created those facts would remain forever unknown. The parts that no one remembers in our lives are the magic. What we do changes the world forever – even something so small as the candy we made possible for that caretaker's son tonight. Well, God might or might not exist but He remembers. And then all we have to do is stand on our hill and work our magic, and let the 'external facts' remember us."

Justine said, "You seem so sure. I came from a very religious, evangelical family, outsiders in this Roman Catholic country. We read the Bible each night, but I was never sure. Maybe the reason I married Dante was because I wanted to wander outside the circle, to know what it was to be without certitude and have someone to talk to about doubt and the possibility of a life of faith even without God."

Alex debated whether to answer. He would have trouble explaining to Justine, who craved absolutes, that most people were happy with half answers. They were content with enough love to get them past the fear, satisfied with the fleeting grace that comforted them through grief. Suddenly he wondered whether Justine was a Communist after all. The Party was full of individuals who wanted categorical answers in place of maybes.

"I think," Alex said softly, "that all revolutions are about faith. In this case it's faith for its own sake, about religion without God. Yes, we are told there could be a paradise on earth. But we're not really convinced and we don't really care for as long as we have some religion and some paradise before us.

152

"That makes it a moral problem, because the paradise we don't really believe in has to be built with the bricks and mortar of people's lives. What everyone caught up in revolution wants to know is whether faith in Stalin or Mao or Antonio Moran Singson is enough to kill or be killed for? Because it would be really funny, now that we are talking about religion – now that it is clear that's what we are really talking about – to exchange Communism for Christianity and Trotsky for Moses. If you find your arms can't reach the heavens, what is the sense to worshipping a model in mud on the ground?"

"So what do you believe in, Alex?" Justine said. "In the old ways?"

"In the unchanging ways, in the human condition. What condemns us to freedom is the chance that God might exist. And if real salvation is real, then freedom is real too."

"Real freedom," Justine asked, "must include the right to choose slavery or even Hell, though I can't think of a good reason for anyone to choose it. Is that part of freedom?"

"It seems that deciding never to choose again is the one act that is forbidden to us," Alex said. "To do that would be to leave the circle of mankind forever."

"Are you afraid of that sin, Alex?" Justine asked. "Despair is comforting because it's definite. And don't be so sure that people want freedom. Many choose slavery, Alex. Many choose to be bad. I sometimes feel as if I could choose it. That possibility of evil was the most terrifying realization about myself; it puts a blemish on my prayer and a shadow over my love."

Alex looked out to the sea. The stars had dimmed. That meant the clouds were back. "The night is well on and some questions have no answers. We'd better turn in so we can get an early start tomorrow."

Justine laughed and scooped up her cassette. She cinched the *malong* securely around her shoulders and stood in the sand with the faint moonlight in her hair.

"You're a funny guy, Alex. I never know where you're going."

"Neither do I."

They went up into their little huts. Morning seemed to come almost immediately. Alex awoke with a start, rubbed the sleep out of his eyes and descended the bamboo stairs. He rapped on the side of the next hut. Justine leaned out and asked, "Is it time?"

"Yes."

He swung the bag which contained the sum total of his belongings over his shoulder and felt his way into the lavatory. He cleaned up in the half-light and went out and watched the road more out of professional caution than anything else. Justine was ready in a few minutes. They had paid in advance so they let themselves out the gate and walked in the dark to the bus station.

The bus ran up the Leyte coast to San Juanico and another ferry carried them across the narrow strait to the island of Samar, where US Army veterans of the Indian wars once battled Philippine insurgents at the turn of the 20th century. Once in Samar, the bus followed the eastern coastal road two hundred miles north until it came, eight hours later, to the last barrier before reaching Luzon. From the port of Allen, the southern tip of Luzon was dimly visible in the late afternoon across the San Bernardino Strait.

These waters had once been traversed by the Imperial Japanese Navy super battleships *Yamato* and *Musashi* on their way to attack Krueger's transports in Leyte Gulf. Never before, and probably never again, would those obscure narrow seas support such a weight of historical drama. But the tides of time had moved on and it would carry nothing more than a small ferry that day. The ro-ro vessel would leave in a few hours. Alex and Justine stayed clear of the dock where a group of passengers sat on the benches around their little piles of baggage, guarding them like the circled wagons of old.

They saw nothing that slow afternoon except the stray dogs of Allen nosing around the dust. Alex bought a ten-centavo cup of sweet coffee to stay awake, but fell asleep under the shade of a tamarind tree. When the ferry was ready to shove off, it was Justine who shook him from sleep.

Alex opened his eyes but he was no longer in Allen. It was cold and dark except for the top of Mount Tennent which flared red in the first light of dawn. He looked at his watch. There was a little time yet to go. He burrowed back down into his sleeping bag and recalled the approach to Manila all those years ago.

RAMON DELGATO

Once across the strait Alex and Justine took a punishing succession of buses and held on without a pause. The provinces of Sorsogon, Albay, Camarines Sur and Camarines Norte flashed past the window in a bone-jarring blur. There were changes at crowded terminals where the earsplitting shouts of hawkers clashed with the incomprehensible din of conductors shouting out their destinations. Occasionally the bus crossed quiet stretches of hilly road when a thin and wet wind whistled softly through the gaps in the coachwork and they settled into a half-sleep. But all too soon the idyll would end and the bus would screech to a halt and they had to change vehicles all over again.

It was an endless lurching ride on hard seats, with frequent stops in small towns picking up passengers who came aboard with livestock or produce. Finally, Alex suggested a stop in Daet, Camarines Norte, about 100 miles short of Manila. He did not want to reach Manila too tired to stay alert.

They found a lodging house near the bus terminal that catered to traveling salesmen and public school teachers. The rooms consisted of plywood cubicles whose partitions stopped a foot short of the ceiling and six inches shy of the floor. To discourage Peeping Toms, the women's rooms were segregated from the men's. The bed sheets consisted of flour sacks stitched together to form a rough rectangle. Alex put his bag under his head to keep it from being pulled from under the divider by bag-snatchers. A daddy-long-legs scuttled across his body and he blew hard on it to make it jump back into the shadows. Then he pushed away the world as if from long practice and slowly the lights dimmed around him and he remembered no more and slept.

Alex and Justine rendezvoused at the front desk the next morning, neither eager to sample the breakfast offered by the ground-floor greasy spoon. They went directly to the depot and boarded the bus for Manila. The ride seemed just as endless as those of the days before. But this time they were filled with a rising tension. The great metropolis was the doorway to an uncertain future that would bring either freedom for Dante Arevalo or capture to them both; which it was to be they would learn soon enough.

The city announced itself long before they got there. The open gaps between the towns got progressively smaller until they vanished altogether. As they neared the great urban sprawl, the network of streets grew progressively denser. Finally, the bus hit its first actual traffic jam. It began to crawl forward in a sea of vehicles, people and street stalls, all intermingled in a cacophonous tide that flowed sluggishly beneath a maze of telephone wires and electric lines that hung from poles and buildings. Alex and Justine bailed out before they got to the bus station. They headed for the sprawling dry and wet goods bazaar in Baclaran where the uproar was great but comforting because they could easily lose themselves in the crowd. They were in Manila.

All that remained was the hardest part: to make contact with the Program. Alex made some telephone calls at a phone rental stall on a side street. Justine watched him speak, one hand clapped against his ear to block out the noise. The conversation was brief. He set the receiver down, paid the woman who ran the stall ten centavos and walked to where Justine was.

"I'll have to call back in two hours," he said.

That call turned into another "call back in two hours" response which turned into yet another. They waited in the heat of the narrow bazaar lanes, occasionally shifting position, but mostly sitting at cheap stalls nursing glasses of sweetened water in which shredded gelatin and coconut cream had been added for flavor. It was nearly dark when Alex made the fourth call. This time, Justine noted that the tone of the conversation was different. Alex jammed the receiver against his ear with a shoulder while he took notes on a small scrap of paper. He put down the phone, gave the woman her ten centavos, looked at Justine and raised his eyebrow rakishly. The meaning was plain: they had a meet.

A short jeepney ride took them from Baclaran to the Remedios Circle in Malate District where they rendezvoused with a middle-aged woman wearing a shirt emblazoned with the logo of a popular brand of cooking oil. She was a trusted domestic servant of some sort. She led them a few streets north to a metal gate set in an angle in a high wall topped with barbed wire. It opened onto a large garden with a gazebo in the center of a very dense hedge. The lady left them but returned minutes later with two glasses of freshly squeezed iced lime juice. They had just put the frosted glasses down when a man, perhaps a year or two younger than Alex, walked out of the brightly lit main house to the gazebo. He was slightly built and wore a T-shirt, blue jeans and sneakers in a careless way that suggested he might have been a college student or a beggar or anything in between. He greeted them in an American accent so perfect it was startling.

"Hello, ma'am," he said to Justine. "Howdy, Alex." He sat down in the gazebo and asked, "What's up?"

"We need a place to stay. Dante Arevalo's union in Mindanao got rolled up by an informer, or maybe they just decided to close his outfit down. At any rate, they went looking for me at a logging camp up in the hills. I'm on the run again from Bobadilla," Alex said. "This is Justine, Dante Arevalo's right hand and wife."

Ramon extended his hand and said, "heard great things about Dante, ma'am." Alex didn't supply a name for the stranger and neither, for the moment, did the stranger. Later, Justine would call the man with the American accent Ramon Delgato.

"We should get some dinner," Ramon said. "We're in luck because this is the right place to get it. It's being laid on now."

Alex and Justine were halfway through recounting their trip north when the middle-aged lady reappeared from the main house with the first of several dishes: an enormous chicken pot pie in a ceramic baking dish, a matching bowl of rice, a tureen of fish stewed with tamarind, tomatoes and vegetables, and a pewter platter of sliced ripe mangoes. There were several pitchers of iced water.

Justine waved a fork at the hedges and the brilliantly lit house which they had not been invited to enter. "I hope you don't mind me asking, but what is this place?"

"It's actually the residence of the ambassador of " – and he mentioned a small country near the Adriatic – "to the Philippines. You'll pardon the host for not being in attendance."

"He a friend of yours?"

"I've never met the ambassador, but I know his wife." There was an awkward pause. "She's not European. She's a Jewish girl from Chicago and was happy to meet a fellow American at a dinner in one of these artist's cafes. It was about an hour into the conversation before I told her that I wasn't American and had never been to the States ever."

"Did that disconcert you?" Justine asked. She leaned back and lit a cigarette. Alex had never seen her smoke before. It must have been very occasional.

"Don't you feel … unnatural?"

"Unnatural is the story of my life," Ramon laughed. "Everything about me is contrived, or maybe the better word is *chosen*. People left me mostly alone growing up so I was free to choose what I wanted to be. Later I met a lot of people who thought there was something wrong not being like everyone else. Maybe they were right. Anyway, she invited me to this house and showed me some rare ethnographic books. After about fifteen minutes, I noticed no one else was at home."

Justine took a puff on her cigarette. "What happened next?"

"I started laughing insanely and it must have been infectious because in a few seconds she was laughing too. When we both stopped, I told her it was a bad idea."

"What's a bad idea?" Justine asked.

"I said it was a bad idea to stop laughing," said Ramon. "When we calmed down, I told her I had to see a man about a dog and she walked me to the door. Just before I turned to go, she asked me if there was anything I had regretted not seeing."

"I said I missed seeing Chicago. And we laughed some more. She's a good kid and *she understands* so I don't want to get her into trouble." Then Ramon suddenly got serious and looked down at the floor. "Look, cool's the only thing I've got."

Justine had a brief glimpse inside the devil-may-care exterior of Ramon Delgato. The door was open for an instant before it closed, leaving nothing again but the smooth outward finish. Alex later told Justine that when he first ran into Ramon before Martial Law he mistook him for one of those Berkeley-educated Filipino-American radicals slumming over the summer break before going back to law school. Only when he noticed that Ramon always wore the same cheap clothes did he begin to realize that he was exactly what he said he was.

One day he met Ramon on his way to visit his mother and tagged along. His parents rented lodging in a decrepit old house that had once been grand and had since been subdivided into a series of rooms rented out to different families. Ramon's mother had a room on the ground floor facing a garden fountain which had been dry for decades and served as a feeder for chickens. A partly disassembled Willy's jeep engine was on a trestle in the center of the living room. There was a large tarp in one corner which turned out to contain a pile of garbage.

Opposite the tarp was a black-and-white television set, the kind with a sliding panel door. That TV set, Ramon explained, had been his teacher, confidante, and portal into the wide world. From the age of eight, he had watched Golden Age TV at every opportunity – after chores and school – until the Golden Age universe and not the ramshackle ruin around him became the place where he really lived. Ramon had probably watched a greater variety of TV shows more often than the average American kid.

There are children in Islamic countries who have memorized the Koran and people who have committed the Bible to memory, chapter and verse. But Ramon could remember the dialogue from *Perry Mason, Star Trek, I Love Lucy, Wagon Train, Have Gun Will Travel, Highway*
160

Patrol, Father Knows Best, Lost in Space, Rescue 8, The Cisco Kid, The Outer Limits, Twilight Zone, Peter Gunn, Sergeant Preston of the Yukon, Laramie, Bonanza, The Fugitive and even programs that had rarely if ever been shown on US TV because they had syndicated so poorly they were dumped offshore. He had watched movie reruns from the 1940s and '50s. He knew the Republic Serials by heart and could recite, verbatim, the dialogue from *Flash Gordon* between Doctor Zarkov and the Emperor Ming. He could tell you what the *Shadow* knew, provided he was played by Victor Jory.

The result was that over the years Ramon Delgato had constructed a private and self-made American personality so thorough it was actually natural. Alex knew that Ramon dreamed in American. When he spoke Tagalog, it was as disguise.

"The key to understanding Ramon," Alex told Justine, "is to understand that he rejected everything in the Philippines except the people around him. He actually has two sisters who trained to become nurses just so they could get away from that horrible place with that wreck of the jeep engine and the garbage pile in the middle of the room. One went to London and the other to Los Angeles. Becoming a nurse to get away to London is what *Filipinos* do. But it isn't what Philip Marlowe does so it's not what Ramon did. Marlowe goes down the mean streets. Everyone in the Philippines dreams of leaving the country. Normally they do that by getting on an airplane. Ramon is the only one I know who did it without moving an inch."

All those explanations were in the future. Right then, Alex and Justine were just two tired fugitives eating a decent meal on crockery and clean linen, courtesy of an improbable but masterful host. When the dishes had been cleared away, Ramon got down to business.

"I've got a safe house available that's due to be phased out. It's secure; it's just been there too long. The cell occupying it has rotated out. But for our purposes it will serve. I'll take you there tonight. That'll solve your problem in the short term. But what are your plans in the long run?"

Justine spoke first. "My priority is to get Dante out of jail. There's a lawyer I will see on Monday who can help out."

Ramon was skeptical. "No offense, ma'am, but your husband was a lawyer and he's in jail. So I don't think Marcos cares much for the workings of the law."

"This lawyer I'm going to is different," she said.

"I tried to tell her," Alex said, "but she wouldn't listen."

"All right, give it a try," Ramon said. "What about you, Alex? You've been a long way and back."

"It's the last network I know that nobody else knows about."

"Let's keep it that way," Ramon said, "for as long as we can. Maybe we're all doomed after a fashion, though ma'am, you may have a choice in the matter if your lawyer is as good as you say he is. But it's getting late. We can't stay here."

Ramon described the route they were to take. Justine could barely follow the instructions, but Alex seemed to understand them perfectly.

"We'll go separately. Alex, I'll go first."

Justine noticed that Ramon felt at something around his waistband before slipping out the door. They followed him five minutes afterward out into the dark street.

CINDY

Their destination was a suburban neighborhood ten miles away called Roxas District, located in a hilly area far from the cafes and restaurants of the Malate District. It was a maze of small streets crisscrossed by watercourses which had since become part of the municipal drainage system and which cut the area almost into moated islands. The topography meant the little streets ran into each other at crazy angles.

Getting there meant taking a jeepney. These were conversions of the World War II Jeep. Passengers sat on benches built along an extended rear chassis. They faced inboard and exited from a small door in the back. Tens of thousands of jeepneys plied the main and secondary roads of the city.

Nothing of the outside could be seen except by turning one's head 180 degrees to look out the low window *behind* you or thrusting forward into the middle of the aisle and looking 90 degrees out the front to see the oncoming road through the windshield or out the back through the receding view in the rear exit.

The lack of visibility did not seem to bother most of the passengers who knew the route literally blindfolded. Alex, anticipating the need to study the route carefully, had squeezed himself into the narrow space between the left hand side of the driver and the running board, one leg hanging literally outside the jeepney. Nobody minded. Half the jeepneys hurtled down the road, with passengers sticking out of the back and the front seat sides.

The jeepney crossed over the Quezon Bridge into the old Quiapo shopping district. At the foot of the bridge was Plaza Miranda, a large square famous as a venue for political rallies. It had not been officially used since the declaration of Martial Law. But that night Justine heard the unmistakeable sounds of a political crowd. They were youthful voices and singing a rousing tune.

> Come on students, wherever you are.
> The field of struggle isn't far.

163

Repel with all your might,
The killers of the light!

The crowd was composed of students from the nearby university belt. Alex knew he was watching one of the flash demonstrations organized by the Communist Party. He also knew what would happen in a few minutes. So did the jeepney driver who put his foot to the accelerator in an effort to clear the scene. Alex leaned out into the slipstream and twisted his body completely around. He was in time to see a large number of riot policemen arrive to take positions all around the square. The "flash" demonstration was in a box. A thin snatch of the song carried over the whistling wind. It would soon change. Some of the students would be guests of Col. Bobadilla tonight. Alex pulled himself back inside the jeep and focused on the road ahead.

Justine and Alex alighted some distance from the given address in Roxas District. There were few people still out on the street but most had bedded down. The people who lived here were low-level employees or junior bureaucrats, people who lived carefully on a small paycheck – early to bed and early to rise. They walked past the address and swung into an alley, waited some moments to see if they had been tailed, then doubled back. Alex and Justine opened a small gate, hardly waist-high, and walked past a bush that hid the main door from the street. Then they went in. It opened on a living room furnished with a fluorescent-green leatherette couch.

Ramon stepped out from behind the angle in the door. "I hope it suits," he said, shutting the door behind them. "This place is called 'Cindy'. From now on, whenever we want to come here we'll say we want to 'visit Cindy', okay?" Then he indicated the couch. "That is our lucky green sofa. It's survived seven transfers of address. No safe house with the lucky green sofa in it has ever been raided. It's our lucky charm. Rumor is that it was manufactured by leprechauns and despite appearances to the contrary the couch is made of genuine leather."

"Leather, my eye!" Justine said. "It's plastic."

"It's leather. Naugahyde to be exact," Ramon said. "Hope to hunt the beast that provides the singular leather someday."

"You can't hunt plastic," Justine said.

"You can. Have you ever seen a nauga hide?" Ramon retorted.

"Ramon's a barrel of laughs," Alex said.

After the lucky green couch, the apparent normalcy of the room ended. Only ordinary furniture could be seen from the open door. Once past that field of vision, it was clear that Cindy was designed for clandestine purposes. Sleeping mats were rolled up against the walls of the inner rooms. A doorway led to a kitchen with a table on which a Remington Noiseless typewriter sat. It was called a "noiseless" because it had four letters to the type bar instead of the normal two. With its reduced stroke distance, the Noiseless did not make the clacking sound characteristic of typewriters, just a muffled thwuck. In a closet opening off the kitchen stood a gleaming mimeographing machine, the heart of any cheap underground press. It was an electric Gestetner model with a manual backup crank. Empty Styrofoam ink-container boxes lined the closet walls to absorb the noise.

The counter beside the sink had a row of empty jars that were used as tumblers in place of the real thing. The available food supplies consisted of a stale loaf of bread, two cans of cheap sardines and what looked to be containers of sugar and instant coffee. A gas stove with a teakettle and a few pots stood in a corner.

Ramon set the teakettle boiling. Then he and Alex poured the seething water over cheap instant coffee and sugar heaped into the jar-tumblers. To Justine's amazement, both began to stir the mixture furiously as if they were trying to whip it up into foam.

"What are you doing?" she asked.

"Making coffee with cream," Alex said, displaying the layer of white froth that formed on the surface of the jars.

"*Café au lait*," Ramon said.

"Café my foot," Justine answered. "It's fake coffee and imaginary milk."

"It's mind over matter," answered Alex. "If you don't mind not knowing the truth, it doesn't matter." Then he turned to Ramon and said, "we saw one of those flash demonstrations at Plaza Miranda on the way here."

"What's the purpose of those demonstrations?" Justine asked.

"To get students beaten up," Ramon answered.

"What on earth for?" Justine persisted.

"To radicalize them, to make them cross over to a place where you cannot go back to being just a student. If you want my opinion, getting people beaten up is the greatest recruiting tool the Communist Party has ever had. Otherwise, it is an exercise in futility." Then he changed the subject.

"This place used to house the admin cell," Ramon explained, "but they've moved on. A cleanup team will pick up the mimeo, typewriter and couch when the lease runs out, which is in another fifteen days. You can have it until then. Let me walk you through the security procedures."

Ramon pulled a backpack from a shelf in the mimeographing closet. From it he removed a Smith and Wesson hammerless .38 caliber revolver with a waistband holster, a cleaning kit and two boxes of ammunition. "The bullets are hollow point." He handed it to Alex, who carefully opened out the cylinder and checked the barrel. It was clean as a whistle.

"The confidential files have all been removed. I went through here to see that no scraps of papers, pocket diaries, or documents of any kind were left behind. Keep it that way. Any new files or notes you generate, any money you have or passports or fake ID you may possess that aren't on your person should be stored in this backpack," indicating the bag from which he had produced the .38. "In the event of a raid, grab it and go. If conditions allow, you are to pull open the venetian

166

blinds in front to the max. They've been closed since this safe house was established. It's the signal to anyone wanting to visit Cindy that this safe house has been blown.

"Then call this number and remember to ask for Danny. They'll say he's not home, but remember the name. It's Danny. Making that call will be the signal warning that no one is ever to visit Cindy again." He gave them a number and made them repeat it until he was certain they had memorized it. He then switched off the lights and took them out back. It was dark but they could see they were in a clear space behind the house with a large tree growing near the edge of the lot. It overlooked one of the creeks which divided the district. From the low back wall to the rapid rush of filthy, frothing water was a good 25 feet down. There was a twenty-foot gap to the other side. Ramon pointed out a coil of rope belayed to a tree near the wall. It was knotted at twelve-inch intervals. The coil was hidden behind a potted plant.

"On the other side, you'll see metal spikes that have been wedged at intervals into cracks in the masonry. The admin team stuck them in on stormy nights when no one would hear them driven. So use the rope on this side to make your way down into the bottom of the sewer and then climb up the other side using the metal handholds. When you get across, take the first street on the right. There's a way through a private gate to a water main you can use as a bridge. Bear right again and you'll be in a fresh produce market. You'll see where the escape route goes from the sketch I'll give you. Know it well. Get it down by heart."

"Aye, aye," said Alex. There was not an ounce of playfulness in his voice. He was all business. "I'll walk the ground tomorrow."

"There's a room for you upstairs, ma'am. Take any mat on the floor. There's probably some toothpaste in the bathroom."

"Just call me Justine."

Their host still didn't offer a name.

"Justine, Alex will man the living room. If you hear him raise the alarm, run. Remember everything I told you. If he can't come, just take the bag and make for the escape route. Don't wait a second."

Justine thought a little bit about what that meant.

"I understand."

"Good."

Alex went back into the kitchen and opened the closet. He took the .38 out of the bag as if by long habit. He slipped it in his waistband and unrolled a mat, placing it where not even the ambient lighting would reach. He sat with his back to the wall in the shadow facing the door, willing himself into the half-sleep wakefulness that people in the Life knew so well. Ramon, not as journey-worn as the two were, sat by the kitchen table and plucked softly at a guitar. It was an old trick he had of singing himself to sleep.

Justine was halfway up the stairs to her room before she recognized the lyrics from *Blind Faith*. She looked at the two and understood that of all the addictions possible, the addiction to freedom was the most dangerous of all. The words came to her at the top of the stair.

> Come down off your throne
> And leave your body alone
> Somebody must change
> You are the reason I've been waiting so long
> Somebody holds the key
> Well, I'm near the end and I just ain't got the time
> And I'm wasted and I can't find my way home.

She was wakened the next day by the late morning sun streaming through the second-story window. Ramon had gone – a note explained there was "trouble in Tondo" – referring to the vast slum area by Manila Bay. Alex was asleep on the green couch facing the door. He had really just returned from recon, walking the safe house escape plan route until he knew it thoroughly and circling the streets of Roxas

District until he had mastered their layout. But to Justine he looked a handsome, vulnerable angel in muddy sneakers with a .38 in his hand.

Justine put some rice on the boil and opened a can of sardines. She ate some and left the rest. Tomorrow she would get some money from friends in the city and go to the Davila and Rodriguez Law Office to see if there was any chance of getting Dante out. She wondered, as she looked at the back of Alex's sleeping head, whether someday anyone would come to call the children of the shadows back into the light and whether they would listen.

Wanted: Dead Or Alive

Alex watched the sun rise over Tharwa. He was a long way from Cindy. Ahead of him lay the Australian Alps. He set the monster pack on the ground and wondered how he had gotten himself into this bind. Until a few days ago, he was a respectable academic with an exciting past and a dull future. Now he was running for his life.

He looked up at the gray-green bulk of Mount Tennent and rolled up the sleeping gear and lashed it securely to the top of the frame. Then he took a granola bar from a side pocket, ate it, and washed it down with half a quart of water. He sat down to strap his pack on. He tucked his knees beneath him and used the force of both legs to straighten himself up. He set his shoulders and made for the high Australian Alps.

Alex's first goal was to loop around the spur of Mount Tennent and bear southeast, heading ever higher into the mountain range. From the map, the best route seemed to be up the ridge, then across a series of small hill valleys until he reached a crest occupied by an old NASA tracking station that had once tracked Apollo missions to the moon. It was derelict now. The entire human spaceflight program was derelict now for that matter. Some motorists probably still drove up to see the dismantled and abandoned site out of historical interest. It was interesting to think of NASA as archaeology.

A motor road swooped around on the hillside between the ridges until it faded into the Orroral Valley beyond Mount Tennent. The valley had an abandoned, historic homestead site that tourists sometimes came to see. For that reason, he would avoid it. He did not want to run into tourists. But that problem was tomorrow's. His immediate goal was to reach the Orroral Valley, about 18 kilometers on the other side of the high ground. At age 52, he could not be too ambitious; he would have to work himself gradually into shape. Getting to the top would be a job.

The pack bit into his shoulders and hips but Alex knew from experience he would get used to it. He tried to adjust the straps so that it would sway with, and not run counter to, the rhythm of his gait. It was a timeless skill that Roman soldiers would have recognized.

170

The mountain slopes were gentle except in parts when the trail forced itself up the sharp rocks. The air was cool. He sweated with the exertion, but when he stopped, the chill rapidly made him shiver despite the bright sunshine. If he stopped for any length of time, he knew he would have to add layers only to shed them again when he resumed the march. To avoid repeated suiting up and stripping off, he decided he would make an extended stop just once for lunch and not again, except for brief rest breaks, until he made evening camp.

The sparsely vegetated Australian landscape sprawled into the distance in that particular shade of brownish-green that set it apart from the bluish blacks of the northern forests or the savage bright greens of the tropics. The Australian bush looked clean in a sand-blasted kind of way as if it had been scoured by the very passage of time. But although the scenery mesmerized him, Alex dared not forget for a moment the trouble he was in. It was not a vacation. The police might soon be looking for him as a missing person or even as an overstaying alien. That was in addition to the professional killers that were after him. Despite the peace around him, Alex knew he could not afford to be complacent. As he neared the top of the ridge, he stopped and scanned the brown and green hills.

Alex forced himself to think tactically. Ramon had chosen gear the color of vegetation and earth because his main defense was to lose himself in the vastness of the landscape. Alone and armed only with a very short-range weapon, his chief protection lay in remaining undetected. The terrain would have to be used to best advantage. He kept off the crests and walked whenever possible through the shadows cast by the changing arc of the sun, traveling on the west side of ridges by morning and on their eastern slopes by afternoon. During the midday hours, when the overhead sun showed up everything in pitiless contrast, he would stop for a meal in whatever cover was available.

Like wary prey from the dawn of time, Alex scanned the surrounding hills at intervals. He divided the landscape into imaginary sectors and focused on each of them long enough to satisfy himself that there was no obvious human movement in each arc. When on occasion some trick of his middle-aged eyes suggested the presence of something unusual, he put the Pentax 8x32s on them. But each time it proved to be just a kangaroo or wombat, he shouldered his pack and moved on.

Alex understood that if that pair of hunters caught up with him, they would mercilessly torture him for information he did not have. They would inflict torments that would far exceed anything even Bobadilla might conceive. He felt the weight of the old .38 in his pocket but it did not console him as much as it did in the old days. What had changed was the weight of 30 years. He would have to compensate with savvy for what he had lost in quickness and strength. So he forced himself back to the mental task at hand. Think tactical. Always think tactical.

Inevitably his thoughts returned to the central problem of Fortunas' secret. Fortunas had said very little of obvious significance during their encounter at the airport but he went over the words anyway. Alex began by recalling the scene exactly as he remembered it: the airport lounge and plastic chairs, Fortunas coming up to him, the two of them shaking hands and the conversation between them. During the noon break, he fished a pencil from his pocket and began to reconstruct every word of the brief exchange as precisely as he could remember it:

> "You know, Australia's a great place to enjoy cattle, horses, honey and fruits. And sometimes you can find the best of it in some nest in the hills. I'll be staying at the Westin Sydney."

They were just ordinary boastful words, a little stilted to be sure, but with no secret meaning he could see. Alex folded the paper and put it in his pocket. When he stopped at a small spring once past Mount Tennent, he took the paper out and looked at the words again. Something in that exchange might hold the key to this whole mess. Either that or there was nothing in them at all and they were all on a wild goose chase.

He examined the text looking for something subtly unnatural and out of place with the rest of the conversation. But a cold wind ripped down the valley and no insight came. Alex considered putting on the R4 windproof fleece jacket but the thought of re-stowing it afterward

172

made him decide against it. He finished his granola bar, put the wrapper in a mesh pocket in his pack and kept going. The walk would warm him up more quickly than the fleece. And maybe the missing piece of the jigsaw would come to him along the way.

He found the dirt road that led to the old NASA tracking station. There were no vehicles in sight, but someone had been up there earlier that day because he could see some fast-food packaging, empty soda cans and the day's newspaper abandoned by the roadside. To the southeast was a climb to another ridge before the final drop to the Orroral Valley. The sunset would probably catch him before he made it all the way down. He would make camp somewhere on the downward trail.

He picked up the discarded newspaper out of curiosity, to see if they had reported him missing. He took the paper across the road, sat behind the bushes and began to read. The newspapers had reported him missing all right, but in a very different sort of way. The headline on the front page said, "Visiting Filipino Academic Sought in Death of Singaporean Scholar".

> "Police are looking to question Filipino academic, Dr. Alex Francisco, who may have information related to the murder of Dr. Marvin Lee of the Singapore National University. The Singaporean's body was discovered in a wooded area in Canberra and is believed to have been the victim of foul play."

Alex's passport picture was included in the news article, with the caption: "If you see this man, contact the police. Do not attempt to approach. He may be armed and dangerous." A related article reported that the government of Singapore had demanded an immediate manhunt for the killer of Marvin Lee, "a well-respected professor whose body bore the marks of brutal torture". The picture of Marvin Lee's widow and orphaned daughter were in the middle of the column. Alex set down the newspaper and took a swig from the water bottle.

"My mistake, my friend," he thought. "I should have never left that laptop with you. Stupid of me to think I knew the worst of human nature. But it's too late now."

He unwrapped another granola bar and gnawed at it absently. Now that he was a suspected murderer, his life had become very simple. There was no turning back. The only way out was to see it through to the finish. There would be no airplane to Manila, no way back to his leaky little apartment by half measures. In fact, there would be no survival unless he and Ramon could turn the tables on the President of the Philippines and defeat his world-class assassins. One side would win and one side would lose. Simple.

He thought about Marvin. What did they do to him? He shuddered at the thought. The Singaporean was innocent, but since when had innocence been a defense against anything? He was getting soft, unable any longer to anticipate people who could kill and torture to gain even the slightest edge.

"I forgot how to be ruthless," he said to himself. "I won't forget again."

Damn the Life. It contaminated everything it touched. Marvin just happened to get too close and caught the infection. Alex shook himself out of the funk. There was no use blaming one's self for the evil in the world. All a person could do was take things as they came and try to make it a little better.

"I told Justine that once," he mumbled to himself. "Everything we do counts for something." He tore up the clippings and scattered them to the wind. Alone, with limited resources on the frigid roof of Australia, unable even to seek help from outsiders if his food ran out or he had an accident, he felt everything was against him. In reality, that very isolation gave him strength. It gave him no option to quit. And if he managed to puzzle out Fortunas' secret, it would drop the floor out from under Licban. Then Marvin Lee would not have died in vain.

Alex reshouldered his ruck and pressed on until he came to a fire trail. It was late afternoon and he wanted to be clear of the NASA station area. Walking down the fire trail was a risk but he would hear any vehicle coming long before it came into view. The afternoon was gone before he was halfway down into the Ororral so he decided to make camp. Water was always hard to find on ridges, but he found a small spring at the base of some rocks. He filled his bicycle bottles with
174

water and scrambled upslope from the dirt road. Some distance above the spring he found a small hollow in the rocks that would hide his camp from anyone not looking straight down at him. There he pitched the one-man tent, feet downslope so there would be no tendency to roll over in the night.

The camp stove fired up quickly. Into it went some water, instant oatmeal, a little salt, some raisins and diced dry sausage. After the long walk, the evening meal seemed hardly adequate. Eventually the trail would pare him down to gristle.

The sun was dropping below the hills and a bitter cold descended. Alex's teeth chattered in spite of the fleece and the Gore-Tex wind layer. So in the last light, he carefully arranged his thermal mat inside the tent and laid the sleeping bag on it. Then he crawled in, pulling his backpack in after him.

There was a moment of panic as he felt the thin walls of his nylon tent press as close to his face as the ceiling in Bobadilla's prison once did. He willed himself to calm down. For a moment, he thought he heard the tormented voices of tactical interrogation again. But it was only the mountain winds. With the surrounding rocks blocking off every thermal signature from his body heat, he was as safe as could be under the circumstances, which was not very safe at all.

VANISHED

Alex need not have worried just yet. His pursuers had no idea where he was. Pierre was on an encrypted IM session to Paris for nearly the entire night. Their "easy" mission had fallen apart and recriminations were flying thick and fast. The target had escaped and the couple had committed a high-profile murder in Australia. Paris was furious. But Pierre pointed out that the entire fiasco had been head office's fault, all of it documented on the IM logs. Head office had told them the target was a middle-aged academic, easy pickings, a piece of cake.

That assessment turned out to be disastrously wrong. Even Paris could not deny that. Alex Francisco was in league with parties as yet unidentified. Even now Paris could not say who they were up against. Pierre and Monique were in a situation where they needed solid intelligence to survive if they were going to keep the field.

"We can't be fighting ghosts. Give us information or let us get it. Give us what we need or pull us out," Pierre said. Paris had no answer to that. They had been humiliated before a major client and nearly dragged him into a fiasco. If Paris could not set things right, their reputation would be ruined. Self-interest alone made it important for them to make an example of Francisco.

"Dumping Marvin Lee's body was intentional," Pierre had explained. "It makes Francisco a murder suspect. Now the question is do you have any assets in the Aussie police departments?"

Monique had suggested to Pierre that the body be dumped where it would be discovered. She said, "Make Francisco a suspect. Let them put out a dragnet on him. If Paris can find a man on the inside, then we can let the cops do the legwork and steal their leads."

It sounded like a good plan to Pierre but he hesitated to push Paris too hard. Their noses had been rubbed in the dirt enough and they might be looking to reassert their control. So he set things up so they would flow the way he wanted. He had no doubt they would double down and reinforce the operation.

176

And indeed they did. The laptop beeped when he was in the shower. Monique had read out the messages as Pierre shut off the water and proceeded to towel himself. Paris admitted that the identity of the opposition remained unknown but believed law enforcement or an official security agency could be ruled out. Paris believed that while Francisco may have used skills learned in the underground to detect the surveillance, he had mostly gotten lucky. Therefore it was acceptable to continue the mission. Sooner or later, the amateur would make a mistake or run out of resources. Then they would have him.

Pierre, now dressed, read on. He believed Paris was whistling past the graveyard but their mission was clear: to pursue and capture Francisco. Failing that, they should kill him. Their contract would be extended and each of them would receive another $200,000. If they had any fears about meeting unknown assailants they were being well-paid to overcome them. Moreover, a major intelligence support effort would be mounted on their behalf, the details of which were to follow. Once Francisco was localized, another man with firearms would reinforce them.

"Do you believe that bit about Francisco getting lucky?" Pierre asked.

"Paris doesn't believe that itself," Monique said. "That's hogwash for the client's consumption. The hope is that the intel will identify the enemy if we draw it out. So the deal is that if they give us more muscle, more intelligence, and more money, we can win round 2. Are you game?"

Pierre nodded. He wondered what sort of "intelligence support" Paris could provide. He suspected Paris had found a man in Australian law enforcement that could siphon off police leads on the Marvin Lee case. Monique's idea to plant Lee's corpse on Francisco was paying off.

Pierre's hunch was very nearly right. With the huge sums it now had, Paris bought a Kremlin asset in Australia by bribing his Russian handler. The mole would receive a request from the FIS but his information would be sent to Paris.

177

Using a system similar to Greer's, the Russians had inserted rogue software into the Australian system. The Russians had been careful to limit data thefts to test quantities that would be unnoticed by the audit software the way stealing nickels and dimes from a multibillionaire would be unremarked. The Russians were reserving their capability against a major international crisis. They did not anticipate one of their own would sell the information to a criminal syndicate for a fee.

Within 12 hours, Pierre was reading the first sanitized gleanings from "intelligence support" on his laptop. It made depressing reading. No one answering to the description of Alex Francisco had left Australia by sea or air. All of Francisco's electronic facilities had been accessed by court order. His credit and ATM cards had gone unused since the afternoon of his disappearance. No one by that name had checked into any hotel. His cellular phone had gone silent. His emails had gone unread. Voicemails and text messages piled up unanswered at his service provider. All his belongings left at the hotel were examined by the police, who found nothing of interest in them.

Pierre saw that every avenue had been thoroughly checked and turned up nothing. Alex Francisco had simply vanished from the face of the earth.

"Gone," Pierre said. He rose from the table and indicated the screen with a head gesture. "There's not a trace. That's impossible. How does he live? How does he eat?"

"You have to have patience," Monique said. "It's the first principle of our trade. We are the hunters, so we wait. The prey is the hunted, so he hides. We wait until the prey breaks cover, wait until a weakness appears. People hire us because unlike those jumpy muscle-bound dime-a-dozen triggermen we know how to sit still. So keep your nerve. Sit still and listen, Pierre. He'll show up."

Monique was right, yet it was cold comfort. How long could he hold his breath? This Francisco seemed unnatural, Pierre thought. They read and re-read the reports, divided the watch on the computer and took turns going to the hotel gym. They would wait and be ready when he surfaced.

178

THE HAPPY JACKS

Alex scanned the Orroral from the edge of the tree line with his Pentax 8x32s binoculars. Nothing human moved in his field of view. He went down into the valley and made for the tree line on the opposite side determined to remain unseen. He had resolved to spot anyone before they saw him and avoid them by ducking into the woods or changing course.

The track ran along the valleys. They crossed a landscape that varied from wildflower-dotted grass and scrub to more wooded terrain. In some places, the trees nearly closed over the trail but even at their thickest, they never attained the solid canopy typical of tropical rainforests. The sun seemed always overhead and there was an invincible gaiety to the Australian bush. It followed him, dancing through the waving branches, bringing out that strange shade of antipodean green in the grass.

But there was little cover and it worried him. That day luck came to his aid. Alex reached the Cotter River valley in the late afternoon as a low mist seeped down from upstream. It enveloped him in cottony vapor while he cooked dinner by the river in the angle of some rocks. He looked up from his oatmeal to see the tops of trees reaching down to him like arms groping through the fog.

Ten years before, a man might be lost in this white-out. But high above in outer space, the US Navy's constellation of satellites patiently broadcast their timing signals and the GPS let him pick up the trail on the other side of the valley just as if he were following a road. Once across, he found a suitable campground on the lower slope of Mount Bimberi and hunkered down for the night. That was what he wanted: cover by day and a sheltered campground by night.

Alex tried to stay as invisible as he could, flitting from cover to cover, walking openly only when there was no alternative. By calculating his pace and planning the legs of his trip on the map, he could time his arrival at open spaces or trail intersections in the early mornings or late afternoons. Once back in the closer vegetation or more broken

179

terrain, Alex would stay below the ridgelines and walk the sun-shadowed side of the path. Where the trail went through the woods, he would "handrail" or walk parallel to the path. As in that long-ago night in the rubber plantation, he would listen carefully to his slow footfalls alert for alien sounds. Whenever the trail made a sharp turn, he paused to listen for anything coming around the corner. Stealth, not speed, was his defense.

In any event, he didn't have much speed. He was still out of condition and tired easily. He would gain stamina from a combination of weight reduction and increasing muscular strength. But it would take time to get back into whatever shape a man of his age could attain. For now the rigors of the trail, even in easy stages, had left him tired.

The map showed he was early to the food drop at Kiandra. So he took the chance to rest and set about looking for a spot. The map showed an area where no one was likely to intrude – a small gully that went off at right angles to the trail, just a notch in the hills. He crossed a short stretch of brush and by weaving and ducking under the matted vegetation gained the entrance to the gully. There was no sign any hiker had ever gone that way. Perhaps no humans, who were so few on this vast continent, had ever trodden it.

Soon, the track descended to a long, shallow depression. Five hundred meters into the gully, far beyond the range of any sound he might make, Alex set up camp not far from a small rill. He pitched his tent inside the tree line beside the small stream-fed glade and gloried in the feeling of perfect safety. After a small dinner, he went to sleep and stayed in his sleeping bag all the next morning, rising only for a short stretch and to prepare breakfast.

Breakfast was his favorite meal of the day. He remembered waking up all those years ago in Moriones Square in Manila. Across from the stairwell where he spent the night was a variety store which opened early. For a very small sum of money, the storekeeper would sell him three hot rolls with a thin pat of margarine in them and a cup of sweet coffee. Then he'd sit in the square and watch the sun come up. He felt gloriously free.

But the call of wild birds brought him back to the present. Alex saw the Australian sun come up over the lip of the hill and remembered where he really was: a fugitive in a strange land. Running away had lost its attractions.

By early afternoon, he felt rested and energetic enough to clean out his gear. The sun had warmed the rocks. Alex took off his clothes and rubbed himself down with a sponge by the brook. He squeezed water from the bicycle bottle onto himself in a field shower. Shivering with the cold, he dried off with the sponge. As soon as he air-dried, Alex pulled on fresh thermal underwear. He washed and rinsed his soiled undergarments in the stream until they were tolerably clean, wrung them out and pinned them to a paracord line he had run between the branches of the trees outside his tent using split twigs for pegs. Then he wiped the mud stains from the shell clothing with a damp sponge, wringing it out and rinsing the sponge by the stream. After adding it to the laundry line, he began the last piece of maintenance. He gave the .38 a once-over with the cleaning brush and rubbed a very small amount of oil all over its surfaces, carefully removing all the excess that he could.

The balance of the rest day passed swiftly. He lounged under the trees looking at the scrap of paper with Fortunas' words on it. He cudgeled his brains to decipher their meaning, but he always drew a blank. Though the sky remained clear, Alex decided to turn in early. He watched the evening throw its long shadows across the translucent roof of his tent. It was the sun waving goodbye to another day. With that he slipped away into restfulness and remembered nothing else for the next 12 hours.

He rose early the next morning and treated himself to some dried sausage to supplement the cereal. Then he struck camp and warily emerged from his private gully and regained the trail to Kiandra. Alex reached it in the late afternoon and slept under cover nearby to make the approach right after sunrise. He had no trouble finding the two distinctively shaped ponds by the Hunger Creek Fire Trail. Between the pools in the high grass were three fox-proof black plastic drums with a food resupply and spare batteries in a Ziploc bag.

His proximity to Kiandra meant cell phone coverage was available. He switched on his prepaid telephone and sure enough there was an SMS from Ramon warning Alex indirectly that he was a suspect in the Marvin Lee murder.

Scandalous murder involving a Singaporean academic. What is the world coming to?

Alex replied to let Ramon know the message was acknowledged and understood.

What is the world coming to indeed?

He restocked his pack with supplies and stashed the plastic barrels behind some bushes. With the sun still low in the sky, Alex crossed the highway after a long look in either direction to make sure no cars were in sight. He headed southwest down the Tabletop Mountain Fire Trail. He had the rhythm now and moved smoothly through down the track. His senses had become attuned to the mountain quiet and his confidence had grown. The desperate journey was becoming almost enjoyable. That night, after supper, he looked up at the stars and for the first time since he began his flight into the hills imagined they smiled down on him.

The next day he came to a wide expanse of open space called the Happy Jacks Plain, a low plateau nearly four miles wide that rose between the Eucumbene Lake basin to the east and a river to the west. Alex tramped across the grassy face of the Happy Jacks, through bands of green sprinkled with wildflowers, before resuming his southwest course. He paused in the middle of the plain and looked out over the eastern end of the plateau onto a blue lake beyond which a town hunched on the far shore. He glanced in the other direction where nothing but higher hills were visible, but the map showed there was a steep gorge where a creek came down from the hills behind the plateau and curled around into the lake. In high heart, a fancy caught him and Alex decided to turn west to explore the gorge that dropped down into the creek.

"I will probably never pass this way again and may as well see what's down there," he said to himself. As he thought those words, he realized

182

they were very probably true of nearly everything that he saw. Once you were on the wrong side of fifty, you saw everything new for the last time.

After giving the expanse ahead a precautionary binocular scan, he walked toward the western corner of the field. There the plateau ended in a shallow drop. At his feet, a long cutting descended like a zigzag stairway to the creek below. He trudged down the gash for a good quarter hour until the whirring of the creek announced he was not far from the bottom. There he found himself in undulating brushland through which a trickle of water coursed. He followed the creek for a few hundred yards but when it led to nothing obviously remarkable, Alex decided to turn back. Then something caught his eye. There was a hut half-hidden among the eucalypts.

The hut was partly burned, in complete disrepair and very old. Since it was obviously uninhabited, Alex felt it safe to approach. On closer inspection, the hut had once consisted of two rooms joined by a common corridor. But the wings had collapsed into a heap from a fire. In the back a rusty, galvanized iron water tank leaned crazily on rotten foundations. Some distance away, a small outhouse in the last stages of dilapidation added a pathetically human touch. Alex wondered who could have lived in so desolate a spot. Then he saw a cloth-bound book held down by a rock in the one intact corner of the shack.

The title of the book said "Visitor's Register for Happy's Hut". It must have referred to the same "Happy" after whom the Happy Jacks Plain indicated on the map was named. Happy Jack had lived here. The book belonged to the "Snowy Mountains Ski Club", and it contained the entries from members who had stopped by it in winter. Most of the entries were one liners with a name, a date and a purpose. But on one page there was a long entry by some pedant who felt compelled to demonstrate his knowledge of local history.

> The Happy Jacks Plain and Creek were named after a miner who found gold here, presumably making him "happy". It is one of several places named after obscure early settlers. Yet most place names in the Snowy Mountains are derived from

descriptive Aboriginal expressions. For example, Adaminaby may have been derived from the Aboriginal word "Adamindumee" which possibly meant "resting place". Bimblegumbie may have come from an Aboriginal word for "spear whistle".

The word Bogong found in many places is actually an aboriginal word for "moth". White settlers, seeing the native inhabitants pointing at something, thought it meant "mountain" when it really referred to insects which the Aborigines roasted for their distinct flavor. The place-name Buchan has no connection with Scotland, as some might think, but is now known to have come from an Aboriginal word meaning "mass of rock with a hole in it". Cootapatamba denotes "a place where eagles drink".

On it went in that academic sort of way, boring explanations of place names running down the alphabet going from "C" to "D" and "E" until it reached "Y". There the unknown author concluded his dissertation.

Alex set down the book and wondered what kind of person would take the time to write that treatise in a visitor registry out in the middle of nowhere. It was probably some dotty old scholar, an Australian version of himself. He was chuckling when suddenly it hit him. Now he understood why Fortunas' phrasing sounded so stilted in English.

"Nest in the hills" was an aboriginal place-name.

The faint oddity in phrasing that Fortunas had used while describing places to visit in Australia was stylistically similar to these place-names. He took out the piece of paper and re-read Fortunas' last words to him.

> "You know, Australia's a great place to enjoy cattle, horses, honey and fruits. And sometimes you can find the best of it in some nest in the hills. I'll be staying at the Westin Sydney."

"Some nest in the hills" was not a phrase that a Filipino politician, let alone a crude thug like Fortunas, would use. It was too flowery, too roundabout to be natural. It was wholly at odds with the distinctive cadence of Filipino speech in English. That was why the phrase seemed out of place from the first. He now guessed that Fortunas was unconsciously repeating a description of a place that he was thinking of but whose name he dared not utter. "Some nest in the hills" was a reference to *an aboriginal place name* out of a travel book or a long conversation with a man who lived there. Alex suppressed his excitement and forced himself to remain calm while he double-checked his deductions.

He ran his finger up the handwritten, anonymously penned page. "Tumut – a camp or resting place by the river. Tumbarumba – sounding ground. Talbingo – corrupted concatenation of the English word 'tall' and the Aboriginal word 'binji' which means 'belly'. Hence, it means 'big belly'. Mount Talbingo resembles the big belly of a man lying down." Alex put his hands to his temples. Who could be sure, but "nest in the hills" sure sounded like it might be one of those things.

Alex remained motionless by Jack's Hut for what seemed a long time, though it was really only minutes. He calmly went over his theory. It was far from certain that the phrase had any significance at all but it was worth putting to a test. At any rate, it was all he had to go on. If he knew anything of importance then this was his best shot at it. He could not remain on the run forever. Sooner or later, he would have to make a guess or keep running. He decided to send the agreed signal to Ramon. Then he would see what came of it.

His first thought was to send a message at the next food drop when he would be in range of a cell phone tower. Then he remembered the town at the end of Lake Eucumbene. Towns had cell phone coverage. His best bet was to re-ascend the gorge and return to the Happy Jacks plateau, then go east to the eastern edge to get within line of sight of the Lake Eucumbene settlement. It would be decent odds that he could raise a signal.

He climbed back to the plateau. As he re-ascended the slope, a breeze rippled through his hair and played on the blue, yellow and white wildflowers that carpeted the flat space before him like a wizard's spell changing the patterns on a magic carpet. He pulled out his binoculars and swept the horizon for signs of any hikers. There were none. Alex took out his cell phone and turned it on. The display blinked a while before returning the "no network found" message. He decided he would have to get closer to the town. When Alex was halfway across the plateau, he tried his cell phone again. The display blinked again as before, finally spitting out another "no network found" message. Finally, he topped a small crest and found himself looking down on the lake. It was shimmering blue beneath his feet and on the far shore tiny houses were visible through the atmospheric haze. He tried the cell phone again. "No network found."

"What the heck's the matter with this phone?" he asked himself. Then it occurred to him that his SIM might not be compatible with the network serving this small town. Maybe it operated on another network. To isolate the defect, he removed the pre-paid SIM chip and re-inserted his old personal one. Again, the "no network found" message was displayed. Okay, so the trouble was not SIM incompatibility, he was just still out of range. He swapped out his old chip for the disposable SIM that Ramon had provided.

He curbed his impatience and decided to get closer. Alex found a dirt road that descended toward the lake. The road was empty as far as he could see so Alex kept walking until the road ended up in a narrow inlet on the lake. He stepped out onto a dock which jutted out into the water. At the end of it, he took out the phone and tried again. The display blinked once more, but this time it found a network. There on the brink of Lake Eucumbene, Alex sent this message: "Let's meet for drinks at the Blinking Bottle".

Then he waited behind some bushes near the base of the quay. It was two hours before a reply came back. "I'll pick you up at Cora's at the usual time." The meet was set.

"Cora's" was the code for the next food drop at the southern end of Lake Cootapatamba in the shadow of Mount Kosciuzko, the highest mountain in Australia. It was done. He had sent the signal. For good or ill, Alex had turned over the card and was prepared to hazard a solution to Fortunas' message. Now he would see if fate had dealt him the winning hand or would show him the Ace of Spades.

PINCER

"We've got him!" Pierre said as he read the message. Intelligence support had intercepted a signal from Alex Francisco's phone. He typed the coordinates provided by Paris into Google Earth and watched the display zoom in on an alpine lake 93 kilometers southwest of Canberra.

"Where is Lake Eucumbene, New South Wales?" he asked Monique. His fingers tapped out a search string to bring up information on the lake and its surrounding area.

"It's in the middle of nowhere, there's not even a substantial town on the lake. More like a vacation trailer park."

The nearest town was a place called Adaminaby, population 230, whose landmark was a 33-foot-tall cement statue of a trout that advertised fishing in the lake 10 kilometers away. Pierre wondered what compelled Australians to erect such bizarre symbols – in one place a giant replica of a soup bowl, here a sculpture of a fish, there a giant marijuana joint to proclaim the distinction of their community. Haven't they heard of billboards? He reined his speculation in and focused on the significance of his discovery.

"What's he doing at Eucumbene? Could he be staying in a trailer?"

"Well, let's find out," Monique said as she grabbed their luggage and called the front desk of their hotel to prepare their bill. In a few minutes, they were on their way south from Canberra. They reached Adaminaby in less than an hour. Paris said their sources detected a signal from Francisco's old SIM at the extreme range of the Lake Eucumbene cell phone tower. The signal was so faint that a reliable duplex connection could not be completed. But the cell phone software logged the failed attempt anyway.

Few people realized that the authorities could use cell phones as tracking devices. The phones automatically checked in to the nearest cell as its owner moved around. While a phone was powered on, it automatically tried to connect to its network via the nearest telephone facility. The log of attempted connections allowed emergency and rescue personnel to locate injured callers by asking the tower where the phone was.

The precision with which phones could be localized depended on the density of the cellular net. In a city, a telephone could be located to within tens of meters. But in the countryside where populations were far less dense, a single cell phone tower might cover a large area. The phone towers servicing Lake Eucumbene could only locate a call within an 8-kilometer radius of the tower.

Paris reported that the Lake Eucumbene tower had received a faint request for connection from Alex's SIM. The Russian system had diverted that result to Moscow, then covered the diversion. The information was further re-routed to Paris. Both the Australians and the Russians were being ripped off so Pierre and Monique could arrive at the bare eastern shore of Lake Eucumbene with a lead.

Their hearts sank as they approached the tiny village. A nearly empty trailer park, a small cluster of vacation homes, and the ruins of the original town of Adaminaby (which had sunk under the waters of the lake) were all that was in evidence. It was unlikely Francisco could be hiding here without attracting the notice of the locals. But the signal placed him here and they were going to find out why.

While driving down from Canberra, they had made an appointment with a real estate agent. As they approached the village, a very young man in a cheap suit was waiting for them by the roadside with a little cardboard sign indicating the name of his company. They stopped and rolled down the window.

"Mr. du Monde?" the man said.

"Yes," Pierre replied. "This is my wife, Simone."

"I'm pleased to meet you. I understand you are looking to rent a property."

"*Oui*, ah … yes. A small house as a base for a small film documentary my magazine will produce about fishing in the Snowy Mountains." The agent perked up at the words "film" and "documentary".

"I'm sure we'll find something suitable," he said, handing Pierre his business card.

"We're unlikely to settle on a property today, but I want to look around and see what is suitable. We can focus on a specific location later. "But," he added, handing the man a brown paper envelope containing $1,000 in cash, "this is a retainer so your firm can keep a lookout for suitable properties while matters are being decided."

"I'm afraid I don't have a receipt book with me," the man said, holding the envelope uncertainly.

"Oh, you can post the receipt in the mail," Pierre said with the wave of a hand, conveying the impression he did not care whether he got the receipt or not. "Can we look around?"

"Of course, Mr. du Monde."

He asked the agent into the car and they drove around the lake and its surrounding. Within five minutes, they had covered every habitation and the agent seemed to know the names of the occupant of each home they passed.

"Now some of my cameramen will be, well, Asians. Will they be welcome in this neighborhood?" Pierre asked. "Are there any of that … sort of person … around here?"

"Oh, sure. Plenty of Japanese and Chinese tourists come here. I am sure they will be quite comfortable, though really there are no persons of … that sort … who live here. They like the cities better. Can't say I blame them as business is not always good in these parts."

"Would a film crew of two or three people be able to pass unnoticed by the locals?"

190

The agent laughed. "No strangers in a place like this can pass unnoticed. Everybody knows everyone else. You could pack the entire population of this village into a bus. But don't worry, we're a resort town. Any visitors would be very welcome and made to feel it."

"But of course. And now, monsieur, I must make my recommendation to Paris."

They dropped the young man off at his little office. As they drove away from the small town, Pierre knew in his bones that he would never find Francisco anywhere in the area. He thumped his fist on the steering wheel. It made no sense for Francisco to hide anywhere in the Lake Eucumbene region while his Wanted notice was prominently displayed in every newspaper and TV show. How long could an Asian remain undetected in an all-white community no bigger than extended family?

They were halfway to Cooma, the nearest major town, before Pierre spoke to Monique.

"What do you think? Was he ever there?"

"I don't think he's there now," Monique said. "But he was. Maybe he was passing through the area while making the call, but there's no sense to hiding there on a long-term basis.

"As in making a call from a car passing through Eucumbene? That would explain why the cell tower only picked up a ghost of a signal." Then Pierre answered his own question. "But it doesn't explain why no other tower picked up Francisco's signal when he moved over to the next cell? We should have a series of signals from a moving car, not just a single, isolated signal."

Monique chewed on that. Then finally she said. "Something's not right in this setup. Or we're not thinking about it correctly. First, why should he be using his old cell phone? He's been smart enough to avoid using it until now. Why use it here, in this god-forsaken place?"

"Why, indeed? Go on."

191

"Someone has been helping him all along. Someone savvy in their own way yet amateur enough to overdo it. Maybe one of his confederates drove out here and turned on his phone to mislead us."

"To drag us out in the middle of nowhere?" Pierre said.

"Well we're here, aren't we? And this is nowhere," she said, sweeping her arm out at the landscape.

"But you think they've been too clever by half?"

"Sure. Before this call, we had nothing. Now we have a nibble at the end of a long line, still something we didn't have before. That's a mistake in my book. Maybe we can turn this nibble into something that will lead us to the fish and turn their cleverness on them.

"To do that we need to stop and set up the laptop. Ask Paris *who else* made a call through the Eucumbene tower immediately before and after Francisco's SIM was detected. We need to find a second phone, the phone of his confederate. Maybe we can find our ghost by looking at the background."

Pierre thought it was a brilliant piece of deduction. He didn't want to waste hours driving back to Canberra so they checked into a hotel in nearby Cooma. Pierre connected to headquarters and asked for a data dump of calls made from the Eucumbene area around the time Alex's signal was detected.

Two hours later, they had the data dump. Poring over the records, they saw that after the faint signal from Francisco's SIM was detected, a number of other calls had been made to the Eucumbene cell. But only one had been to another pre-paid cell phone in the Sydney area about 35 minutes after the Francisco failed connect. The message was "Let's meet for drinks at the Blinking Bottle". After two hours, it received a reply: "I'll pick you up at Cora's at the usual time".

Monique searched the Internet for information on any pubs, restaurants or bars in Sydney called the Blinking Bottle or Cora's. There were none. She didn't expect there to be. Her instinct told her that someone was sending a coded message to a contact in the Sydney area.

"That was probably his decoy signaling base that the dummy signal had been sent," Pierre said. "Now if we can find either end of that pre-paid cell phone, then maybe we could close in on his support team. They're probably using disposables."

Pierre could see Monique shaking her head and laughing under her breath. Finally she spoke.

"Pierre, that wasn't a decoy call at all. Strange as it may seem, that was Francisco himself calling. And 'Cora's' is a meet."

"What? But we already figured that doesn't make any sense. He's avoided using his cell phone all this time. Why should he use it now and purposely give away his position?"

"The key to understanding the situation, Pierre, is to note two things. First, no decoy would wait two hours to receive an acknowledgement that his decoy message had been sent. Second, anyone sending the fake message had no way of knowing that it had even been monitored because his phone would have read 'no connection'. He had no way to know his half-call had hit the emergency services database for us to pick up. The follow-up call to Sydney could not have been to report success because there was no way to know it had succeeded. Therefore, the signal was no decoy. It was the real thing."

Pierre nodded his head. He saw the force of the argument but didn't know where Monique was going with this new line of reasoning. "Go on" was all he could say.

"So if it wasn't a decoy effort, what was it? Let's try Occam's Razor. The simplest explanation for this set of facts is that Francisco was signaling his base. He wanted to come in. Maybe he's finally remembered what Fortunas said. Maybe he's sick or injured or scared of something. In any case, he's in a hurry and he whips out his phone from long habit to call, perhaps even switches it on for a few seconds until he remembers he isn't supposed to use it. But his cell phone finds no network, so there's a sense of relief that his momentary carelessness hasn't given him away. Or so he thinks. He does not know the cell phone signal tickled some tower. Then he walks closer to where he thinks there might be a tower and makes a second call on his disposable phone to Sydney. But he needs confirmation for the meet. So he waits for an answer. That explains all the facts."

"But why did it take him 25 minutes to get close enough to connect to the same cell phone tower? Because that's the time difference between the first and second call."

"Because he's walking," Monique said. "He's on foot." She turned to stare out the window of the hotel. The huge gray bulk of the Snowy Mountains rose to the west, mottled by a pattern of sunlight and cloud shadows that drifted across its face. She put her fingertips to the glass and moved her face forward until her breath was misting the pane.

"He's out there. We were fools not to realize it," she said. "In the mountains, hiding in the open air. That's why there's been no record of a hotel occupancy, car rental, credit card purchase. That's why there's been nothing from the Australian police informers. They'd be useless. Our quarry has been hiding where there are no people, not even any cell phone towers to give him away – until now. Now he's reached out. Wants in. He's going to 'Cora's' which must be the code name for a food drop or rendezvous where they will pick him up. We have to hunt him down quickly before he gets to the pick-up point."

Pierre was struck by the force of her analysis and acted at once. He told her to take the car back to Canberra to buy hiking gear and supplies for both of them. In the meantime, he would contact Paris and ask for a map of the cell phone coverage in Eucumbene.

"I'll figure out where the call came from to plan a pursuit route. Get what we need for a week on the ground."

Monique knew exactly what to get. She and Pierre were experienced outdoorsmen and had climbed 7,500-meter Himalayan peaks. In comparison to those vertical cathedrals of frozen rock, the worn-down Australian mountains would seem as flat as a billiard table. She would be back in the Cooma motel room within a couple of hours with the right gear. If Pierre could find his trail, they would be on the scent before many hours had passed and easily overhaul him.

In the meantime, Pierre was looking at a graphic sent from Paris showing interlocking circles representing cell phone coverage in the Lake Eucumbene area. There was only one place where the circles did not overlap: northeast across the lake from the Lake Eucumbene dam. That was where a signal might be picked up by one and only one tower.

Acting on a hunch, he looked up a map of popular Australian hiking tracks on the Internet. One, the Australian Alps Walking Track, appeared to pass on the other side of the lake starting from Tharwa on the outskirts of Canberra and running unbroken until it finished near Melbourne hundreds of kilometers away. No detailed maps were available online because these were held back by the government survey agency that sold the paper maps by section. He looked at his watch. It was too late to buy a map until morning, but he could not wait that long.

Pierre went to the front desk and told the night hotel manager that he was a filmmaker interested in doing a documentary about the Australian Alps Walking Track. He explained that he needed a sectional map of the trail urgently and persuaded the young lady to calls to her friends in Cooma to see if he could buy a map from someone willing to sell it second-hand. The front-desk lady called around and finally got in touch with the head of the local bushwalking club. Pierre was called to the phone and he offered the president of the club $500 for his maps.

"Is this a practical joke, sir? That's ten times what you would pay at the Lands office when it opens tomorrow."

"Oh, monsieur. Tomorrow will be too late. I am preparing a film proposal for my head office – you understand it is another time zone in Europe – and I must submit a logistics plan to go with our proposal. It is a matter of urgency that I have these sectional maps at once. If you would do me the honor of selling me your maps you will save me not only time, but money – even at that price."

"I will lend them to you for nothing," stammered the club president. He was not accustomed to people buying maps at extravagant prices.

"Nonsense, monsieur. I may have to cut some sections from the maps for illustrations, you see. I will ruin them. Don't worry about the money. I have a budget for such things."

"I'll be at your hotel in 10 minutes." And sure enough, a tall wiry man walked into the hotel lobby inside of a quarter of an hour and put a packet of maps on the front desk.

"Fifty dollars," he said, "and not a penny more."

Pierre took the maps, handing him a fifty-dollar bill and thanked him effusively in rapid-fire French and English. The bushwalker beat a hasty retreat from the hotel to get out of the line of such Gallic effusiveness.

"A thousand thanks, monsieur," Pierre called after him.

A minute later, Pierre had laid the relevant map sections out on the double bed. He traced out the route that ran southwest from Tharwa all the way to the Dead Horse Gap through the main range of the Snowy Mountains, running his finger along the track until it came within a few miles of Lake Eucumbene. There, it crossed the Happy Jacks plain. This must have been where Alex Francisco had let his guard down and made his call.

Pierre looked at the exact time of the intercept. There, he had Francisco's location from 12 hours before. Where was he now? To answer that, he had one more puzzle to solve. In which direction had Francisco been heading since he made the call? Was it north to Tharwa or south towards the main range of the Snowy Mountains? Or did he simply get picked up at Eucumbene? He looked at the intercepted message again:

"Let's meet for drinks at the Blinking Bottle".

196

"I'll pick you up at Cora's at the usual time".

No. He was heading for a rendezvous codenamed "Cora's". If that was Eucumbene, he would not have needed to send the signal to begin with. It was another place and the phrase "at the usual time" meant it was at a regular food or resupply point located almost certainly at a prearranged point on or near the trail. Pierre estimated the food endurance of a hiker between food drops and figured Cora's would be from two to three days away. So was it north or south? The team could split up, start from Happy Jack's, and cover both possibilities – have Monique sweep to Tharwa while he went southwest towards Dead Horse Gap – but that was dangerous and unprofessional. Split up, they would be vulnerable. No one could watch while the other rested; no one could watch while the other bounded forward. They had underestimated Francisco and his allies once before. It would be foolish to underestimate them again. There was a more logical solution.

He would trap Francisco.

He estimated the maximum distance an unfit man in his 50s could walk in a day, then measured off how far from Happy Jacks Francisco could be in either direction. His informed guess was that Francisco could not possibly be further north than Cooleman on the road to Tharwa by nightfall the next day.

The operational plan he presented to Paris was simplicity itself. He and Monique would join the track near Cooleman the next day and sweep south toward Dead Horse Gap. With their superior foot speed, they would either intercept Francisco on a meeting engagement or overtake him from the rear as he trudged toward the Gap. And just to further ensure they got Francisco this time, Pierre made arrangements with Paris to send the reinforcement – a weapons expert – to Thredbo in the south to sweep north. One group would come up from ahead and another would come up from behind. They would catch Francisco in a vise.

Paris readily agreed. To avoid a "friendly fire" clash, they decided to send someone already known to Pierre and Monique – Emile Landrieu, formerly known as Emilio Landicho, a Paraguayan who had become a naturalized Frenchman after serving in the Foreign Legion. He was on standby in Bangkok and would fly to Australia within a couple of hours. Pierre knew Emile from previous jobs and respected the droll, handgun specialist. Paris would arrange for Landrieu to get a Glock through its underworld connections and he would collect it on arrival in Sydney. Now Pierre's team would consist of three professionals and one of them would be armed.

There was a knock on the door. Monique had returned from Canberra with tentage, food and sleeping bags. With typical foresight, she acquired a satellite phone, and told Pierre to ensure that Emile got one too. The satellite phones would allow both teams to stay in contact even in the depths of the wilderness where no cell phone coverage existed at all. Not only would they have a weapons and numbers edge on Francisco, they would have comms independent of the cell phone network. Every advantage would be theirs: numbers, weapons, comms. Any way you sliced it, Francisco was finished.

In Sydney, Ramon was waiting for an answer. Two hours before, he'd been out checking messages and received a signal asking to meet for drinks at the Blinking Bottle. That signified Alex had a solution to the Fortunas puzzle. Ramon contacted Bill Greer immediately about how to proceed. The answer was in the IM window.

> **Bill:** I've asked for a safe house and Alex's extraction. Washington want me to do a risk analysis. They're taking no chances with their careers.
>
> **Ramon:** We have three days to Cora's.
>
> **Bill:** We'll do it then. That ought to be enough time to get the authorization and send a man.
>
> **Ramon:** Great.

Ramon grabbed his helmet and rode his bike away from his home until he was just on the north side of Sydney Harbor. That was far enough to conceal the true location of his home base. He pulled out his disposable cell phone and sent a text message: "Meet you at Cora's". He went to a café to wait for the answer and was halfway through a double espresso when his phone vibrated. It was a reply from Alex. "Looking forward to it."

Things were moving to a close. Maybe they would pull it off after all. Ramon paid his bill and rode back to the apartment. He had just parked the bike when his real phone vibrated. Who could be calling his real number, he wondered? The message was from Bill Greer. It was peremptory. "Get on IM, quick."

He ran down to his basement office and switched on the computer. The login screen popped open on the monitor. A minute later, the secure IM session was up and running.

> **Bill:** Alex has been compromised. Your SIM number is also blown. Don't use it in any circumstance that would let them track you.

> **Ramon:** They won't locate me from the SIM. I always displace before I send or receive signals. How did the break happen? How were we blown?

> **Bill:** We looked over the data and we think he accidentally used his old SIM card before he sent you the Blinking Bottle message. Why, we don't know. But he realized his mistake and switched to the safe SIM. But the enemy caught the first message and did traffic analysis on the subsequent messages to the same cell phone tower. They figured out what SIM IDs both of you are using and read your message.

> We also know they've told the client they believe he's on the Australian Alpine walking track, but they don't know whether he's headed north or south. So they have asked for reinforcements. Two enemy teams, one coming up from the north starting today from the vicinity of Cooleman and another starting early the day after tomorrow from the Thredbo area, will converge on him. We think they will be close to him one way or the other within 36 hours near the Cora area.

> **Ramon:** Cora's near Thredbo. When will he come into cell phone range so we can warn him?

Bill: He'll be out of range for about 24 hours. Our analysis shows that if he is on the planned track he won't be in range of any cell tower until he is 12 hours out of Cora's.

Ramon: What are the options?

Bill: Get up near the Cora vicinity quick and stand by. I'm working on getting someone over who can provide you with some support on an ad-hoc basis even without a decision from Washington. He'll be restricted in what he can do because the Rules of Engagement are going to be very tight. But he'll do everything he can under the authority we have, which is not much. Nobody wants to do anything remotely illegal inside an Allied country. So you will be the only person with complete freedom to take a risk. You're the only guy who can go all the way. I don't know how much help we can give if things go bad.

Ramon: I knew the limits from the start. Do your best Bill. I'm starting now and will check back in on clean comms.

Ramon shut down the IM session. He took the battery out of his compromised cell phone and stowed it. It would be needed one more time to warn Alex *en clair* near Cora's.

He began the short ritual of packing for the trip. In five minutes, he had loaded everything he needed and sat astride the Suzuki. It seemed an age since the night he started high-hearted with excitement to rescue his friend. Now he was simply tired and afraid. Somewhere in the southern mountains, another middle-aged man was hobbling toward a rendezvous with enemy teams before and behind. What did Bill say? *"I don't know how much help we can give you if things go bad."* He felt for the bulk of the .38 in his pocket and pulled the motorcycle out on the road to start the first leg south.

SIXTH SENSE

Alex was also heading south. Now the trail to Cora's ran across the western face of a line of peaks. At the end of it, Mount Jagungal rose like a giant tower more than a mile high. He felt like a bug crawling on the side of a sloping roof toward a huge steeple at the far end. Then the bug looked around him, satisfied at his progress. At this pace, he would make the rendezvous with time to spare, and for a moment he was tempted to leave the trail and make for Jagungal's peak. It would not take more than half a day to climb to the top.

What a view there should be from there! He would probably never walk these mountains again. But he fought the temptation to turn aside and deliberately held on. As he moved past the ridge that led to the peak, he looked back with a kind of wistfulness, remembering Tolkien's lines about the roads we are destined never to travel: the secret gate, the hidden paths west of the moon and east of the sun. The gate that led on and on.

Right after the declaration of Martial Law in the Philippines, Alex had adopted the cover of a street vendor, hiding in plain sight, while others opted for the immobility of safe houses. But he thought he made the better choice. Peddlers were part of the scenery and therefore universally ignored, like waiters at a restaurant. Alex took up the trade in earnest and sold boiled duck eggs, pork crackling and peanuts out of a wicker basket while walking from one end of the city to the other. That he attended underground meetings and couriered messages was almost a fringe benefit.

But he was sometimes overtaken on the road by the midnight curfew and, like other vendors, forced to sleep where it caught him. The beat cops enforcing the curfew left the vendors to sleep undisturbed in alleys and on pavements. Once the patrol turned the corner, the vendors would sit up, talk among themselves and look around. It was the best way to see the world.

Alex saw things as a street vendor that he would never have noticed from a bus, jeepney or car. There was a mother looking old beyond her years who was feeding her child something thin and unrecognizable out of an old tin can. Looking through open windows, he had glimpsed a family gathered around a meal of fried fish, vegetable soup and candied yams as well as a group of teen-aged friends clustered around a black and white TV set watching a basketball game. One man was crying for no apparent reason on a curb with an open bottle of gin beside him.

Each was a world he could have stepped into. For good or ill, he had chosen this path that had now taken him to this mountain trail. Alex pushed on, driven by a feeling of urgency he could not shake. The sixth sense that had saved him in the past was now vibrating with increasing force. He felt a strange foreboding even when logic told him there was no reason to be afraid.

Despite the harder going, he forced the pace and planned to reach the rendezvous as early as possible. Once near the lake, he could lie hidden watching and waiting for Ramon to arrive. He would be safe under cover from anyone who didn't actually stumble over him. But in transit he was exposed to any threat within line of sight. He began to dread every moment on the trail.

Alex remembered the last time his sixth sense saved his life, the day they lost the lucky green sofa. Justine had gone down to the Davila Rodriguez Law Offices located a few blocks from the US Embassy. The principal partners of the firm were two ex-Senators who, since Marcos declared Martial Law and abolished the Senate, had become the *de facto* leaders of the legal opposition. Though no longer in government, they still wielded influence, and on that hinged Justine's plan to spring her husband, Dante Arevalo, from jail.

Like Dante Arevalo, ex-Senators Davila and Rodriguez had become in Marcos' era both hero and pariah to many people, spoken of in awe but at the same time avoided like the plague. Their former clients had been captains of industry; now the only people who came to their offices were an assortment of opposition leaders, radical churchmen and disgraced academics.

Despite the sign saying "law offices" outside their door, few actually came hoping for a legal remedy for their problems since there was very little hope of winning a case in the Marcos-controlled judiciary. Some came in order to turn their foreordained convictions into a public drama. Others because they couldn't think of anything else. The atmosphere in the waiting rooms was redolent with nervous cigarette smoke and resignation.

But the two eminent lawyers still had ways to get a select few off the hook. One of these was through their contacts in the foreign press. Marcos, like most dictators, worried about the profitability of the companies he controlled, which in turn depended on his image among international investors. Davila and Rodriguez exploited this weakness by turning their premises into a kind of press club for foreign correspondents. The two lawyers offered journalists steady grist for their mills by introducing them to highly-placed "sources". They might have lost access to Marcos' courts, but for the duration of Martial Law, they could still subject him to a trial by publicity.

Marcos' security forces refrained from any obvious surveillance of the premises on orders of the dictator. But they continued to watch from cover. They had also recruited a person on the inside to spy for them, someone to cue them in on real subjects of interest among the hundreds of visitors who came in on any given day. They might not be able to trap the roaches inside, but they could follow them back to their nests.

A battery of 16-mm motion picture cameras with telephoto lenses covered every approach to the offices. When Justine, wearing a baseball cap, blue jeans and a white blouse walked in, three of these cameras positioned at different angles recorded her entry. The "receptionist" also noted the vague answers Justine gave her when asked the reason for seeing Rodriguez as well as the friendly and familiar terms with which Rodriguez received her.

Once inside his office, Rodriguez offered Justine a seat and asked what was the matter. "Dante's been arrested by Col. Bobadilla," she said. The older man's face fell at the news. He at once recognized the seriousness of the situation and gave her his full attention. Justine told him everything she knew, which as in most other Martial Law arrest cases, amounted to nearly nothing. Arrests were made on the basis of secret files, without witnesses present, and in which no warrants were served. It was a system in which nobody knew what was going on.

To Rodriguez, who was following Justine's recount closely, it looked like Arevalo had been arrested simply because he was a Marcos political opponent. He was not targeted for any particular offense and that offered the former Senator a glimmer of hope.

It was obvious, he told Justine, that there was no chance of obtaining Arevalo's release by writs or court orders. No judge would defy Marcos and order his release, no matter how trumped up the charges. Ordinarily, all they could do was wait for Arevalo to pass through the byzantine toils of the system and hope for his release some time in the future. But just now, there was an opportunity they might seize. Rodriguez said he might be able to interest a visiting American congressman from California – Frankie Barnes – into intervening for her husband.

Rodriguez sounded so confident he could persuade Congressman Barnes to bring up Arevalo's detention with Marcos that Justine was mildly surprised. Had she been willing to look a gift horse in the mouth she might have asked why it was so easy. But few people glance twice at good fortune and she took it on faith that the American congressman would act out of principled solidarity, nothing more, nothing less, and happily accepted Rodriguez's assurances.

Rodriguez told Justine to check back with him after some weeks and asked the receptionist to escort her to the door. The old man returned to his office. He had not told her the whole truth about Barnes. Despite his image as a human rights advocate, Barnes used his position in the Congressional Foreign Relations Committee to set up lucrative deals for his American cronies in "developing economies". His specialty was negotiating equity participation in businesses located in countries run by autocratic regimes. Normally they would be too politically toxic for many American investors to touch. But Barnes had a way of getting around that. He would convene hearings on "human rights abuses" or threaten to block foreign aid to a particular country. Eventually the dictators would ask Barnes what it would take to get him off their backs.

Frankie Barnes' answer was "a little drama". He would negotiate the release of some "prisoners of conscience" with the regimes and portray it as a "step in the right direction" which should be matched by a little foreign investment. In the afterglow of the prisoner releases, it was easy to slip in his cronies into the "wedge of freedom in the wall of tyranny". It was a no-lose setup: by acting the guardian of human rights, he burnished his image and created business opportunities along the way.

To Barnes' way of thinking, this was pragmatism. You had to act the crook to deal with crooks. Jobs for some, freedom for a few and fortunes for his friends. What was there not to like?

Rodriguez knew all this from his contacts in Washington. They had tipped him off to Barnes' latest interest in a series of factories in the Bataan Export Processing Zone. Marcos badly needed investors for the project but there would be protests from human rights activists. If Manila could throw in Arevalo's release as a sweetener, then the human rights lobby might be placated. In exchange, Barnes would guarantee smooth sailing in his committee when the foreign aid bill for Marcos came up. It was the wicked way of the world, and Rodriguez figured that Justine didn't have to know it.

The "receptionist" accompanied Justine not just to the front door but out onto the sidewalk. She waved an enthusiastic goodbye with a hand gesture that resembled a person wiping a pane of glass. Across the street, the watcher peering through the spotting scope saw the pre-arranged signal. The "receptionist", in reality also a security agent, was indicating a subject of interest. He alerted the tail team to follow Justine as she headed south on Apolinario Mabini Street.

A three-man surveillance team swung out of nearby alleys and took up position behind her, two behind and one across the street, switching positions periodically to avoid being detected. But Justine was so happy with the result of her meeting with Rodriguez that she failed to notice three shadows tailing her. She hailed a taxi. The leader of the tail team spoke into a radio and handed the tail off to the vehicle surveillance team, who were soon right behind the taxi and headed northeast.

A nondescript Nissan followed the taxi. Ordinarily, they would have had no trouble tailing it all the way to the safe house. But the traffic was so heavy Justine's cabbie tried for a detour after they had passed the Nagtahan Bridge. He moved off the main road into the side streets thronged with motorized tricycles and pedestrians in an effort to outflank the traffic on the main road. The Nissan team did not follow for fear of being trapped by the alleyway traffic. They stayed on the main road, radioing ahead to a second vehicle to wait at an intersection that Justine's taxi had to cross when it regained the highway.

It was then that Justine's taxi had a flat. A rusty four-inch nail drove through its worn tire treads and brought it to a pavement-thumping stop. The cabbie cursed but there was nothing he could do but push it to one of the many tire-vulcanizing shops in the area. These shops had in fact sown the nails themselves to drum up business.

Justine saw from the flat that her taxi ride was over. She paid off the driver and continued by jeepney. Her jeepney and a hundred others like it passed the spot monitored by the intelligence agents without being remarked.

It was nearly a half-hour before the vehicle surveillance team decided to go on foot into the alleys. They found both cab and driver at a vulcanizing shop. Flashing their badges, they questioned the surprised cabbie and hit him with a tire iron and shoved a gun in his face to make him talk, but all they could get from him was a stammered explanation that his passenger had told him to head for Roxas District, a suburb four miles away.

Their subject was too far ahead to intercept, so the agents radioed for a saturation team to close in on Roxas District immediately. The safe house had now been localized to an area just small enough to canvass house by house. The procedure for smoking out safe houses was for teams to knock on the door of each house in a suspect group of blocks pretending to be census takers or door-to-door salesmen. They would work one street at a time looking for telltale signs of clandestine occupancy: too many young people at home during working hours; the absence of ordinary family furniture; indications of a complete lack of normal life. With any luck, the canvassers could narrow things down to two or three likely addresses. Then the combers would call in the raiding teams.

Justine's jeepney got to Roxas District 15 minutes ahead of the first team of door-knockers. It was a ten-minute walk from the jeepney stop through a succession of narrow alleys and small streets to the safe house. She opened the rusty metal gate and walked past the hedge that screened the front door, turned the key and walked in. It seemed empty until Alex stepped from the shadow of the side room out into the light.

"How'd it go?" he asked.

"Better than I could have hoped for!" she said. "Atty. Rodriguez thinks he might be able to get an American congressman to put pressure on Marcos to get Dante out!"

"Well, that's great," Alex said. "Are you sure you weren't followed?" He glanced out past the curtains into the street.

"Well, I wasn't as careful as I might be but my taxi had a flat and I changed vehicles coming here. So, I should be all right."

"What did you take coming here from the law offices?" Alex asked.

"A taxi until just past Nagtahan Bridge. Then a jeepney till the corner. I walked the rest of the way here. Why?"

Alex looked a little reproachful for a moment. Then he looked out once again into the empty street and smiled.

'Tell me about this marvelous deal Rodriguez is cutting," he said. He asked her into the kitchen, where there was some bread, instant coffee and a can of tuna.

"There's a lot to tell."

"It seems like good news and calls for a celebration. But all I've got is Tuna Extreme."

Justine laughed. Tuna Extreme was what they called canned tuna on cheap bread.

"Then Tuna Extreme it is. Frankie Barnes, a congressman from California, is starting a fact-finding tour of Southeast Asia in a couple of months. Senator Rodriguez thinks he can get Barnes to ask Marcos to release Dante."

Alex listened and put the kettle on the gas burner to heat water for coffee. The match to the gas ring had just started a circle of blue flame when the rusty hinges of the garden gate outside grated open. Alex froze. That was when the rest of his sixth sense kicked in.

"Are you expecting a visitor?"

"No."

Footsteps crunched across the gravel path from the gate to the front door. Now there was an urgent rapping on it.

"Philippine Census Bureau. Is anybody home?"

Alex put his finger to his lips and both sat stock still in their chairs, making neither a move nor a sound.

"Census. Is anybody home? Open up! Open up!"

Alex put his palm down to warn against sudden movement. He knew that the next few seconds would determine whether they would be captured or not. He eased himself out of the chair, silently switched off the gas burner and grabbed the backpack containing the confidential documents and the gun from the mimeograph machine closet. Justine knew they were in a race against a raiding team. The hopes of just a few moments before had been replaced by an adrenaline rush of fear. In one smooth movement, Alex took the .38 Smith and Wesson from the bag, opened the cylinder to see it was loaded and shoved it into his waistband.

Still using hand signals, he directed Justine toward the back door. The knocking in front of the house had stopped but he sensed that whoever was at the door had not gone away but was standing just outside the threshold. More footsteps could be heard coming in from the street. The door-knocker wasn't going away, probably acting on a hunch too. Alex was now certain that a raid was imminent.

There was no time to lose. He opened the back door and quickly guided Justine out back to the knotted escape rope. Without prompting, she went over the back wall and down the rope into the fast-flowing sewer water 25 feet below. He could hear shouting from the front of the house now. It was now or never. He went over, sliding rather than climbing down the rope.

He heard footsteps clatter in the safe house above. Alex splashed his way across the filthy, knee-deep water with Justine. A decomposing dog borne by the sewer water hit him square across the legs. It spun around, and continued floating down the stream.

When they reached the opposite wall, he indicated the metal spikes driven into the rock wall. Justine grabbed the first and swarmed up them as quickly as she could, with Alex right behind her. She rolled over the top. He was just going over when out of the corner of his eye, he saw two heavy-set men come around the corners of the safe house. He followed Justine over the top but they had spotted him. The two men ran to the ledge on the far bank they had just left. They grabbed the knotted rope and made to follow.

"Wait over there," Alex hissed, "crouch below the level of the ledge and run," pointing in the direction of the escape route. "Wait for me around the corner."

He knew that Justine had never reconnoitered the escape route as he had. In a chase, she would lose her way and be overtaken. He had to delay the pursuit.

Alex heard a splash as the first of the intelligence agents lowered himself into the putrid water below. He pulled the gun from his waistband, moved a few feet to one side so he would emerge from behind cover in an unexpected location. He heard another splash. He drew back the hammer of his revolver and counted to five. He could hear the labored breath of a man clambering up the spikes scant feet below him, almost certainly using both his hands to climb.

Alex popped over the edge and lined up the sights on the second man in the center of the canal who was covering his partner's climb with a Colt Model 1911. It was pointed at the wrong place, where he had ducked down. He fired twice into center mass. The sound of the shots was deafening. The man dropped into the stream and began to float after the dead dog. In the next split second, he shifted his aim squarely at the face of the climbing man only three feet below. The agent's mouth was open in an "O" of astonishment. He fired and a puff of white smoke and sparks blurred the target. The man lost his grip on the wall and fell with a sickening thump into the hard rock below. It sounded like a flowerpot being dropped from a second-story window.

Dropping to a crouch to get below the parapet, Alex ran bent over after Justine. He had killed two cops. Now there could be no surrender or prison, the only options were death or escape. It would be the same for Justine, only worse, should she be captured. Therefore, he wouldn't let it happen. She was waiting around the first corner, her blue jeans, soaked to the knees. Alex pulled himself erect and slowed to a walk, while he led her with deliberate calm through a loosely latched gate, down an alley and over the two-foot diameter water main that bridged another but wider creek in the crazy quilt of Roxas District. On the other side of the creek was a narrow, climbing way that led to a small fresh food market. They went over and crossed a space of stalls where fish, vegetables and cuts of meat were being sold in round woven palm-leaf trays. The chatter of haggling filled the air. Alex pulled his shirt over the butt of the gun hoping no one had seen it. At least in this bustling wet market, with its shirtless porters and yelling hawkers, no one would notice their wet and smelly clothes.

Alex walked straight up to a passenger motorcycle with a sidecar, called a tricycle, and gave the driver twenty-five pesos to start straightaway for the main road without waiting for other passengers. The driver stamped on his kick-starter. The two-stroke engine sputtered twice, caught and they roared away. Alex allowed himself a look back. There was no pursuit.

After the tricycle, more jeepney rides and an extended walk, Alex and Justine came to a cinema on Santa Mesa Avenue, a low-end commercial street some miles from Cindy. Justine entered the movie house while Alex called the alert number to ask for "Danny". "Danny" was of course not home but the signal that Cindy, the safe house, had been blown. Alex thought briefly of the loss of the talismanic green Naugahyde couch. It had finally run out of luck.

The plan, Alex had told Justine, was to hole up in the movie house until dark. At the moment, they were the two most wanted fugitives in Manila. It was too dangerous to move around by day.

They sat in separate rows of a second-run screening of "Shaft" doubled with "The Ten Commandments". Some drunks slumped in their seats, others snored. In Manila, anyone who bought a ticket could sit through as many screenings as he liked and air-conditioned theaters made the best places to nap. Only a handful were watching Richard Roundtree portray Shaft. Maybe some of them actually understood English. What mattered was nobody noticed them.

At 8:30 p.m., Alex tapped Justine on the shoulder. Both slipped out of the cinema at intervals just as Moses was parting the Red Sea. Outside, a heavy tropical downpour came down in sheets and saturated the air with a heavy wetness. Tendrils of mist rose from the hot asphalt only to be beaten down again by raindrops the size of corn kernels. The night turned into a pane of muddy glass that hissed so loudly one could not hear oneself talk.

They edged along the side of buildings, skipping over the dry spots on the sidewalk, facing from eave to eave. Office workers on their way home ran with their heads down, some holding sodden newspaper sheets above them. Alex leaned back against a dirty cement wall and yelled.

"We're in luck. Rain. Lots of it."

Since neither had eaten since breakfast, Alex led Justine to the Sputnik Café, a hole in the wall with a glass counter display of bad food. A jukebox with a blown speaker provided atmosphere for the half-dozen formica-topped tables scattered throughout the diner. He told Justine to sit away from the entrance at the corner table. Then he went to the counter and bought some fried fish, a bowl of congealed vegetables and a large plate of rice for their supper. He tried to consider his next move, but his mind was in turmoil. He was a cop killer. He had killed two people.

"My mother spent her life savings to send me to college," Alex said to no one in particular. "She wanted so much to see me graduate. My grandma gave me her rosary. See, I still have it." He produced a small wooden rosary from his pocket. "It was to keep me from evil. I left school because it seemed like the 'moral thing to do'. And this is where I end up: shooting two men in a single afternoon."

Jeepney radios blared news of the cop killings as they drove past the cafe. The phrases "death in Roxas District", "murder gang at large" faded in and out with the Doppler effect. He looked out at the wall of rain lit by the passing headlights. It looked like a crystal prison.

"Alex," Justine said. "Don't take it so hard. How many people have those intelligence agents taken to Bobadilla's house of horrors? How many have they tortured and killed?"

Alex said nothing. He knew more about torture chambers, including ways to escape from them, than he cared to tell. Finally, he said, "I put two men in a coffin with a .38. A slug in the face ends every argument. It ends the cop and the dad, the intelligence agent and the man who

212

bought treats for his kids on Sundays. It ends all that was and all that might have been. Helluva thing, a .38."

"Maybe guilt is the price of freedom," said Justine. She couldn't think of anything else to say.

"Guilt is the price of living," Alex answered. "Sometimes I wonder if it's worth it." A silence fell across the room, broken only by the rain drumming down on the galvanized iron roof. Then suddenly, Justine knew.

"You're in love with me, aren't you?" she said.

"More than I can say."

There was a silence before Justine answered.

"Dante told me once the day might come when I might love someone else besides him. If that day came, he wanted me to understand that the choice of whether to love back or not was entirely up to me. He just wanted me to remember that he would always love me. He wanted to give me both love and freedom. Oh, Alex, what should I do?"

"Do? Why, stay where you are. Stay a little beyond the reach of what, God help me, I feel just now. Keep a little distance from that terrible animal triumph and desire and the knowledge that with a word – well, you talked about love, didn't you? From the grasping that comes all too easily when you're high with the power from two empty chambers in the cylinder and a woman who's asking you what she should do. I'm a reptile, Justine. A hissing mass of hatreds and desires. Or, at least, right now I am. There's nothing I can know about love and freedom and sacrifice in this state."

"Or is it something else?" Justine asked.

"What?"

"Pride."

"And don't forget the fear," Alex said. "The fear of the day when you come to your senses and remember the man of decency and honor who loved you so much he would not take your freedom if it meant his happiness, when you think about a career and a family. That's a whole lot to set against two empty cylinders in a .38. Whatever you feel for me, Justine, it's the rain and rush and the Café Sputnik that weaves the spell. It all fades in the sunlight.

"If Rodriguez is right, you've got a chance at life. All I've got is the underground. Let me keep it rather than wait for the day when you walk away. So sit where you are, Justine. For all the wrong reasons and for all the right ones, too."

He looked out at the sheet of rain. It wasn't going to let up. The café radio resumed its tinny sound. The announcer reported that a tropical depression was hovering over Luzon. The downpour could go on for days. It was a hell of a time for confidences but nearly a perfect opportunity to move.

"It's time to go to Tondo," Alex said.

The only way to get there without risking identification was to walk the entire distance. While the dragnet was out in full force, it was too risky to show their faces for any length of time. They walked out into the rain. It was like stepping under a bathroom shower. Both were thoroughly soaked within seconds. He could feel the water pouring down his pants into his sneakers. It didn't matter. Everything important would be kept dry by plastic or gun oil.

THE PROMISED LAND

Alex and Justine crossed Santa Mesa Avenue and left its bright main thoroughfare for the murky labyrinth of Sampaloc District. Sampaloc was a tangle of residential streets that extended unbroken for nearly two kilometers until it petered out on España Street. He moved with the confidence of a former street vendor. He knew every twist and turn and even when his knowledge failed his sense of the general topography of Manila was so encyclopedic that they invariably progressed toward their destination. They kept to the shadows and used the smallest streets for as long as they led in the right direction. Ordinarily, that would put them at risk of running into street gangs and petty criminals. But the rain had kept even the thieves home, which was good because Alex didn't want to use the .38 again.

Once, they emerged from a narrow way to find their path blocked by an island of trees and vegetation growing in the middle of the urban warren. Justine blinked at the unlikely sight but there, towering incongruously over the densely packed homes of the district, was a fairy-tale forest filled with faintly lit houses that resembled relics from the Spanish colonial period. "That's Jungletown," said Alex, but did not explain. They pressed on and Justine watched the small forest city recede with fascination.

After a time they came to a disused rail line that once ran through the heart of Manila. The ruinous roadbed stretched before them, barely visible in the near-darkness. Its trace was crowded in by shanties on both sides. The rails or what was left of them had been converted into an interminable pedestrian walkway that disappeared in the distance. It was covered with slime for much of its length and cluttered with makeshift stalls that by day sold food, newspapers or flavored water. Now they were covered with scraps of plastic.

The shacks on each side seemed to lean inward until they left only a ribbon of sky above the alley. Dim lights peeped through the wooden window slats on either side.

"This leads to Tondo," Alex said. "We could take the street, but there are fewer prying eyes this way. This is the old Philippine National Railway line. Normally, it is crowded even at night with residents sitting on their doorsteps but with this storm on and the hour we'll have it mostly to ourselves. We might leave it every now and again where it's blocked and use the side streets. But we'll use it whenever we can. It will take us most of the way and cut down on our exposure. Stay close," Alex said.

She looked at the menacing surroundings and did not need to be told twice.

An hour's walk over the squishy mud and rusty rails eventually took them to Retiro Street. The street was now flooding so badly that Justine saw a Volkswagen Beetle floating down into an alley. She watched the apparition disappear into the night. Alex held the backpack above his head and waded through the chest-deep water. Soon they came to a vast square that was like a shallow lake of floodwater. A small hill of fermenting vegetables and decaying organic matter rose above the water. It was the day's garbage pile; it would not be collected that night.

They had reached Blumentritt Market. Thousands of vendors laid out their wares in that vast space each morning but it was deserted now except for one or two hardy traders selling mysterious-looking herbs and amulets on dark wooden tables. The amulets bore Latin inscriptions and were decorated with symbols that might have been traced from the Tarot deck. Justine would have wanted to look closer but Alex ignored everything and pushed on.

They turned into an alley and regained the railroad track. It looped south for a seeming eternity and ended in the market district of Divisoria, the commercial heart of Chinatown. Dark warehouses loomed on either side. The narrow streets were dotted with shuttered stalls that crammed every inch of sidewalk.

They were cold and footsore by now. Alex saw a small shop selling homemade donuts and brewed coffee. The enticing aroma almost made him want to risk a cup but he decided against it. They would
216

push on. In half an hour, they were walking down Juan Luna Street and passing the last outpost of the regular city before the streets dissolved into the crazy quilt of the Tondo Foreshore.

Justine had heard a lot about this fabled place. Now she was about to see it for herself. The Tondo Foreshore was a strange beast, a mutation created by the huge urban explosion that followed World War II. Dickens might have recognized it, but even he would have been taken aback.

Old Tondo – which Alex and Justine had just left – was a dingy, working-class area dating back to Spanish times, but the Tondo Foreshore had formed by a cancerous process of accretion into a dense mass of shacks with no parks, public squares, residential districts or city centers and no streets in any recognizable sense. It was a formless morass inhabited by 200,000 people without a trace of water, electrical, sanitation or sewage systems.

The Foreshore simply had none of the substructure familiar to modern cities. It grew from a process resembling cellular reproduction, starting from a small group of settlers from the Visayas and refugees from the Battle of Manila who built hovels in a mudflat along the shores of Manila Bay. Gradually, they were joined by displaced persons and migrants arriving by ship. The original nucleus spread outwards like a malignancy, stopping only when some physical barrier – a block of concrete buildings, a river, or the sea itself – stopped the sprawl.

This heaving mass of urban tissue communicated with the outside world through little trails that wound through it like capillaries in the vascular system of an organism. Some trails were wide enough for only one person to edge through sideways. The little pathways snaked past clumps of shanties made from cardboard, scrap iron and waste-wood. They were the organs of supply of that fantastic ecosystem, and on wooden planks, duckboards and ferry boats over stagnant waters, a stream of people and supplies flowed in both directions.

Tondo covered the foreshore like a fungus and like a fungus it gnawed at the geographical features themselves through the intensity of human use. Ocean inlets became lakes of sludge. The old waterways were so choked with vegetable matter, plastic bags, cans, rusted machinery, dead animals, and rotting timber that no one could say where land ended and the water – if it could be called that – began.

What the residents of the Tondo Foreshore actually did for a living has never been determined by scientific survey. But Alex knew the answer well enough. There were petty thieves of all descriptions: bag-snatchers, pickpockets, laundry line filchers, confidence tricksters, card sharps, fake beggars, cheap buskers, mountebanks, counterfeit merchandise salesmen, and grifters of all kinds. Then there were the broken specimens of humanity: the mentally disturbed, homicidal maniacs, the religiously insane and the plain insane. There were drunks and drug addicts, glue sniffers and pill droppers. There were prostitutes of the lowest category. There were deadbeats and workers on starvation wages so that many wandered around nearly stupid from hunger, the worst cases staggering in short stages and sleeping in doorways in the broad day to conserve their energy.

A number of unusual trades were plied. From time to time, a shack would be blown sky-high, the result of someone in the dynamite fishing business unsuccessfully trying to saw open a stolen artillery shell with a hacksaw to obtain the powder. There were professional ghouls who, when not otherwise employed in digging up the recently buried to extract gold teeth, were engaged in raiding wakes and mortuaries in order to sell the cadavers to medical schools.

But if one type of person typified the Tondo Foreshore, it was the garbage scavenger. Each night as darkness fell, thousands of them ranging in age from the teens to their early sixties swarmed out of the maze of hovels pushing homemade wooden carts in search of garbage. They mined trash for valuable material like a Forty-Niner might pan for gold. The light industrial districts yielded copper wire and scrap metal. Office districts produced large quantities of waste paper while others generated quantities of glass bottles or wood waste of various kinds. Anything of value would be plucked out and sold on the recycling exchanges. Scavengers competed for lucrative scavenging routes and once in possession defended their territories against all comers.

218

Each morning saw the fleet of carts return to Tondo to sell the night's pickings in garbage exchanges called "bodegas". These marts resounded with the thump of cans being beaten flat, bottles being smashed into shards and paper and wire being baled.

But the scavengers were not the only ones out for the valuable scrap. The city garbage collectors coveted the same waste that scavengers scrabbled for and whenever the collectors got the chance they muscled the scavengers away, as did lions to hyenas in the African plains. Both the scavengers and city sanitation workers co-existed in an uneasy *modus vivendi*, with neither gaining a permanent advantage. Though between them they extracted nearly every item of value from the garbage, enough residual material was tipped into the landfill to sustain those at the true bottom of the barrel, the absolute bottom of the rung -- the people who actually lived on the landfill itself, the denizens of "Smokey Mountain".

Smokey Mountain was the common name for the Manila city dump. It was a hill of garbage 10 stories tall, its top bulldozed flat into a plateau 22 acres in area, as large as the flight decks of five aircraft carriers. A switchback road carved in the face of the garbage pile zigzagged from street level to the summit, bearing hundreds of garbage trucks in a continuous line, each tipping its payload onto a monstrous ziggurat of trash rising to the skies. But no sacrificial smoke on any ancient ziggurat could compare with the fumes from countless subterranean fires generated by spontaneous combustion from organic matter fermenting and bursting into flame. Around fissures that constantly belched noxious fumes, dozens of trucks weaved, seeking a path over that infernal plain, eagerly pursued by dozens of people clad in rags like imps in hell.

The people of Smokey Mountain lived in terraces hacked into the side of the hill of garbage. They were born, raised and often died in these terrace towns, rarely visited even by the residents of the Foreshore itself, in a universe as far from the outside world as a planet on another solar system.

Some hours after midnight, Justine and Alex reached the heart of the Foreshore after a journey of twists and turns in the pouring rain. Justine followed Alex across the huge sewer of the Vitas, dark as the Styx and as viscous as a river of mud. It was spanned by a tottering bridge of rusty metal that carried vehicular traffic long ago, whose ruins were now a pedestrian pathway of rickety planks over the remaining girders. Beneath the bridge was the municipal meat works. Yet it was neither the river, the bridge nor the abbatoir that arrested Justine's attention but the sight on the further bank. Her gaze rose upward to take in a tower of darkness and flame – a vast, evil-smelling man-made mountain that blazed even in that tropical downpour.

Alex looked at Smokey Mountain in happiness and relief. "We're nearly safe," he said. He pointed to a clump of huts growing like a rash from the side of the dump and told Justine that Ramon maintained his private safe house in one of them.

As they crossed the walkway over the rusty bridge, she glanced down at the meat works below. The stench of decaying flesh rose from it. There was a small building to one side of the abattoir from which jangling music still issued, even at that late, stormy hour. A door opened in the side of the building and in the flare of red light some men could be seen stumbling out.

"That's the *Boteng Umiilaw* – the Blinking Bottle – a bar for slaughterhouse workers and petty criminals," Alex said. He scarcely gave it a glance. "They drink mostly *Marca Demonyo* gin down there, the one with the label showing St. Michael and Satan fighting for the soul of man."

Justine looked back down at the *Boteng Umiilaw* and wondered how Alex knew about it. "Have you ever been there?" she asked him.

"Yes," he said, "and didn't quite fit in. Maybe I'll keep coming back until I do."

They were now across the sewer and entering a narrow climbing path through the winding lanes that led to the terraces of Smokey Mountain. They stepped over carts, sleeping figures, stalls draped in cloth or plastic, all in the uniform shade of gray with which the constant rain of wet ash coated everything. They snaked their way through alleys and teetered across elevated single-board walkways until they finally came to a little courtyard with corrugated iron washbasins hung up on nails. Alex knocked at a door in coded staccato. It opened after a few seconds. As he and Justine stepped out of the rain into the safe house, their eyes adjusted to the darkness and they saw Ramon in the corner lighting a small oil lamp.

"Howdy, I've been expecting you. Too bad about the green couch," he said. "Pick up any company on the way over?"

"Nothing I've noticed in the last ten kilometers or so."

"Good. You're all over the news. What about a cup of coffee and you tell me all about the raid."

He lit a kerosene stove in the corner and put a kettle on the fire. The burner was fed from a small reservoir of pressurized kerosene that forced the fuel up a needle into the burner. It burned red and smoky. When the burner head got hot enough to vaporize the kerosene instantly, it would burn clean and blue.

They sat in the dark on the floor, soaked to the skin, watching the flame turn blue. In a few minutes, they each had a cup of sweetened instant coffee and a small plate of cheap biscuits before them. Alex took the confidential papers out of their wrapping and handed them over to Ramon. He told the story of the last hours from the knock on the door to their arrival in Smokey Mountain. Ramon sat listening without comment. He knew, even in the dark, that the two were near exhaustion.

Ramon simply nodded in acknowledgement after Alex had finished and opened a sliding panel set waist-high in the wall. It opened on a small extension built half a level higher than the rest of the room. The floor was made of small strips of bamboo beneath which the muddy ground could be seen. A rusted sheet of galvanized iron formed the roof.

"Here's your room, Justine," Ramon said. "I think you'd better get some sleep, though I must confess the accommodations here leave much to be desired."

Justine stepped up into her quarters and saw the room overhung the slope of the garbage-hill, jutting out like a low balcony from the side of Ramon's safe house. A small pivoting wooden board, hinged at the top by a nail driven through each side of the frame, tilted up like a window. She opened it and gained a view into the outside world. Dawn was breaking and it lit a serried row of hovels that descended in a jumble that ended on the shores of the Vitas sewer. She realized she was looking at the Smokey Mountain version of a view across Central Park: the best vista from the best address in town. Just then, the sun broke through the overcast and touched the rusty rooftops with fire. Even the dark waters of Vitas were momentarily imbued with magic.

"Quite a view, huh?" Alex was leaning with his elbows on the shelf beside her.

"A river Jordan and across it, a Promised Land."

"The Promised Land is on this side of the Vitas," Alex said, "on a hill flowing with scrap and garbage." He paused, then said, "We've come as far as we can. For me it's the end of the line. I'm not running from Bobadilla any more. Get some sleep while you can. There's no telling what happens next."

Alex turned and half-closed the sliding door. He picked out a corner in the larger room where he could get some rest. There he lay, half-sitting against the wall with the .38 in his waistband. It was then Justine understood the terrible freedom of the underground, where your life was free of the encumbrance of addresses, names or plans. It was devoid of all responsibility, devoid of anything that needed a tomorrow. Here, everything was contingent and anything was possible provided it happened today. She shut the hatch and lay down on the bamboo slats to sleep.

THE LAST VALLEY

Whenever Alex came to an open stretch, he would stop, find a vantage and scan ahead with his binoculars. Only after nothing turned up did the landscape throw off the shadow of apprehension that seemed to rob the snow gums, wildflowers, rocks and grass of their color. He would hurry on to the next vantage, moving ahead by bounds in the best compromise he could make between speed and caution.

Alex chose his evening encampment with even more care, selecting corners hidden from view or angles where rocks screened even the tiny blue flame of the camp stove. Instead of drifting off to sleep, he sat outside the tent alert for any approaching sound until he was convinced he was alone in that bleak landscape. Only after constant watchfulness had exhausted his nervous energy did he grope his way back into the sleeping bag. Through the tent flap he left open to hear nearby sounds, the sky seemed so alive with stars they were like a swarm of fireflies just above his head. He drifted off to sleep amid those lights only to wake with a start to find that dawn had not yet come. Even in half-sleep, that sixth sense was urging him on.

Dawn gave him the light to make a hurried breakfast, break camp and hit the road. The country began to rise steadily. He was reaching the approaches to the Main Range of the Snowy Mountains. The snow gums and grass were changing with the increasing altitude, dressing as it were, for winter. Alex looked up at the clear blue sky between the peaks but knew their placid promise was deceptive; snow could come without warning at these heights.

He stopped, tucked himself behind a bush and looked at the map to visualize the terrain ahead. It showed that after Mount Gungartan some distance away he would begin climbing the Main Range, a series of peaks separated by a deep valley on either side from the smaller ranges to the east and west. From here on, it would be like climbing a ridge flanked by two lower ridges on either hand. The eastern, or left hand, ridge was heavily dotted with ski camps, lodges and resorts, all connected by the Kosciuszko Road. Alex realized that from the high

223

ridge road it would be a mere seven kilometers across a valley to the resort-studded and lower eastern ridge. That meant the opportunity to check in with Ramon since a signal could probably reach the cell phone towers near the resorts. And he would take it.

Ever since he used his old SIM to test for a connection at the Happy Jacks, Alex had been haunted by the possibility that he might have given himself away. The fact that his cell phone reported no connection did not entirely dispel his misgivings. He realized now that he must have been at the fringe of coverage. Could his old SIM have been momentarily detected by the tower? The momentary excitement of discovering the possible meaning of Fortunas' words had made him careless but if he had made an error, then Ramon would warn him. The risk was remote and he was probably worrying about nothing. Nevertheless, he would check for messages or warnings once he reached Mount Tate, just in case. Just in case.

He finally reached a position where his cell phone could connect. He turned it on and downloaded a single message. It hit Alex like a hammer. He had turned on his cell phone as soon as he cleared Mount Tate. Once past the crest, he had a direct line of sight to the cell phone towers serving the ski resort of Charlotte's Pass. As soon as he switched on the phone, the message was waiting for him. It was direct and to the point:

> Enemy knows you're on the trail. And this channel is
> compromised. Evade to Cora's.

As on that long-ago day at Roxas District, he knew survival depended on clear thinking and quick action. The enemy could read his phone traffic but they could not decipher messages completely because they lacked the crucial context. He knew – and they could only guess – where "Cora" was located. As long as they did not know the rendezvous point and his location, they could not completely block the way. If he could get off the trail and find another way to Cora's, there was still a chance.

Alex had gamed this possibility in his mind during the long nights in his tent. His best bet was to get off the main trail and proceed by an indirect route to the rendezvous. But the problem was time. Time brought the enemy closer. Hours, perhaps minutes, now counted. The enemy was younger, stronger and faster. With the cold weather beginning to set in and his food supplies limited, he could not lie up and wait for the hunters to go away. In fact, they would probably reinforce. Time was not his friend.

The trail on the high central ridge was by far the fastest and easiest way to the rendezvous. If he left the main walking track and proceeded cross-country down in the valley to either side, he would be slowed by ridges and the punishing hill contours. That would exhaust him but more significantly it would slow him down. Staying on the trail brought danger, but so did delay. If he left the trail too soon, it would give the enemy the chance to close.

Besides, the sheer barrenness of the hills at these high elevations meant that going down into the valleys gave scant protection to a foe on the ridge that could look down with binoculars, as a hawk does, for its prey. He might escape notice when the morning or afternoon shadows darkened the valleys, but once the sun rose, he would be as obvious as a ball on a billiard table.

His best bet was to take a calculated risk. Alex pulled out his topo map and ticked off the distances. He would risk staying on the trail another ten kilometers – three to four hours hard going – until he passed Lake Albina to his right. Then he would descend left off the trail into the last valley before Lake Cootapatamba – also known as Cora's. He would go down into the valley just as the light was beginning to fade. From there he would be close enough, if he had the strength, to cover the last five kilometers on the valley floor by a single night's march.

He moved up the trail, supercharged with adrenaline. But the ground stared back at him. The landscape for miles around was open, broken only by clumps of rocks, lichens, grass, and the occasional snow gum. There was not enough cover by day for a rabbit. Fighting the instinct to keep looking behind him, Alex picked up the pace until his breath started to come in gasps. Then he slowed down bit by bit until he found his level of sustainable effort. He kept at it. Every five hundred meters, he would look behind him for signs of pursuit. There was nothing so far.

The day was waning when he saw the blue surface of Lake Albina down in the hollow to his right. The trail crossed the western slope on the same side as the lake, tempting hikers to go down to its shores. But today Alex had no interest in the languid waters. His attention was focused on the low saddle barely a kilometer ahead where the trail dipped before rising again to another ridge. He would bear left on reaching the saddle and instead of climbing the ridge descend into the valley to its east. He would leave the trail at that point.

He looked up at the gathering clouds. A light snowfall appeared to be in the offing; he hurried on. Maybe it was a trick of his imagination, or maybe it was the effect of his overwrought nerves, perhaps it was even the proximity of the turnoff, but each step closer to the saddle raised Alex's anxiety to an even greater pitch. He looked at the ridge behind him, but there was nothing to be seen. Nevertheless, an unreasoning conviction that he had to reach the turnoff as soon as possible gripped him. He pushed himself harder than he had ever done in the past week. He could feel the impact on the soles of his boots travel up his old bones.

Although it seemed like a long way to go, the turnoff was barely minutes away. He fought the feeling that he had to *disappear now* and held on to turnoff. Yet he did not see the point of waiting: it was bare down to the valley floor. Even when he left the trail he would not disappear. Then he saw a clump of boulders, boulders big as cars, 250 meters down into the valley. He knew from experience that they often had crevices in which a single hiker might hide. He abandoned the trail where the ground was least susceptible to boot prints and made for the rocks.

Five minutes later, he wiggled into a space about two and a half feet wide in the gaps between two of the largest boulders. Alex wedged himself in and crouched down. He sank into the deepest shadow and pulled the dark parka hood over his head to blend in as far as possible.

226

Then, as if he were waiting for something, he sat perfectly still and watched.

The human eye is instinctively attracted to movement. Alex learned this lesson first-hand when, while moving through a trail in the Cordilleras, he evaded a platoon-sized group of armed men – he did not know who they were since the Communists often wore Army uniforms to stymie recognition – by sitting completely immobile only eight feet off the trail, very partially screened by some bushes.

Now, movement attracted his eye. Two dots topped the rise and came down the track toward the saddle. Even though Alex knew he was invisible in the shadows, he felt the hairs rising on the back of his neck. Each passing moment brought the familiar athletic couple into closer view. For the first time in his life, Alex fought back a panic attack. The two assassins were moving down the trail he had just left at an unbelievable pace. They were running effortlessly. Their heads were swiveling purposefully as they trotted along, like a pair of predators scanning the veldt for their evening meal.

Then, as suddenly as it came, the anxiety left him. The impulse to duck down vanished. He came to himself and concentrated on watching the approaching duo. The old habits of mental discipline reasserted themselves and he hoped they would remain with him one last time. Suddenly the pair stopped in their tracks near the point where he had left the trail. For a moment, he wondered whether they would notice the boot marks he had left. But the ground was hard; besides, they were not interested in looking for boot tracks. They were waiting for someone.

HEAD ON

Alex watched the couple intently across the 250-meter gap from his hide in the rocks. The man pulled a satellite phone from his backpack and spoke into the receiver. Alex could hear nothing but he saw the man put down the handset after a few minutes and speak to the woman. They conferred and dumped their packs by the side of the trail and waited. Neither seemed winded. A few minutes later, Alex heard a shout to his left, from the direction in which he had been going. From a place just outside his field of view a small, wiry man loped down the trail and into the scene. He shook hands with the man and woman. Then, Alex understood. The enemy had sent two elements at him from opposite directions to close on him like a pincer. He wondered what they would do now that their vise had closed on nothing. He watched as they took out the satellite phone again and a map.

Pierre made another call on the satellite phone. Alex watched, straining to interpret the body movements which were his only clues to the conversation. The satellite phone conversation lasted some minutes. When Pierre put the receiver down, he gathered Monique and Emile Landrieu into a circle.

"That was Paris. They say Francisco switched on his phone again at coordinates near here. They are not exactly sure where he was at the time but from the relative strengths of the signal from different cell phone towers, their best guess is that he downloaded a message from five to ten kilometers back."

"What was the message?" Monique asked. Pierre read out what he'd written on a piece of paper:

> Enemy knows you're on the trail. And this channel is
> compromised. Evade to Cora's.

"So, he has received a warning. It's just a warning. It doesn't change anything."

"Yes, but the message confirms crucial things we weren't sure of," Monique said. "First, our enemy knows we've broken their comms.
228

That means they've broken our comms. Can we still believe we're up against mere amateurs? Amateurs who have SIGINT capability? Francisco's not just a target. He's a threat running for the safety of powerful allies. Allies powerful enough to hurt the client, perhaps destroy him.

"On the other hand, they are desperate because they don't care if they reveal they've broken our comms. We can infer that they cannot physically help him. He has to make his way to 'Cora', wherever that is, alone. We are on a knife's edge. They've thrown everything in. If we get Francisco now, we win. If we let Francisco reach his powerful friends, they will take his secret and finish – absolutely finish – our client. Do you understand the stakes?

"So let's get him. We know he was moving south toward his rendezvous and we're going in the right direction. We can safely say that at the time he got the message, which was only four hours ago, that he had not *yet* reached the rendezvous. Otherwise, there would have been no point downloading the message. He would already have been safe with his helpers."

"Monique, that's brilliant analysis," Emile said. "He was on this trail recently but left it after getting the warning we were on his tail. The question is, where did he leave the trail? Four hours ago or did he wait awhile? "

Pierre stood up and gestured to both sides of the trail. "That means he's somewhere out there to either side, he may even be nearby, but where?"

Monique had the topographical map out. "Put yourself in his position. What would you do if you knew you were being hunted on the trail? I would leave the main route on the ridge and go down into one of the valleys and handrail south."

"Of course," Emile said. "But the ground is too broken to the west. For my money, he's in the eastern valley." The trio looked straight at the clump of rocks.

"OK," said Pierre. "That means he's down there somewhere." The trio stood up and looked in Alex's direction almost as if they knew where he was.

"It will soon be getting too dark to go down into the valley to search. Our best move is to stay up here and scan. Did you bring the thermal sight?"

Alex watched as Emile produced an object that resembled a small rectangle from which a lens and eyepiece protruded on opposite ends. The newcomer attached it to a headpiece and gave it to the woman to try on. Alex guessed it was some kind of night vision device. He wished he knew more about such things.

"It's accurate to half a degree centigrade, but it can only reliably resolve man-sized objects out to 500 meters. It will pick him up only if he's nearby. Any further out and we'll need daylight to see him."

Pierre spoke up. "He can't be far. There are three of us and my guess is he's in that valley down there or in a place we've overlooked a kilometer behind or ahead of us. We'll scan from this ridge and either he stays under cover or we spot him. It's been a good game, Alex Francisco, but it is the end. I will almost be sad to get him. He's been a good hare."

Alex could hear nothing of the conversation. But he knew the subject of their conversation and when he saw the new arrival produce the night vision device, he could guess the rest. They gestured along the track. He figured they were going to scan from the high ground. What was the range on those things? How far could night vision devices see?

These hunters were professionals. Alex now realized the full weight of the odds against him. The escape had been a lucky break. This fully alert enemy was far more formidable. They could read the terrain better than he could. They had devices to pierce the darkness. In a little while they would be looking right down on his escape route and he would be pinned to this pile of rocks while they square-searched the whole valley for hiding places. Before too long they would find him. Suddenly he noticed small white flakes drifting down. It had started to snow. Relief washed over him.

Snow blinded electronic vision devices. The snow would change everything.

WINCHESTER

Bill Greer's reinforcements had arrived.

Ramon was waiting on a bench by the shores of Lake Jindabyne, a town in the Australian Alps, when a man about 28 years of age, five feet six inches in height and in good physical condition walked from a motel parking lot down to the lakeside path. For all his diminutive size, Army Reserve Captain John Winchester was shaking Ramon's hand so vigorously it threatened to come loose from its socket. Winchester was getting ready to enter Harvard Law School in the fall term, but for the moment he was the whole proverbial Cavalry.

"So you're the guy who helped me get the Arabic blogging software when I was deployed in Iraq," Winchester said. "Pleased to meet you after all this time."

"Pleased to meet you. How are the sheiks at blogging?" Ramon asked.

Winchester laughed. He looked at the Asian man who was in his early 50s and said, "Man, this is a hoot. Why, you sound completely American!"

"Long story," Ramon said. "Welcome to Australia. C'mon, forget the sheiks. We've got no time to lose. Bill told me three hours ago that you were coming."

Winchester knitted his brows. "I might as well level with you. First off, my role is limited to getting him into a safe house *if you get him off the trail.* I'm not authorized to actively intervene. But I'm allowed to advise, observe, provide intelligence support and, if necessary, defend myself. I'm sorry for all the restrictions but it's cover your ass all the way in Washington."

"Fair enough," Ramon said. "How closely can you advise and observe? Here's the situation. Alex is on a stretch of trail between Kiandra and Lake Cootapatamba, which is the next food drop point. Cootapatamba is 'Cora's'. I reckon he's nearly halfway there. Should be getting to

Mount Tate soon where I hope he retrieves my warning message. The question is can you observe at the actual drop-off point?"

Winchester thought before answering, "Yeah."

"My basic plan is to get to the drop-off point – Lake Cootapatamba – as soon as possible and lie up. He's got a .38 snubby and, if someone else shows up beside myself, he'll assume a hostile and we'll have a potential fratricide problem. So I will make visual contact with Alex because he knows me."

"OK. That sounds reasonable. Where do I come in?"

Ramon produced a Google Earth color printout from his pocket. "This is what Lake Cootapatamba looks like. It's a short valley with a small lake in the middle. It's like an oversized football stadium with the lake standing in for the playing field and hills to either sides like the bleachers."

"Gotcha." Winchester sat down on the bench so that he could study the printout more closely.

"What I want you to do is observe and advise."

Winchester nodded. He knew what was coming.

"I want you to be my spotter from the high ground. The drop is at the northern end of the lake. I want to lie up in a hide near the drop-off point. But since I can't see over this small ridge, which is the next valley from ours, I want you to stay up on the hill – in the bleachers – and be my eyes. You'll have the God's-eye view. I will rely on you to provide me with situational awareness and maneuver me to best advantage."

"Are you armed?"

"Another .38 snubby."

"Those things have a range of what, 30 yards?" Winchester said.

"On a good day. But it's too late for me to qualify on something else now. The best scenario is if Alex arrives alone. Then all you have to do is make sure there's no pursuit and we waltz out of there easy as pie. At the other end of possibility, Alex doesn't make it at all. Then we wait as long as we can until we accept what we've got to accept."

"What happens if Alex makes it to the drop with the enemy in pursuit?"

"That is the problem I want to work out with you. In that case, I want you to get me into the best position and let me handle it because I know you can't get involved."

"You won't have much of a chance with that little gun."

"Then we'd best make it count. If you are good eyes, it will count."

Winchester thought about it for a moment and said, "Well, it sounds like it's all within the rules of engagement. I'll observe and advise and do my best."

"Now, let's get there as soon as we can so you can show me where I should position my hide. You're the infantry officer. I'm just an old blogger. So you tell me what to do."

Winchester chuckled. He looked at the map for a moment before speaking.

"We'll select several alternate locations for hides so we can adapt depending on the situation. Get ready for different scenarios. But we can do that later. The main thing is to get to the site as soon as we can and set up."

"OK," said Ramon, "You said you had the authority to defend yourself. What does that mean?"

Winchester said, "Let me show you."

They walked up the path to a row of lakeside motels. Each room had a door to the parking lot and another to the back which led down to the lake. Winchester took a motel room key from his pocket and opened the door. Ramon followed him in. The Captain took a tubular object about three feet long out of a nylon stuff sack from a closet. He drew all the room curtains closed and put the items on the bed.

What seemed like a stuff sack for a tent turned out to be a 36-inch tube of hard foam rubber that split into two half-cylinders. Embedded into the foam was an M4 carbine. It had the usual folding stock and a 4x32 ACOG optical sight. The ACOG was not a sniper scope but an aiming aid which allowed rapid and accurate pointing at fast-moving targets out to 500 meters. A separate nylon bag contained four 30-round magazines of 5.56 mm ammunition, an AN/PVS-7B Night Vision Goggles with spare batteries, a brace of secure tactical squad radios and Steiner 8x30 binoculars.

"I can carry this rifle around concealed as a tent strapped to a hiking pack. Nobody will be the wiser unless they examine it physically."

"That's a heck of a lot of firepower. How did you get that into Australia?" Ramon said.

"It came out of a hole in the wall and will go back into that same hole. I told them it was too late for me to qualify on something else. So it's you with your snubby and me with my carbine."

Winchester repacked the M4 in its foam tube. Ramon took out the map and indicated the route to Lake Cootapatamba on it. They studied the map briefly. In a half-hour, both men were on their way to the blue lake in the mountains.

THE LAST REBELS

There was nothing to do but watch the snow drift down and wait for darkness, nothing to do but wait and remember. Alex thought back to Smokey Mountain when Justine had to lie low and learn to blend in. She sorted jars and bottles into baskets and pounded cans flat at a scrap yard nearby. She must have found it repulsive but self-discipline kept her at the task. Before long, she was processing scrap with the best of them and even acquired a taste for the sago and syrupy water peddled by a vendor who passed that way each afternoon.

After a couple of weeks, she began to accompany Alex and Ramon through the trails that crisscrossed the Foreshore. They talked to small groups along the way, on house-steps, stalls and variety stores. They were mostly free-flowing conversations and from them, Justine began to learn the secret life of the Foreshore. The chaotic mosaic around her resolved itself into a series of clear images. No longer did Justine simply see "variety stores" but knew who owned them, who supplied them and at what prices. No longer were there just "fishermen", Justine knew their factions, what parts of the sea they fished in and to whom they sold their catch. The world around her slowly drew into focus.

Before long, she saw the bones beneath the skin of the underground. She noticed that some of Ramon's contacts were special. They passed little notes and engaged in furtive confidences. She recognized these apparently random contacts as part of a series of overlapping networks. Some formed a defensive ring to warn of informers who were getting too close. Others were part of a courier system or message exchange. Some just provided support in the form of a meal, money or weapons.

Nearly all the energies of Alex and Ramon were devoted to the offense; they were not merely surviving, they were attacking. Whenever they found a grievance, the two started a conspiracy. There was no injustice too small to start a fight over; no ideal too trivial to encourage. To Justine, these efforts seemed aimless and curiously apolitical. She had expected to meet modern Lenins in the underground and instead had fallen in with a bunch of Robin Hoods. Instead of a continuous process of group consciousness-raising for the classic general strike, Alex and Ramon seemed as willing to organize against the Communist Party as anyone else. Instead of bringing unions, homeless people, fishmongers, garbage scavengers, vendors, housewives, even criminals, under one revolutionary vanguard, the two seemed happiest when their every man was a leader.

Occasionally, the trio left Tondo to meet with cells in other parts of the city, at safe houses reminiscent of the lost Cindy. One day, after returning from a meeting in the factory town of Valenzuela, they stopped at a small coffee shop in the university belt. It was mid-afternoon and the three had the little café to themselves.

It was the sort of setting where English could be spoken without attracting attention. Justine was surprised to hear Ramon order coffee and cake in a thick Filipino accent. She looked at Alex quizzically.

"He sounds different," she said.

"The man of a thousand faces," Alex said.

"Are you even Communists?" Justine asked. "Can you explain what you're playing at?" Alex looked towards Ramon.

"The answers are 'no, we are not Communists' and to the second, the answer is, 'we don't know'." Justine looked puzzled.

Ramon continued. "First of all, there are many undergrounds, not just one. Underground life is as much about competition between revolutionary factions as it is about fighting Marcos. We are united in our disgust for him. Otherwise, we hate each other's guts.

"This is perfectly normal. The most famous of all the modern undergrounds, the French Resistance of World War II, was simply the collective name for a whole bunch of groups engaged in fighting Nazis in some form when they weren't fighting each other. Cooperation among them simply took the form of an agreement not to disagree.

237

"And here it's the same. Only the setting is less romantic. Instead of the Seine, we have the Vitas; instead of the Eiffel Tower, we have Smokey Mountain. But allowing for differences between the Gaul and the Filipino, it's the same dog with a different collar. It's a mess. Charles de Gaulle's greatest frustration to the end was his inability to unify the Resistance.

"In fact, De Gaulle ordered one of their most senior leaders, Jean Moulin, to establish a National Council of the Resistance to bring the factions together. You know what happened? Moulin was captured and tortured to death by the Gestapo shortly after arriving in France. To this day, it's thought that Moulin was betrayed by Resistance factions for whom loyalty to the sect was more important than victory over the Nazis. When Malreaux described that era as 'the great battle in the darkness' the description cut both ways. In the dark, all cats are gray."

"I guess you can say that we haven't any definite ideas about what happens after we get rid of Marcos," Alex added, "and personally, I think the answer is best postponed. I don't much care what, so long as it leads to a society where people are free to choose. What I'm not willing to do is swap one dictator for another."

Justine looked at the two men, "OK, so you're not Communists. Then, what are you? From what I can tell, you are either anarchists or lunatics. Which is it?"

Alex answered this time. "Well, the Communist Party calls our network 'The Program' – pejoratively, I might add – because it is dedicated to a process, not a definite end-state. Our goal is to ask the questions without supplying a definite set of answers. That doesn't make us anarchists, exactly. But I'm not sure it makes us lunatics."

"But that's irresponsible," Justine persisted. "If you ask questions, then you have the responsibility to supply the answers. I can see that you are professional revolutionaries. But what is your revolution about?"

Ramon gestured for quiet while the waitress brought the coffee and cake. As she moved away, he took up the answer.

238

"Not revolution but rebellion, a perpetual rebellion against authority, a constant effort to prune away the weeds of tyranny that grow up so easily in us. 'The earth,' Thomas Jefferson once said, 'belongs to the living ... the dead have neither powers nor rights over it'. That means that we can never decide anything for always except that people ought to be left free to decide – *and to always remain free to decide*. Either that or the world belongs to the dead. Most revolutions are about the dead telling the living what to do. All I want to do is sip my coffee and eat this cake."

"Without ideological guidance?" she asked.

"Don't need but a fork and cup," Ramon said.

"Madness," she said. "Those goals are too small and petty to expend clandestine resources on."

"And what would be a worthy use of resources?" Alex interjected. "Holding teach-ins? Training for six months to kill a town mayor so someone can pin a note to his chest saying 'enemy of the people'? Holding revolutionary tribunals? Launching purges? Holding arcane discussions about the superiority of Marxism-Leninism-Mao-tse-tung thought over Trotskyist revisionist capitalist roading? That's what other people actually expend clandestine resources on."

"It's a time-tested method," Justine insisted.

"Power always promises to save us from itself," Alex said. "It wins either way. I took two guys into the first safe house I ran; they were the sole survivors of the Communist Party purge. The last of twenty who were led to a cane field for a meeting and instead met a .30 caliber Browning machine gun. I know enough to understand that both sides want power at all costs for different reasons. But eventually it's not the reasons that matter but the power. And while I don't mind power, 'power at all costs' is too high a price to pay for it because sooner or later one of those costs is going to be freedom itself. Ramon thinks the underground is a competition among ideologues. But I disagree."

"How would you define it then?" Ramon asked.

"It's a collection of cults trying to survive," Alex said. "I don't want to be part of a cult. The basic reason we don't supply answers is because we don't know what the answers are."

"But doesn't that make you a cult yourselves?" Justine asked. "The church of professional doubters, the brotherhood of confirmed skeptics."

Ramon considered the question for a moment. "No, because we don't supply what every cult provides – something to belong to. We're not another kind of roof because there is no roof: it's all sky. The real dilemma is whether any revolutionary activity that doubts itself can survive. Uncertainty is a serious handicap in this game.

"People don't become Communists from conviction. Most will never read Marx or Engels. They join the Party to belong, because they need a new family and meaning in their lives, something to replace the God they have killed. That is why the Party can never understand us. We acknowledge a God outside of us that we don't want to describe, while they've created a God inside the Party who they deny exists. When you join the Party, it is to join a revolutionary elite. When you join the Program, you get the right to seek the answers yourself."

"That's us," Alex said.

"How many are you in The Program?" she asked Alex.

"Three dozen, the merest handful, without any apparent prospect of rapid increase."

"Do you have a leader?"

"We take turns being leader," Ramon answered. "Right now, our leader is an ex-Redemptorist priest who we call 'Y'."

For a moment, Justine wondered whether they were playing a practical joke on her. Her mouth formed an "O". Then she saw they were serious and her eyes flashed.

"Y? It's like a kid's game played with real bullets. You know, I'm very fond of you both. Maybe I owe my life to you, but I have to say you have wasted your talents by making a decision to stay on the margins. Consider whether your aversion to power – your reluctance to become Bolsheviks – stems from reason," she looked at Alex, "or from vanity."

The two laughed, but it was Alex who answered.

"Well, we're no joke in the practical sense. No Communist cell has the influence that we have. We are the core of the metropolitan underground. As to pride or vanity, why, that's no dirtier a word than power. And paid up, too. With our lives as down payment. Don't you think I am scared of growing old and being left with nothing but a fund of pointless stories about events that no one will care about? You cannot eat pride. But power buys cars, and villas and Rolexes. It is this lack of ambition that makes us unworthy to be taken seriously. Do you like Albert Camus?"

"Yes," Justine answered, "he's a great revolutionary writer."

"Well, he wrote that the only serious problem in life was whether one could be 'a saint without God'. My problem is very similar. I would like to be a revolutionary without ambition. Can I fight in the underground and go home at the end of it, to an ordinary job?"

"You shouldn't be in it for the philosophical consolation," Justine replied. "You should be in it to win and that requires accepting the risk of power. Don't go into the casino if you fear the taint of money."

Ramon looked at his watch and gestured for the check. "It's getting late, guys." They paid for their coffees and started back for Smokey Mountain. Within the hour, they were climbing the flaming hill of garbage, the dark ash falling all around them.

In the week after the debate at the café, events at several bus companies that Ramon was organizing picked up pace and fed on each other. "Metro Manila's stopped," Ramon said, walking into the Smokey Mountain safe house after monitoring the ratlines. "The major bus

241

lines have stopped running. The NE union made the decision last night after the new conductor's quotas were announced.

"By dawn the JX lines had joined in, then Vivo Transit. The whole of the Highway 54 ring road is empty of public transportation."

The sudden seizure of the metropolitan transportation system was magical, and yet there was no magic. It was simply the result of building up cells in NE, JX and Vivo and planting an idea in each. Now the seeds were sprouting like weeds. The individual networks were acting on their own initiative, each touching off the others.

"It's spreading to the jeepneys. That's Buboy's group. They picked up the idea at Baclaran and Monumento. That lit up the Taft Avenue line which stopped, I think, at around 7 am. Then Mabini and Del Pilar followed. Now it is general. The whole thing is spontaneously combusting."

Alex added his information. "Bobadilla is investigating the hell out of everybody, according to 'Oscar', one of my contacts. But he can't find a mastermind."

"There is no mastermind because there is no mastermind," Ramon added drily. "Truly, cross my heart."

"What about you two?" asked Justine. "You look guilty to me."

"Only of suggestion and fostering debate," Alex said, "innocent of all else. But here's the thing: the whole episode is turning into a crisis for the Party."

"I would have thought they'd be delighted," said Justine.

"Oh, they are – it's just there are no Party cells behind the unrest. The foreign press is badgering them for information on what they are going to do next and there's nothing they can say because they're completely in the dark. So, they've announced a general strike the day after tomorrow. That way, they can pretend to be in control."

There was a rhythmic rap on the hut door. Alex went out and came right back holding a note which he handed to Ramon. As he read it, two completely different expressions passed briefly over his face.

"Well," he said at last, "it looks like the Party isn't completely clueless. They smell a rat; namely, the Program. The Metro Manila Party Committee wants to see me and Y. You can guess what about."

"Is it safe?" Justine asked.

"Archbishop Barretto has set up a neutral venue. It'll be safe enough with Barretto around. Alex, I'd like you along to provide distant cover. We're leaving right now. Justine, you might want to come along too."

"What for?" she asked.

"There's another item in this note. Says there's a message at the drop from the Davila Rodriguez Law Offices. I don't know what it says but I can guess."

No one said anything. By common consent, they shut the hut behind them, walked down from the terrace and across the rickety bridge to Barrio Magsaysay. Justine looked down through the floorboards at the black waters of Vitas and the *Boteng Umiilaw*, poor and shabby in the morning light. They went down to the water and came to a small dock in one of the inlets with large tin fish buckets piled all around it. Nearby was a chapel dedicated to Christ the Nazarene and, beside it, a variety store. Ramon went up to the store and purchased a few menthol candies. He was handed the candies and a small brown envelope. He thrust the envelope into his pocket without reading it.

He walked back to the dock where a small motorized outrigger canoe sat bobbing on the rising tide. Ramon spoke some words to the boatman, who went off and returned with a jerrycan of gasoline. Alex looked up at the sky and stepped over into the boat. He felt, rather than saw, Justine take a place behind him. The boatman boarded, followed by the final arrival, whose footfall he knew to be Ramon's. The boatman wound a cord around the starter flywheel and pull-started the two-stroke engine with a vigorous tug. It caught after a few tries and pushed the little boat out on the waves.

When they were five hundred yards from shore, the ocean air began to win the battle against the miasma of Tondo. The water lost its diseased appearance and regained a healthy tinge of green and blue. The boatman opened the throttle and the bow planed up into the waves. The wind sang through the nylon lines which acted as stays for the outriggers. Justine looked back and saw the Tondo Foreshore with its mountain of smoke receding. Then the boat turned south and zigzagged through the huge freighters moored in the port.

In a short while, the little outrigger entered the mouth of the Pasig River near the old Spanish city of Intramuros. They passed under the shadow of its forty-foot-thick walls. At first, the river was choked with garbage, watercraft of all descriptions and huge clumps of waterlilies which floated by like small islands. With the two-stroke engine dinning in her ears, Justine watched as they passed under the dark arches of the city bridges. She noticed there were people living in the girders.

They came along a clear stretch of water lined with dilapidated warehouses, rusting factories and huge tank farms. Beyond that was once a genteel district whose grand but decaying homes had steps that led right down to the river like some echo of Venetian grandeur. All these sights reminded Justine of the mysterious Jungletown, places whose history would forever remain unknown to her. The little boat passed under a modern bridge and sped past Malacañang Palace.

Alex and Ramon looked straight ahead as they sped past the Palace river wall. Justine thought to herself that this was where Ferdinand Marcos lived and controlled the country. Neither Alex nor Ramon seemed interested.

After a short while, the river seemed to broaden. The boat passed another major bridge and several smaller ones as they forged continually upriver. Finally, the city thinned out and the houses gave way to mudflats and fishponds interspersed with occasional marsh. Then they turned a corner, cleared the mouth of the river, and entered the second largest freshwater lake in Southeast Asia. Laguna de Bay

244

washed the shores of three major provinces, including Metropolitan Manila. From the small boat, it seemed like an ocean, but an ocean divided into a checkerboard of fish traps built of bamboo palings driven into its shallow bottom.

After an hour's hard pounding, they arrived on the banks of Calamba town in Laguna province. The boatman beached the outrigger on a gravel shore. Alex jumped out and helped Justine make her way over the bow and hop onto the beach. Ramon clambered around the boatman, who gave him a nod. He pushed the boat back into the water and watched as it planed away. The three walked up an embankment onto a road that led to a town in the distance. They stopped beside a small variety store. Ramon took the letter from his pocket. "About time we see what this letter says," he said. He opened the note and, with Alex and Justine behind him, they read it together:

Dear Mrs. Arevalo:

Congressman Frankie Barnes of the United States House of Representatives has had the kindness to bring up the subject of your husband's imprisonment at the Bicutan Detention Center with President Ferdinand E. Marcos. He impressed upon the President the feelings of concern and apprehension that his constituents in California have expressed for the totally unjustified detention of Atty. Arevalo.

The President told Congressman Barnes they had indisputable proof of your husband's participation in seditious plots against the duly constituted government. Moreover, the President maintained that police reports have identified you as being in league with persons unknown, notorious cop-killers and public enemies, which I think is preposterous.

But as a courtesy to the Congressman, and in view of the historic and cordial relations between the United States and the Republic of the Philippines, the President has decided to grant executive clemency to your husband. Moreover, he has overruled any derogatory information the police may have against you.

At the meeting with Congressman Barnes, President Marcos dictated and signed a release order for your husband and a safe-conduct pass for yourself, and provided a copy to the Congressman. You are now covered by this pass.

Congressman Barnes informed me that Harvard University has awarded a fellowship to your husband, with employment for yourself at the United Nations a distinct possibility. I am sure that Congressman Barnes' friends have helped secure these appointments. I am glad to say their influence is not misplaced.

All law enforcement officials have been notified of your safe conduct and will on no account ask you any questions. But for formality's sake, please make your way to my office to claim a certified, true copy of your safe conduct pass. Should you encounter the least difficulty, refer all inquiries to Colonel Zosimo Villegas of the Presidential Guard Battalion. Your passports with US visas and airline tickets departing for Boston are ready for collection at my office.

Yours truly,

Casimiro Rodriguez
Attorney-at-Law

"A jeepney comes by here every hour and you can connect to Manila from that town," Ramon said to Justine, pointing into the distance where the road went round the bend. "You don't have to leave just yet. We are early for the meeting and I'd like to stretch my legs. I'll be back in a half-hour."

Alex did not say a word. He turned away from Justine, went up to the girl manning the store and asked for two bottles of Coca-Cola and a package of crackers. He opened the caps by levering them against the edges of the store counter. Then he sat by the lakeside, handing Justine one of the Cokes and an open package of crackers.

"We were interrupted that last time in Roxas District. This is my other specialty, Crackers Extreme."

There was a fresh breeze on the lake. In the distance, the bulk of an extinct volcano raised its head above the green country. Far off, by some flats, children's kites could be seen reaching up into the blue sky. A bird gave a solitary cry from somewhere in the marsh.

246

"I've never been abroad," Alex said. "Send me a postcard."

"Where should I address it?"

"Why, I never thought of that," Alex said, and laughed. "Address it to whom it may concern."

"Alex."

"This should be the happiest day of your life, Justine. And I want you to believe that it's mine too."

"There are no shadows now, Alex."

"None at all. Today I can answer you truly. For all the right reasons."

"Then let's make an oath of it, Alex." She took his hand, and pulled him close, almost as if they were to be wed. And there by the shore of the Lake, the two recited in unison from memory a verse from the Old Testament, from the Song of Solomon: words as ancient as love and hope and despair.

> Set me as a seal upon thy heart,
> As a seal upon thine arm:
> For love is strong as death;
> Jealousy is cruel as Sheol.

When Ramon arrived some minutes later, Alex and Justine had finished the Coca-Cola and the crackers and were laughing at some absurd joke.

"It's time," Ramon said.

The scheduled passenger jeepney came. Without hesitation, Justine got into it and sped off. Alex never saw her again.

The two men checked their weapons and started off down a side road until they came to an isolated house with a number of cars parked at random distances in the nearby lane. Alex took up a position 100 meters away and watched Ramon walk up to the door. He knocked, and the familiar figure of Archbishop Barretto opened the door. Y was beside him. For a moment, he saw a little crowd gathered in the hallway behind the prelate. The entire Manila Party Committee must have been there. Before the door was closed, Alex glimpsed an unnaturally short figure. He recognized it as the son of a former senator, Ulysses Q. Licban.

NIGHT MOVES

Alex knew the snow would reduce the range of night vision devices to almost nothing. He lowered himself behind the rocks waiting for his chance – when the hunters had been fully blinded by the darkness and the snow. An interpretation of Fortunas' message – its connection with an aboriginal place-name referring to a "nest in the hills"– was in a small square of paper in his pocket. If Ramon found him wounded or inarticulate at the rendezvous, then the message would still get through. He transferred the set of rosary beads his late grandmother had given him to his shirt pocket. Then he took his GPS unit and set the destination coordinates to the drop-off by the Lake. He would need it to find his way in the total darkness. The snowfall was a blade that cut both ways; it blinded the enemy but it also blinded him.

He readied for the last lap. Every article of clothing was buttoned up or zipped to show the minimum of skin. That would reduce any thermal signature that the enemy electronic devices could detect. Then he tightened the straps and redistributed the clothing until he was sure nothing would rattle in the pack. All he needed now was to wait for full darkness and more snowfall.

Meanwhile, Ramon and Winchester were finalizing their hide positions around Lake Cootapatamba in the gathering dusk. Winchester chose a spot on the left side of the valley that overlooked the ridge which Alex would have to cross on his way in. From his vantage, Winchester could cover targets out to the far side of the valley 500 meters away. It was far from ideal, but it was the best that could be done under the circumstances.

Winchester dug a shallow hole among clumps of tall grass and produced a ghillie suit made by sewing netting onto an All Over Brush Pattern Army jacket and hat he had bought in a Canberra surplus store. Into the netting, he inserted strips of grass-green cloth and foliage cut from the surrounding area. Once he lowered himself into the hole dug amid the grass, he would be nearly invisible except at close range. Winchester hunkered down and yelled.

249

"How am I doing, dude?"

"Awesome, I can't see you unless you move."

"Great."

Ramon's hide positions were pre-made by glacial action eons before. The bottom of the valley was littered with clumps of boulders over which Winchester guided Ramon by radio from his vantage until they found two positions: one they called "west" and another on the opposite slope called "east". Ramon could hide crouched in the crevices among the rocks, and, with a little help from an extra All Over Brush Pattern shirt that fitted over his smaller frame like a smock, remain practically invisible.

They would assume position before last light while remaining in contact over the encrypted individual squad radios, each equipped with earpieces and boom mikes which Winchester had brought along. Acting as the spotter, Winchester would direct Ramon to the best position on the valley floor once Alex – or his pursuers – was in sight.

Some distance north, the other actor in the drama finished his final preparations. Alex waited until he could no longer see the hand in front of his face and crawled out of concealment. He moved with the deliberate slowness of a man groping his way through a lightless cave, reckoning the enemy's position only from memory and calculation. He had seen them set up camp higher up the road. They could have patrols out, but he doubted it. He inched downward until he was clear of the rocks, then consulted the luminous dial of his compass under his parka flap, and struck for the bottom of the valley.

He was traveling so slowly that the GPS could not compute his direction of march, just his position. For direction, he would rely on the compass to keep his heading and the rosary beads to count his pace. It was an old trick he learned in the days before GPS. The compass gave you a bearing and the rosary beads let you pace off distances on the map. Alex had estimated his stride length in darkened conditions to be half a meter per step. One circuit of the rosary would be 50 beads, hence 50 steps. That worked out to 25 meters per rosary.

The GPS told him it was 4,500 meters to the ridge beyond which was the lake. That was 180 complete rosaries. He began his first step and bead.

Back near the road, the three pursuers had set up a hasty camp. They pitched a tent and ate cold food. Pierre reasoned that with the night as dark as the inside of a cow and the snow falling heavily, even the thermal sight was useless. There was no point searching in the pitch dark, which would likely only tire them out or result in a cracked skull or a broken leg. The best course was to rest and wait for morning.

Out in the night, there was no rest for the quarry. For Alex, the march in the dark seemed an eternity. The blind stumble in the cold and broken ground with a heavy pack would have been challenging for a man of 25. At fifty-two, following a day of maximum exertion, it was pure punishment. It was nearly an hour before he reached the bottom of the valley and his first indication was his boot going into the icy water of the stream. The stream would lead him south. He carefully stepped back from the stream and followed it south.

Finally, the rosary count began to hypnotize him. It took a conscious effort to keep track of the circuits. Sometimes, he would stub his toe on a clump of rocks in the dark and feel his way around them until he was clear and start the pace again. It was 23:00 – an hour before midnight – when he found himself in a huge depression he did not remember seeing on the map. What had seemed like a short walk on the map was turning out to be much longer in the dark.

Worse, he was falling into total exhaustion. He found his boots slipping as his leg muscles expended their last reserves of strength. It was hard to stand without shaking. Finally, he stopped to rest. To go on would be to risk injury. He was so exhausted it felt like nothing mattered but sleep. But there could be no sleep.

Alex sat down on the cold ground. He ate a granola bar and drank a liter of water. Then he lay down on his side, opened his fly and urinated as nearly directly into the ground as possible. A stream of urine would stand out in the cold air like a beacon if he stood. He lay there for fifteen minutes. Again, he found himself fighting the urge to sleep despite the cold. He knew that if he slept he would never wake again. So he forced himself up.

He reshouldered the pack and began a new decade of the rosary. Then another and another. He was walking so slowly now that he could mentally count the words of the Hail Mary as they passed out on his breath. Hail Mary, full of grace. Okay, there was the next foothold. The Lord is with Thee. And the next. Blessed art though among women. And another step.

It occurred to Alex that unless Ramon had found some way to bring the Cavalry with him, he would achieve nothing by reaching the rendezvous but getting the two of them killed. Ramon would be waiting there with his little .38, stolid as ever. But even the two of them together would be helpless against the three professionals on his tail.

Then, he was dimly aware that something had changed. It took his tired mind nearly a minute to work out what it was: the snow had stopped. There was something else too: it was starting to get brighter. Dawn was coming on.

LAST STAND LAKE

Winchester peered again over the ridge into the adjoining valley. Till now, darkness and snow had thrown a solid curtain across it. Now the slight brightening in the east let him pick up the outlines of the further crests. Ramon was sitting nearly frozen near position west, closely monitoring his headset for updates.

Pierre, Monique and Emile had risen an hour before dawn, struck the tent and were peering from the edge of the trail down on the shadowy valley below, waiting for the light to give them a chance.

For Alex, dawn was a mixed blessing. With color and detail now returning, he could see where to put his feet. In fifteen minutes, his stride almost resembled what might be described as a normal walk. Then he saw the ridge as a dark line against the sky. He pulled the GPS from his pocket and looked at the display. He had 455 meters to go to the rendezvous.

It was Winchester who saw Alex first. He had been scanning across the ridge with the Steiners when he saw something moving in the shadows. He keyed his radio.

"One unidentified in sight, moving south, can't tell how far yet."

"Roger."

At nearly the same moment, Emile, using Leica Ultravid 8x52s binoculars with greater light-gathering power, spotted the small figure in the valley. He shouted out the sighting to Pierre and Monique. "He's down in the valley bearing 175 magnetic."

"Let me see," Monique said, taking the binoculars from Emile.

"We can cut him off by going south on the trail, then going east over the ridge dividing the two valleys," Pierre said. "We'll make better time that way. Let's go." The three started off at a blistering trot.

By now, it was light enough for Winchester to use the reticle on the Steiner military binoculars to estimate the distance. The information came in over Ramon's earpiece.

"I think it's Alex, 400 meters from the ridge."

"Should I go out to him?" Ramon asked.

"Negative. Maintain position west. If you leave your position, you will lose tactical advantage if there's pursuit behind him."

"Roger."

"Wait. There is pursuit. I see three, repeat, three unidentified heading south over the trail at the double."

"Roger."

Ramon knew it could only be one thing. Alex was in a race for his life. He fought the urge to ask for more information; he knew Winchester would keep him posted. After what seemed like an interminable time, but was probably only three or four minutes, Winchester spoke again.

"The three unidentified are two males, one female. No rifles visible. Here's the plan: if they cut Alex off before he crosses the ridge, the enemy will be between you and Alex. I will maneuver you for rear attack. If he crosses the ridge first with them following, you will take them in the flank. Maintain position west."

He acknowledged the radio message, pulled his camouflage hood off and forced himself to remain calm. Not long now. Winchester's voice came over the earpiece again.

"The three are dropping packs. Boy, look at them go! Alex is scanning. He sees them! He's dropping pack. It's a footrace now."

But it was a very unequal footrace. It was obvious to Winchester from Alex's weaving run that he was in the last stages of exhaustion. The three, on the other hand, were coming along like racing greyhounds.

254

When Alex scanned behind him and saw the three sprinting figures on the track above him to his right, the last of his adrenaline kicked in. He shucked off his ruck. Survival would be measured in minutes now if there was no help beyond the dividing ridge. He lumbered clumsily up the slope.

"Stand by," came the voice on Ramon's earpiece.

"Standing by."

Alex topped the crest and saw Lake Cootapatamba's shimmering gray-blue ahead of him past a nearby line of large rocks. There was no sign of Ramon. His heart sank as he looked to his right. Two men and a woman were turning left to run across the crest of the ridge he was just crossing, coming at him at right angles. In a minute, they would be right on top of him.

His only hope was to use the element of surprise. The enemy's strength gave them confidence – perhaps overconfidence. Instead of encircling him, they were coming straight on. He would make them pay for underestimating him.

The three were angling down the ridge to cut him off even as he made for a gap between the line of rocks. Alex ran, waiting until he could hear the drumming of footsteps to his right before pretending to stumble. The distance should be about right. He rolled over and came up pointing the .38.

He swung the snubby up and found Pierre in the center of his sight picture. An expression of horror flashed across the Frenchman's face. The .38 bucked once and the bullet flashed across the short distance through Pierre's diaphragm, exiting two inches to the left of his spine. Pierre did a half spin and thudded to the ground. He would bleed to death in the next five minutes. Pierre's last thoughts as he lay on the cold ground were about the money he had saved up for retirement and the dive resort he planned to visit. He wondered to himself why he preferred one room type to the other.

But in the land of the living, the action continued fast and furious. Monique and Emile dove to either side and flattened themselves against the folds in the ground. Emile drew his Glock but was too low on the ground to get off a return shot and too close to risk raising. Monique was on the other side of the dying Pierre. She had flicked open a spring-loaded switchblade.

From his Legion experience, Emile knew their best chance was to rush Alex from both sides. The quarry's advantage in surprise was gone. Now, they would outmaneuver him. Emile yelled to Monique in French.

"Stay put. He can't get a shot at you without standing, and I'll kill him if he raises. Got it?"

"Yes."

"I'll crawl outward to the right. His gun only has a range of 15 or 20 meters. When I get farther than it can accurately shoot, I'll stand to get enough angle to shoot down on him. He'll have to turn to face me. I've got the gun. When I stand I'll yell 'go', that's your cue to rush him from the left. He can't be more than eight meters away. One of us will get him."

"Got it," she said and began to edge to her left.

Ramon heard the shot but could not see what was happening. He was tempted to look, but relied on Winchester up on the hill to act as his eyes.

"Alex shot one male. I think he's down. The other male has produced a handgun." There was a pause. "They are going to rush Alex from opposite flanks. Primary threat is the man with the handgun. Come to the top of the rocks. But don't stand before my signal. The man with the gun will be at your 11 o'clock, range 20 meters."

"Roger."

Ramon's heart was pounding as he levered himself from his hide and positioned himself below a rock shelf. According to Winchester, when

256

he stood up, the man with the gun – probably an expert – would be 20 meters to his left front. He would get one shot or none at all.

He heard Winchester's warning through the earpiece. "Looks like the gunman's getting ready to stand. He's up!"

Ramon heard a yell in French from beyond the rocks and forced himself to stand and extend the Smith and Wesson. As he laid the bottom of his wrists on the stony surface, he realized the rock shelf gave him one final unanticipated advantage. Not only did it protect him from the chest downwards, it provided a nearly perfect bench rest for the little J frame .38.

In that instant, Emile detected movement to the rocks on his right and switched his target to Ramon. Ramon saw Emile swivel faster than he believed possible. But as he brought the Glock up, there was a shout from the hillside above. Emile moved his head in time to see a clump of grass seemingly rise straight out of the ground. Although the Glock remained pointed in Ramon's direction, Emile was distracted for a crucial half-second.

Ramon fired.

The ex-Legionnaire continued to raise his Glock in a two-handed Weaver stance. Ramon fired again. He thought he had missed both shots completely because Emile's automatic barked in reply. But the aim was high and that was because both arms went up and up until they pointed at the sky as the gunman's right leg collapsed behind him until finally he toppled over.

Then Ramon saw a sudden flurry of activity where Alex was. While everyone's attention focused on the gunman, the third assassin had rushed Alex. He saw her deliver a series of swift, economical jabs at a figure on the ground. It was too far for a shot so Ramon jumped down from the rocks and closed the distance.

Monique raised herself from the prone figure and came charging low with the speed of a cobra, a bloody switchblade in her right hand. Ramon fired two shots at fifteen feet through center mass and she went down like a sack of sand. He stepped over her and fired one more into her head as he passed to where Alex lay looking up at the Alpine sky.

"Alex."

"In my pocket." He tapped his shirt pocket. "Ramon, it's so dark. Is it night again?"

"No, my friend, it's dawn."

But there was no answer. Ramon sensed a figure approaching, but it was only John Winchester in his ghillie suit.

AND LAST

Together they policed up the battlefield, which was how Ramon wanted to remember it: the Last Stand Lake. Ramon read the little square of paper and handed it to Winchester. Then Ramon took his friend's effects while the former captain of infantry walked over to retrieve Alex's rucksack where it had been abandoned during the chase. They took everything of intelligence value from the bodies of the assassins and left the field.

In the vast Snowies, where wild horses ran, where mountain springs roared down in cascades and thunders sounded in the sky, the sound of men's struggles went unremarked. Earth took no heed of joy or sorrow. It took other men to do that.

When they got to Canberra, Ramon slipped another pre-paid SIM into his disposable phone and sent a text message to the tips line of the Australian Federal Police, telling them where they could find four bodies in the Snowy Mountains.

Because of their prior familiarity with the case, Wilkinson and Ward were assigned to investigate the deaths of Marvin Lee, Alex Francisco and three Frenchmen believed to be traveling under assumed names.

"Where do we begin?"

"With one garroted, one stabbed and three shot – by two guns, plus suspected involvement from parties unknown. Or you can add it up another way: two academics, three professional hit men and no apparent motive. It gets more complicated if we add politicians poisoned on airplanes."

But the two detectives didn't have to furrow their brows for long. Following a back-channel tip from US sources that the Russians were reading Australian law enforcement wiretaps, the Defence Signals Directorate ordered a security audit of their computer system which revealed that a system administrator was siphoning off classified information to shadow terminals. The traitor admitted to spying for

Russia and was sentenced to life in prison. One of the numbers that the traitor had been monitoring was Alex Francisco's, so Wilkinson and Ward were told to close the case under some pretext for national security reasons.

"So the Russians are in it, eh? The instructions are to make up a reason to close the case. You're better at that sort of thing. What do you suggest?" Wilkinson said.

"Let's see. Maybe we should say that the murders were committed by rival drug gangs and the deceased were victims of mistaken identity," Ward suggested.

"And appeal to members of the public who may have pertinent information to come forward," Wilkinson added.

"Do we really have to say that? It might bring out the conspiracy nuts," Ward said. Wilkinson snorted and began to type out the report.

"Just let me keep typing, mate, I want to get home early to watch the footy."

At about the same time, a junior American diplomat visited the country estate of Filipino billionaire Cris Atienza in Moolegee, New South Wales. The name Moolegee was derived from the aboriginal Wiradjuri term *Moothi,* meaning "Nest in the Hills". The term "estate" understated the magnificence of Atienza's holdings. It was really a complex of vineyards, stud farms and cattle breeding stations under one handy name. The billionaire greeted the young American who bore the title of commercial attache, an appellation which covered a multitude of possibilities.

"Come in, Mr. Soames," Atienza said. "My lawyers in New York advised me to see you."

"I believe we can do business," Soames said. He opened his briefcase and took out a three-page printout of the overseas accounts, assets and shell companies that Atienza had failed to tell the Australian Taxation Office and the Australian Securities and Investments

Commission about. He laid the pages in a neat row on the polished mahogany coffee table and sat back.

"What do you want?" Atienza asked.

"The DVD or disc that Johnny Fortunas left with you."

"It's encrypted. Only Fortunas had the password. You can't read it."

"Why don't you leave the problem of breaking passwords to us," Soames said smoothly. Then he leaned forward and said, "Mr. Atienza, we're not unreasonable. If there's a change of administration in Manila, we'll put in a good word for you." Atienza smiled and said, "You have a great future in diplomacy."

President Ulysses Q. Licban held on to the bitter end. The DVD which Atienza handed over to the Senate, explaining it had been entrusted to him "for safekeeping" by Johnny Fortunas, was aired in session and subsequently broadcast on every radio and television station in the Philippines. Licban clung to the hope of bribing enough Senators to escape impeachment but that hope crumbled after the Supreme Court, using the precedent that Licban himself established, declared him incompetent. The Senate, now sure that Licban had lost all political support, returned a verdict of guilty. He was impeached and the US Ambassador, having satisfied herself that Licban was no longer the constitutional President, advised him to go. She brokered a deal under which Licban was allowed to go into exile where he eventually found employment as head of a major international environmental organization devoted to preventing global warming.

Dean Rodolfo Barcelon retired from the Institute and devoted his time to raising scholarship funds for orphans of the Mindanao campaigns. He withdrew from active life, but occasionally organized speaking events for the Harvard Club of Manila.

Three months after the Licban administration collapsed, and with it the threat to the US Task Force mission, Greer sat in his high-rise Manila apartment watching the movers pack his furniture. The new American President, a former politician from Chicago, believed the time was ripe for the Communists and Muslim rebels to be brought into the "political process". He had proceeded to browbeat the new Philippine President into suspending all military operations against terrorist groups as a "confidence-building measure". He called it "hitting the reset button". And reset things it did. Within weeks, Camp Abu Bakr was taking shape again.

Greer was busy filling out every claim he could – drapery allowance, hardship allowance, relocation allowance – not because he needed the money but out of spite. The Special Forces mission to the Philippines had been suspended until the "situation clarified". Greer would do his level best to squeeze every penny he could out of a government bureaucracy that made a habit of squandering the best years of its servants' lives.

Eventually, Alex Francisco's remains were returned to the Philippines. They came as cremated ashes in a sturdy half-gallon plastic urn with an identifying plaque and an attached death certificate. The old priest from the parish in Albay, with whom Alex had once sought shelter long ago in the underground, came out of retirement to perform the graveside service.

The ashes were interned in the same family plot in which Alex's long dead father, mother and grandmother were buried. The old priest mumbled his way through the service, but his voice did not have to carry far. There was only one mourner, who had arrived on a motorcycle. After the service, the mourner put the old priest in a chauffeur-driven rental car for transportation back to the chapter house. But the sole mourner was in no hurry to leave. He stayed until the shallow grave was filled in and a headstone placed. The epitaph read:

Alex Francisco
See you at the *Boteng Umiilaw*

Some children rode bicycles through the lengthening shadows while gardeners trimmed the grass. Still, the man with the motorcycle waited. He knew she would come.

Finally, a Mercedes sedan driven by a uniformed chauffer arrived. In the passenger seat was a woman in late middle age. She was still slim and beauty had not wholly left her. She was now a senior career bureaucrat in the United Nations. But Ramon knew her as Justine.

It was the first time they had met in over 30 years. They regarded each other with the surprise of those who return to a familiar place to find it changed nearly beyond recognition.

"Hello, Ramon."

"Hi, Justine. He's over here."

She had forgotten how American he sounded. They walked a little way and stood over the grave. She bent and brushed away the dirt and small pebbles that had scattered over the newly placed headstone.

"Alex was afraid of growing old and poor, with nothing but a fund of stories that no one would care about," she said. "How did the last story go? There was nothing in the news, but I can guess."

"How did it go?" asked Ramon.

"Along the lines of once upon a time there was a man who knew the secret of toppling a wicked sorcerer. And though it was sought by his many evil servants, he kept it safe through the darkest roads armed only with his pride until at dawn on a hilltop he turned the sorcerer's spell against him and the world lived happily ever after."

"Alex would have liked the story to be told that way," Ramon said. "I think that is nearly the truth, but the fear of growing old left him before that last hill."

"Were you there?"

"Yes."

"Then you know what happened."

"I don't know exactly what happened; I will remember what I saw. Of the whys I can only guess. All we can ever know, Alex used to say, were the 'external facts'. But we were together in this last enterprise and I think I'm right to say that on that final morning he had caught up with himself and come to terms with his talent for this one great thing.

"And he gave this gift, sure that he would be preserved in all things and honored in the life he gave the woman he loved. He had come to a place where the need to be cherished and remembered counts for less than the desire to give. Justine, the sun still shines even when nobody looks. It's the love that's given in secret that brings us home."

"You're a good man, Ramon Delgato."

He silently shrugged in that familiar, boyish kind of way. Then she saw that he was preparing to go. He extended his hand and she shook it.

"What are you going to do?" she asked.

He walked over to his motorcycle and said, "Do? Well, just one more thing."

She was about to ask him what that was and decided against it. And then he started the motorcycle and was gone. She watched until his rear lights, now vivid against the gathering darkness, were lost in the glare of the road outside, like a star twinkling out.

Afterword and Acknowledgements

I wrote the draft of this book in a two-month period in 2008. In the process, the story acquired not just its basic structure but accumulated innumerable errors. Narratives were related out of order, names interchanged, continuity errors and problems in tenses and formatting abounded. Most, but inevitably not all of these defects have been weeded out by my wife Susan Pe, who edited the manuscript and improved it in many ways. If this book is readable at all, it is due to her. Any errors that remain were mine to begin with.

Others have helped better the manuscript in various ways. AC pointed out shortcomings in descriptive passages. JM reviewed the action sequences. PD made suggestions for improvements which, if omitted, were due to my negligence. LL pointed out the shortcomings in the plot.

There is the debt of gratitude to all those who inspired elements in this story. My thanks go out to Benjamin B, Francisco F and Fernando Y, brothers always. David D, Elsie E, David B and Fred R are still the stuff of legend in Tondo. Ray R, Sonny H, Manny Y and Carlos T are perhaps in some Valhalla, sitting on the lucky green sofa.

Yet this remains a book of fiction. No story can be told after 35 years and be faithful to the facts. Time has so softened memory that all that is possible is to spin a tale as it should have happened, to people who should have lived.

And perhaps they did, in circles I did not know; or in places I have never been been. But I hope one day to hear the originals tell their stories at the place beneath the bridge, after St Michael, I trust, shall have won his battle against the devil for the soul of man. May we meet again for all the right reasons at the *Boteng Umiilaw.*

Made in the USA
Lexington, KY
12 December 2010